REBIRTH

LEGION OF DRAGONS

BOOK 1

RC DRAKE

TABLE OF CONTENTS

CHAPTER 1 – THE PROJECT
CHAPTER 2 – GRAVITY
CHAPTER 3 – IT BEGINS
CHAPTER 4 - THE LAIR
CHAPTER 5 – THE MYSTERY
CHAPTER 6 – PHASE ONE
CHAPTER 7 – THE MEETING
CHAPTER 8 – BONDING
CHAPTER 9 – MEMORIES
CHAPTER 10-TIME PASSAGE
CHAPTER 11 – THE CHILDREN
CHAPTER 12 – BUMBLE
CHAPTER 13 – THE CREATION
CHAPTER 14 – THE ORB
CHAPTER 15 – THE BALCONY
CHAPTER 16 – SHARING
CHAPTER 17 – PROTECTION
CHAPTER 18 – THE PROPOSAL
CHAPTER 19 – THE AWAKENING
CHAPTER 20 - THE PLAN
CHAPTER 21 – DEAD ZONE
CHAPTER 22 – THE UNKNOWN
CHAPTER 23 – THE RETURN

 All characters in this book are fictitious, and any resemblance to actual persons, living or dead, is purely coincidental.

PROLOGUE

Humankind has overstepped the boundaries necessary for global balance. This horrific mistake has set into motion a catastrophic event of monumental proportions. Through research and experimentation, "The Project" is conceived. Many anticipate this experiment to fail, thereby setting it up for sabotage. The debacle that is to follow will cause a cataclysmic chain of events that will change everything as we know it.

CHAPTER 1
THE PROJECT

My name is Protecus Magannis, and I was a professor at a small college in Stirling, Scotland when The Project was conceived. I never dreamed that one day I would have the task of saving the universe.

For many years, we abused our natural resources, but our atmosphere had suffered through more negligence than it was capable of handling. Over time, humanity's extreme misuse has slowly degraded our ozone layer. When the actual degree of damage was finally revealed to the public, it became ominously apparent that a solution to the problem was imperative. Many ideas were developed to resolve the issue, but no solution was found. The ozone layer thinning had reached a point of peril. It was now critical that something change. All other scientific climate work was put on hold, and the primary focus was directed toward solving the problem. Government grants for a reversal to the depletion came pouring in. As many did, my college accepted the challenge of finding a solution and applied for a grant. Once our funding was sanctioned, my department began working on a possible solution to the problem.

I was excited when I first developed nanorobots. After almost a year of dedicated development, I finally achieved my goal. The official department, The Commission for Critical Development, or CCD as we had begun to call it, acknowledged my idea as the top-rated choice for The Project.

I never dreamed that I would be the one to discover the compound that could save our planet.

After receiving approval, more funding became available to expand my original discovery. The government relocated me to a military base outfitted with a state-of-the-art lab. There, I was to mass-produce my compound to a quantity capable of equipping one hundred capsules that could release upon command. That meant I would require assistance.

To meet the deadline of my benefactors, I enlisted three of my scientific co-workers from my hometown college to join my team. I solicited Reese, Malcolm, and Harry. Once they joined me at the base, we began our work to mass-develop my nanorobots.

Once the development phase of The Project was complete, we were to begin the expansion phase. Several more scientists from around the world joined our team to help us expedite the mass production of my nanobots. The Project quickly became an enormous undertaking.

When the day finally came, and we were ready to announce to the world the expansion phase was complete, we were thrilled.

"Well, Protecus," Harry said as he approached me on the day we finished everything. You should be proud of your accomplishment."

"I am proud, Harry, but you should be saying we instead of just me because it was a group effort, and I'm proud of all of us."

"Well, you can share the glory if you feel it's necessary, Protecus, but as far as I'm concerned, and I think everyone here at the base would agree with me, this baby is all yours."

Several other team members had joined us in the lab by then and began clapping. The extraordinary display gave me a real sense of pride. I could see Malcolm standing across the room from me. He was smiling from ear to ear and clapping. Another development partner, William, began to pat me on the back. He then loudly announced, "Since Protecus was the person that originally discovered the nanorobots, I think it should be named *The Magannis Project*."

That was a nice thought, but I knew it would never happen. It was an honor just the same to have been a part of something so noble and to have the admiration of my friends and colleagues, as well.

My fellow professors were glad their part of the endeavor was over and they could return home. However, as the department head, I was required to stay until its completion. The production phase of The Project proved to be a massive undertaking, taking several more months to complete.

I missed my co-workers and wished I could have left with them, but I was anxious to finish our work. It felt good to know that everything was handled appropriately at the base.

The nanorobots were now ready for launch. After supervising them being retrofitted inside the rockets from which they were to be launched, my part of The Project was finally complete. I was required to remain at the base until a launch date was set. Then, I would be allowed to return home.

However, while waiting for that notification, I became aware of several threats against the participating nations involved in The Project. They were all played down as idle by the base administrators, so I blew them off as radicalism and the drama that incited.

The day finally came when the launch date was set, and it was time for me to return home to the family farm in Scotland. At that point, I had been working on The Project for almost three years, but while away, marauders ransacked my family farm and murdered my brothers. I had also lost my parents the year before in a deadly car accident.

I had not been informed of their deaths, so I had no idea I had lost my entire family while I was away. It was a shock to learn the truth. I was now all alone in the world. It was hard for me to be enthusiastic about the upcoming launch after that.

My teaching position at my old college had been filled in my absence. All my previous associates had lost their jobs as well and relocated. So much had changed while I was away.

My only means of communication with the base station was through my cell phone, and at the farm, or what was left of it, my cell service was spotty at best.

I decided to get a small apartment in town while I searched for a new job. I had decided to sell the farm because I knew I couldn't live there alone. There were just too many memories there for me.

I drove to town and headed for the real estate office. I would have them help me look for an apartment and speak to a realtor about placing the farm for sale. I picked up a newspaper while waiting, and that is when I read the latest information about the launch.

There were more threats against The Project.

I had been out of the loop for a few days while trying to reorganize my family home, so I was unaware of the new threats.

I couldn't understand why there were so many people against the launch. Top scientists worldwide had agreed that with the continued thinning of the ozone, the nanorobots were our best hope for halting the depletion.

However, with so many diverse groups threatening The Project, it became apparent there could be a launch delay.

Many people believed switching from gas-powered to electric cars and transferring our homes to solar power would allow the atmosphere to cleanse itself naturally. They believed that, given time, nature would heal itself. However, that had not happened, and it had been several years since the enactment of the *Desist Law* requiring all the updated changes.

All businesses were required to have zero emissions and stop contaminating the air, or they would be closed by government mandate. Oil production had ceased, causing many to lose their jobs. You were only allowed a driver's license if you owned an electric car. No gasoline-powered engines were permitted, which put a lot of farmers out of business too. So many new regulations, however, the wait-and-see method had not worked, and abuse of our natural resources had finally caught up with us.

Conversely, several factions had disproved all efforts toward interfering with nature and began audaciously protesting that fact. Many seemed highly suspicious of all actions to alter anything in the atmosphere. They vociferously verbalized multiple threats. The group wanted the entire project canceled and promised dire consequences would befall the launches if they took place.

Many worldwide were still eagerly awaiting the day of the launch. Everyone knew about the planned date of the rocket launches. It had been relayed over the world net for several years. Most of the world's population was praying for it to be successful.

While Protecus sat in the lobby at the realty office, one of his friends, Barrett, from the base station called him in a panic. He told Protecus he feared the launch would be sabotaged as threatened and for Protecus to get as far away as possible. He said they had been told that the nanobots could be toxic if they escaped into the atmosphere, which Protecus knew to be true. Barrett said, "I'm leaving, and you should too. Get as far away as you can. The rockets are on the launchpad, loaded and ready to go. They are scheduled for launch, and the countdown will begin in two hours."

Protecus knew that Barrett was right. The nanobots could be toxic if lost in our atmosphere. With his friend sounding so frightened, Protecus believed Barrett was also right about the threats. He heeded Barrett's warning and immediately left the office without saying a word to anyone.

Back at the farm, Protecus quickly collected his journals, books, and the few belongings he could find, leaving the only home he had ever known. He didn't know where he was going but knew the danger they would soon be facing and feared there was nowhere safe to go.

CHAPTER 2
GRAVITY

Barrett had been correct. When the final countdown for the launch began, there was a sudden explosion. By the time everyone realized what was happening, it was too late.

The group that had promised to sabotage the mission had followed through with their threats. The launch station was destroyed, along with some of the rockets. The entire population stationed at the control center was dead. Some of the rockets launched and were able to clear our airspace, but many others crashed back to Earth. Chaos ensued.

The United States wasn't the only country in the world that was hit.

Worldwide threats had been made against all participating nations. Any of them involved with either the creation or the execution of the testing would reap dire consequences.

Not all the countries of the world agreed to the experiment. Many had felt it was better to do nothing than intervene with nature.

It wasn't until later that we learned that all the nations participating in the experiment were struck simultaneously.

The rockets carrying the nanorobots were their primary targets, but the base stations were also destroyed. It wasn't immediately evident exactly where the retaliation was coming from. With no control over the direction the rockets were to fly in, there was no prediction of where they would land. There was also no way to prevent the release of nanobots.

The nanobots must not be allowed to return to Earth at all costs. However, many of the rockets exploded in midair and released their capsules. Others, with no guidance control, drifted aimlessly toward their targeted areas. Once they came into contact with the sun's gravitational pull, they were drawn toward it. The sun's extreme heat combined with the chemicals inside the capsules caused a catalytic reaction, prompting them to rupture and release the nanobots. The sun's gravitational pull drew the nanobots toward it, causing a slow chain reaction that would have catastrophic results.

Hundreds of people were killed by the fallout debris. The timing mechanisms on the rockets were not designed to release on impact, which meant the capsules that returned to Earth didn't release their contents the instant they crashed. It could be several days or even weeks before they released their contents.

No backup plan had been designed to recover the capsules should an event of this magnitude occur. With the launch station destroyed, there was no way to locate the fallen rockets anyway. Our natural balance in the universe has been destroyed, and no one can predict the final outcome.

Once the gases became airborne, the nanobots began their devastation. Anyone unable or unwilling to evacuate the affected areas will soon face exposure to the deadliest gas that man has ever known. Thousands will quickly perish.

Within only a few hours of being inhaled, the nanobots began their assault. They had been designed to oxidize with the ozone layer and prompt it to "re-thicken" itself as they were slowly absorbed within it. They were then to remain there forever, like icing on a cake.

The chemicals used to create the oxidizing agents were poisonous to any living thing. They were never meant to mix with Earth's airspace.

After the natural and manufactured gases conjoined, the nanobots were intended to be absorbed by their host, the ozone layer, and begin reproducing themselves.

However, with the destruction of the base stations, all means of controlling the rockets were lost. That meant all the unfortunate living things in their path would soon feel the effects of the gases.

At the onset of inhalation, all victims would begin to develop uncontrollable spasmodic shakes. Then their nervous system would start to shut down. They would then experience difficulty breathing as the soft lung tissue and internal organs slowly dissolved. The final assault, before death, was festering boils as the nanobots slowly ate their way out from the inside, leaving only skeletal remains and the hair of the victims. A few people lingered on for days, but with extreme pain and grotesque disfigurement, death was imminent.

This horrible "Plague" would later be called "The Great Disaster." Not only will Earth feel the effects of this catastrophic event, but the entire universe will eventually feel the effects.

The Project was doomed. What had been designed to be our knight in shining armor and save us all will ultimately cause our destruction.

The chemical Protecus had created caused widespread destruction and death on a scale no one could ever have imagined.

Mankind has accidentally initiated its own destruction.

Many prayed for help, but they prayed for selfish reasons. Humanity must now face the probability of total annihilation if a miracle does not occur soon. God is weary of man, though. He has forgiven our mistakes for centuries and given us many opportunities to change, but we have failed.

One little girl, however, an innocent child of three, begs for help. She begs not for herself but for someone else. She prays for her mother's sadness to go away because she doesn't want to see her cry anymore. Her mother cries because she is unable to get her daughter to safety. They tried to flee the devastation but got caught in bad traffic, and their electric-powered car was almost dead. This child's unselfish prayer is heard.

CHAPTER 3
IT BEGINS

It has been three years since The Great Disaster, which is what that ill-fated launch day is known as by the remaining survivors. Millions died that day, and millions more perished in the aftermath of the poisonous gases released within the fallout. Few survived, and now those few live on a thread and face imminent danger around every corner.

A miracle must occur soon, or Earth and the entire universe may change forever, and humankind will no longer be a part of it.

Adolla is awakened from her long sleep. The great dragon hears her summons. Her rider, Harwin, has called her, and she rises to the call. Her awakening was long coming. It was prophesied that a young girl would be born with the power to save the world, and Adolla was to be her protector.

The great dragon slowly spreads her enormous wings to shake herself from her lethargic state. She has been sleeping for a very long time.

Adolla must now prepare for the arduous journey ahead of her. She knows what she must do and does not hesitate. Harwin also knows what will unfold but does not relish the upcoming task.

When Adolla arrives at Harwin's side, she immediately senses his dread. After he places the harness on the dragon's back where he is to ride, he straps a small basket onto the front of it. Their journey will take a long time for their destination is far away. After securing the precious cargo. Harwin climbs onto the great dragon's back and mentally commands Adolla to fly.

There is a telepathic bond between rider and dragon with no need to speak words aloud.

Once Adolla nears her destination, she slowly begins her descent. Passing over the small town of Sirus, or what is now left of it, the smell of death permeated the air. The remains of all that have perished there still hung in the air. Scavengers had long since picked apart everything else after the initial onslaught of destruction, and the fires devoured the rest. The winds of time then slowly swept through the once thriving little town, reducing it to rubble.

Greystone Manor was Adolla's intended destination, and it was now in sight. Adolla took in her surroundings as she slowed her descent. Nothing could be seen below her for miles except devastation. Everything was either dead or dying. Nothing of substance was evident. The scene before her was most foreboding.

Adolla had witnessed death and destruction many times during her lifetime, so this was not new to her. However, what she was now seeing was somehow different, harsher, and much more definitive in its scope.

Somehow, the Manor had remained intact, to a degree anyway, possibly due to its remoteness. The air seemed to clear somewhat as Adolla drew nearer. She knew it wouldn't be long before the totality of destruction would also bear down on this place. Soon, nothing would be safe. Not even this little haven.

The hour was early when the sun should have been bright, waking up the day with its warmth. However, it was now a dull grey, as if the clouds had taken up permanent residence and shadowed everything with its gloomy presence. There was an ominous chill that seemed to hand over everything.

As Adolla leveled out for her landing, the only sound heard was the whisper of her great wings as she raised and lowered them. Harwin gazed down at the desolation below them and thought how cold and dreary this place was. The scene before him only made his task grimmer. His mission was not difficult, but the emotional enormity of his duty would take every ounce of strength he could muster to complete it. He would achieve his mission no matter the adversity and do what he must.

As Adolla landed, placing her large, clawed feet upon the brittle landscape, she quickly took in the harshness of the terrain. Few living things were visible for miles. Only a few splotches of green dotted the ground here and there. No trees, no flowers, absolutely nothing of substance was visible. There was just devastation. The air was thin and difficult to breathe. The sky was a dull, lifeless greyish-purple hue, making it appear bruised like it had fought a difficult battle and lost. It was apparent that Earth could no longer replenish itself. It was slowly dissolving into dust and taking everything in its path.

Adolla let out a long, haggard breath.

Harwin said, “I know, girl, they’re in desperate need of help, and we are the only ones that can provide it.”

Harwin slowly unstrapped the basket from Adolla’s back and turned toward the crumbling gates at the front of the degrading stone wall. Harwin then gently placed the little basket he had been charged to deliver in front of the gates. Then Harwin grasped the precious sword from within its sheath at Adolla’s side and thrust it into the hard ground beside the basket. A loud humming reverberation began to resound, enveloping the entire area. He fought back all emotion as he turned back toward Adolla and climbed onto her back.

Harwin dared not look back at the basket, lying alone on the cold hard ground. He knew looking back would weaken his resolve to do what he must.

Adolla was anxious to complete her task as she waited for her rider. She, too, was feeling pangs of remorse for what they must do, but she knew the necessity of their task.

Harwin turned, and Adolla knew it was time for them to leave. She bowed low for him to climb on. As soon as Harwin was on the dragon's back, Adolla looked upward and lifted them in a burst of brilliant light. They were out of sight within seconds, with only a whisper of sound.

Adolla would take Harwin to his home in the stars and then return to Earth to wait for her next summons. She would sleep there until her master called to her.

Something jolted Protecus awake that morning. He was unsure if his vivid dream was the cause of his awakening so abruptly or if something else had all but shaken him out of bed. He checked to see if his wife, Devant, had also awakened. She was still sleeping, snoring as usual, rather loudly. He slowly crept out of bed to ensure everything was as it should be.

The upstairs area seemed fine, so he decided to go downstairs and check there. The staircase was in an extreme state of degradation, so it loudly creaked as he descended, but Protecus had to ensure everything was in order, so he continued onward. As he proceeded down the stairs, he recalled his dream from the night before. That dream had recurred several times and frightened him, but at the same time, it had given him hope. It had seemed so real.

Protecus could see nothing awry downstairs but still sensed something was not right. He slowly proceeded outside to check the grounds as well. As he stepped out into the courtyard, he surveyed the fenced area but could see no one up and about. Multiple tents dotted the yard forming the temporary housing for the many homeless that Protecus had provided refuse. It seemed the noise he heard hadn't awakened any of the residents. Everything was quiet on the grounds, so he decided to look outside the gates to check further. There was a dreadfully loud creak as he opened the massive gates that led outside the courtyard.

The iron gates that had stood for many years protecting the Manor wobbled on their hinges. The rusty, worn-out hinges that held them gave way, and they fell to the ground with a mighty thud. When the dust finally settled, Protecus cringed as he thought he heard what sounded like the whimpering of an infant. That was when he noticed the small basket lying on the ground beside the fallen gates. One of the gates had barely missed landing on the basket. As he approached, Protecus quickly realized that the sound he heard was coming from inside the basket. He cautiously reached for the basket, unsure of what he might find inside. He found the most striking gold and silver cloth he had ever seen there. Protecus slowly began to peel away the layers of fabric to reveal what lay inside. He was amazed at what was inside the basket. It was indeed an infant wrapped inside the cloth

As Protecus gazed down at the baby, he recalled his perpetual dream from the last few weeks. He could remember it vividly. In his dream, which was always the same, he was to receive a most precious gift. He was to treat this unique gift as the most precious treasure one could ever receive. As Protecus lifted the baby from the basket, he immediately noticed the beautiful chain wrapped around its little neck. Suspended from the chain was a large medallion. Emblazoned on the front of it was the symbol of a golden sphere. He read the words engraved upon it: *Let there be light.*

Since the day of The Great Disaster, Protecus had prayed for help, as had all the people under his care. He knew a miracle was needed to save them, for nothing less would do. Their food supply was becoming increasingly scarce, and with the slow fading of the sun's life-giving rays, his seeds could no longer thrive in the soil outdoors. The only food that Protecus could grow now was in his hydroponics garden he built upstairs inside the Manor. It was evident that if something miraculous didn't happen soon, they would all starve.

Protecus looked down again at the tiny infant in his arms, and a slow smile upturned the corners of the older man's face. Was it possible that this child could be the answer to all of their prayers? What could an infant possibly do to reverse Earth's current degrading state?

At that instant, the baby let out a little giggle that snapped Protecus back to the here and now. Protecus must get the baby indoors quickly because this was not the right place to be asking questions. The baby was probably cold and hungry. He was uncertain how long it had been exposed to the elements, possibly all night. Protecus gently laid the baby back inside the basket and was about to grab the handle to carry it inside when he began to hear a loud humming sound. To his amazement, there, on the ground near the infant's basket, was a sword stuck in the dirt. He hadn't noticed it before. It made him gasp in awe. He had never seen anything so unusual.

Protecus pulled the sword from the ground, and the humming sound ceased. The blade was so bright that Protecus could see his reflection in it. It was encrusted with jewels of spectacular color. There were Rubies, Emeralds, and Sapphires inlaid in the handle. The sword was magnificent. The blade's edge had an inscription, but the print was so small it was hard to read. It appeared to be in Latin. Protecus' language skills were not as honed as they once were, and his eyes weren't so good anymore either,

Protecus knew that soon everyone would be waking, and he wanted his discovery of the sword to remain private, at least for the time being. He tucked the sword under his arm and lifted the basket with the baby resting peacefully inside. Then he carefully carried both the sword and the baby around the broken gates and into the confines of the Manor.

Once he was inside, Protecus went straight to the great room. He then placed the basket on the sofa in the middle of the room. After checking to ensure the baby was asleep, Protecus hid the sword behind a group of loosened stones in the wall he had found the day before. He felt it must have been fate that he happened upon the loose stones and saw it as a sign of what was to come. Protecus was at a loss, though, as to what to do with the infant. As he pondered his options, he was in deep thought when he was startled by Devant's sudden entrance. She burst into the room with her usual dramatic flair. Devant was an enormous woman, excessively loud and incredibly pretentious.

"Husband, where on Earth did you find that?" Devant said as she pointed toward the baby. Then she totally ignored the infant and changed the subject.

"I waited for you in my bed this morning to bring me something to eat, but you never returned, so I came to look for you."

Devant never let Protecus out of her sight for long. She was very possessive of him and very jealous. She monitored his every move.

Entering the room in her usual ostentatious manner, she made so much noise that she woke the baby. The infant began to cry, which drew Devants attention. She turned toward the sound, and Protecus could have sworn for an instant he saw a smile cross her hardened features. It was fleeting, so he assumed he must have been confused. The two of them had no children, of which Protecus was glad. He didn't think that Devant was the mothering kind anyway.

As the baby lay helpless before Devant's probing eyes, her outward demeanor quickly changed. She turned on her husband like a viper. She began pointing her finger at him, loudly accusing him of bringing another stray cat home, as she called any newcomer to the Manor.

"Not another mouth to feed!" she shouted. "Protecus, what were you thinking?" She then wheeled to face the infant as she continued to rant and throw angry insults back at Protecus. Suddenly she stopped short, and the entire room fell silent. She had spotted the necklace around the infant's neck.

Devant bent lower to get a closer look at the shiny chain draped around the baby's neck and immediately spotted the unique golden medallion suspended from it. The corners of her mouth slowly turned upward as she quickly reached to extract the chain from the baby's neck. However, in her hurry to snatch the necklace, she accidentally pricked the baby's skin with her extremely long fingernails. The infant never made a sound. A drop of the infant's blood touched Devant's hand, and she let out a blood-curdling squeal the instant it did. The blood had burned her flesh like fire. She immediately turned loose of the chain and sneered down at the infant.

Protecus had heard Devant's scream and quickly reached for the baby. He was unsure what had caused Devant's cry of pain but sought to protect the baby at all costs.

Devant promptly hid her hand from her husband's inquiring eyes. She didn't want him to see her injury and tried to cover up the uncomfortable moment by saying, "Oh my, I broke a fingernail. "Seeking to change the subject, Devant quizzed Protecus about where he had found this new guest. She tried to hide her suspicions about this newcomer, but her manner had changed, and it had not gone unnoticed by Protecus.

To ease the tension in the room, Protecus quickly began to explain. "When I came downstairs this morning to get you something to eat, I heard crying outside, and when I checked, I found the baby. "

That explanation was a lie, but he was grasping at straws and unwilling to divulge the truth, not yet anyway.

"One of the iron gates on the perimeter wall fell off its hinges, so I'll need to fix that as soon as possible."

"Well, good luck with that, you old fool. You can't see two feet in front of you without your glasses, and you lost those months ago. Plus, there isn't one person among the vagrants strong enough to help lift that gate. Most of them can barely stand up."

She was right about part, for sure, so Protecus dropped his head and fell silent. Devant didn't expect a retort from him anyway. He never argued with her because he knew it was a lost cause. She turned her back to Protecus and again glared down at the baby. She didn't believe for one instant this infant just happened upon their doorstep, nor did she care. Devant knew that she must possess that pendant that lay around the infant's neck, and once she had it, that baby had to disappear.

That tiny creature could not be allowed to live because its presence interfered with her plans. Devant had to figure out how to safely extract that pendant from around its neck first, then she would do away with it, as she did all things that did not please her. The baby would merely perish without a trace.

Protecus didn't like the way his wife was eying the baby. He was afraid that, in some way, she was going to harm it. Devant had a mean streak about her, and anything that displeased her always managed to disappear. She hated children most of all. The truth of the matter was that Devant didn't care about anything or anyone except herself.

Protecus decided his best course of action, at least for now, was to reassure his wife that the child would not be a problem. He hurriedly clarified his intentions, "The baby will be no bother at all, Devant. I plan to forage extra hard and leave earlier every day. I'll stay out as long as it takes, searching for food, and I'll take care of all its needs myself. You won't have to do a thing."

Devant laughed out loud, "You crazy old fool. A baby requires milk, and the last time I looked, we were fresh out of milk cows around here." She then sneered at him and leered back down at the infant once more, "You are going to need far more than luck with your new bundle of joy, Protecus, or that baby is going to die. You better find me some meat soon, or I'll have Miranda cook me donkey stew for supper."

As she spat those words out, her actions were palpable. It was apparent her warning was a serious one. Proteus knew that she was not making idle threats. She had killed his beloved horse, Lady, earlier that month and forced Miranda to cook it. It had saddened Protecus greatly to lose his horse, but the donkey was his last means of transport. Foraging and hunting would be impossible without the animal to carry him to and from his destination. He would now have to venture further from the Manor to find the few remaining berries and roots for everyone to eat. He had to be more successful on his hunts because he knew Devant would not hesitate to follow through on her threats.

Devant was suspicious of this new visitor that Protecus had brought into her sanctum. This infant made her very uncomfortable, and she felt intimidated by it. Devant had never felt inferior to anything or anyone, and she didn't intend to start now. She needed to take control of the situation before it got further out of hand. She quickly turned to Protecus and began shouting at him again.

"You can't take care of an infant. You can barely take care of me. I'll call Miranda. She'll know what to do."

With that proclamation, Devant began to yell for Miranda to come to her aid. Miranda was never far away for fear of upsetting Devant. So, when she heard Devant's boisterous summons, she responded quickly.

Devant was the one that discovered Miranda in the city at the very moment Miranda had all but given up.

While trying to escape the city as it burned down around them, Miranda and her three children were trapped in traffic when her electric car ran out of power. Many had already given up their vehicles and started walking. She, too, was forced to gather her children and the few belongings they could carry and strike out walking. It didn't take long for thievery to begin, though, as people became thirsty and hungry. Many were murdered in the streets for a drink of water.

As desperation set in, Miranda's two sons were forced to search for drinking water too. When they didn't return, Miranda searched for them. Sadly, she found them both murdered in the street.

Her daughter, Solarian, was very young then, and Miranda was desperate. She was destitute, out of drinking water, and hungry. That is when Devant, in her horse-drawn wagon, happened upon Miranda. Miranda humbly accepted the hand outstretched to her. A few weeks later, Devant and her entourage seemingly happened upon Greystone Manor, Protecus's newly acquired refuge.

Knowing Miranda's dire situation, Devant selfishly took advantage of the young woman's predicament. She said, "I think it would be in your child's best interest if you keep quiet and allow me to do all the talking."

Of course, Miranda agreed. She was at Devant's mercy. She feared Devant's implied threat if she didn't follow her instructions.

Devant told Miranda that she planned to tell Protecus that Miranda was her maid. She explained that he might be more apt to allow them to stay if he felt they could be useful. Miranda feared for their safety, so she followed Devant's advice and said nothing.

Devant told Protecus that Miranda would happily take care of his household and cook for everyone at the Manor. Protecus agreed, not realizing he had been duped.

Devant told Miranda, "You'll do whatever I tell you to do without question. Otherwise, the two of you can take your chances on the outside. Out there, you'll both probably starve or be killed by marauders."

Miranda felt she had to agree to do Devant's bidding for the sake of her daughter. But now, several months later, Devant was still taking advantage of Miranda. Whenever she barked a command, she expected Miranda to jump to do her bidding, and she was not patient. She was short-tempered and quick to anger if things weren't to her liking. So Miranda was never far from earshot of Devant for fear of upsetting her.

The instant Miranda was at Devant's side, Devant began shouting orders at her. "You are to take this baby and bathe it. It stinks. Then dress it in something more suitable than those filthy rags it came here wrapped in.

Devant then walked directly in front of Miranda. She quickly toned her barking to a whisper, saying, "Undress that child and be sure to remove the chain from its neck, along with the attached pendant. Then place both of them inside my special box; you know, the one that sits on the top of my bedside table. That necklace isn't suitable for an infant. It's far too heavy for a baby to wag around. It's too large and could strangle the poor little thing. Then as soon as you finish putting those items away, come and let me know."

Protecus couldn't hear what Devant was saying to Miranda because she was talking too softly. Still, he felt safe entrusting Miranda with the infant's care. He had no fear that she would treat the baby as if it were her own.

When Devant stopped whispering to Miranda, she flounced off toward the kitchen, muttering something unintelligible.

Protecus then quietly told Miranda, “I truly appreciate your help with the baby.”

Miranda smiled and cooed at the little one as she lifted her into her arms. “No problem at all, Protecus. This little thing is the bright spot in my day.”

Then she headed toward the kitchen to heat the baby’s bath water. Devant was leaving the kitchen just as Miranda entered. As she started up the stairs, she turned to face Protecus one last time. She shot him a very unpleasant look. He noticed her expression and quickly said, “I’ll go now and forage. I promise I’ll not return home without something the baby can eat.”

“I don’t care if that baby ever eats another bite Protecus. I’m hungry NOW. There is nothing decent in that kitchen to eat. Don’t bother returning at ALL if you don’t find something decent for me to eat, and it better not be berries again or those nasty rotten roots!”

Protecus was always amazed at the utterly horrible things that came out of Devant’s mouth. He couldn’t understand how she had turned into such a shrew, but she had never been pleasant.

“Not to worry,” he said, as he tried to reassure her, “I’ll hunt all day if necessary, and I’ll not stop searching until I find something decent for all of us to eat.”

“You’d better!” Devant brashly shouted as she nonchalantly waved him away like she would a mosquito that was bothering her. Then she abruptly stormed up the stairs, grumbling the entire way to her bedroom.

Protecus was always happy to break away from Devant any chance he could get.

He quickly seized that moment with everyone gone from the room to retrieve the sword from its hiding place. He would now take it to where his dream had instructed him to place it. Protecus was told to take the sword to the place no man dared go.

CHAPTER 4
THE LAIR

Once Protecus retrieved the sword from its hiding place behind the bricks, he went to the barn to ready his little donkey for the journey he was about to undertake. He knew he must return with something edible and enough to feed everyone, or he would have to contend with Devant's wrath.

Protecus must travel down to the coastline and past the beach area below to reach the place in his dreams where he was to leave the sword. The place where no man dared to go meant only one thing to Protecus; he must put the sword inside the dragon's lair.

Protecus had heard many tales about the dragon's lair, retold to him by the old ones now living under his care. Some of the stories were ominous in their context, but all were difficult to conceive as factual.

As Protecus set out on his journey to the cave, he recalled one of those stories and mulled it over while he traveled. According to local legends, the dragon's lair was a place where no one ventured for fear of death. It was said to be a maze of several interconnecting caves that had once housed many dragons. Protecus had never ventured anywhere near that location before. It was reportedly beneath the Manor, but he had never noticed any entry point while on his foraging trips before. The legends were frightening, though, so Protecus had never made a point to search for the entrance.

Many years before The Great Disaster, there were stories of mythical dragons that lived in the caves beneath the Manor. That was supposedly why there were no houses anywhere near Greystone Manor because no one was brave enough to go against the legend.

The way Protecus heard the story, the property's original owners, a wealthy young couple with two small children, had inherited the land from an eccentric aunt upon her passing. The couple fell in love with the place the first time they saw it and immediately decided to build their dream home on the panoramic cliffside. They had heard the tales of the dragon's lair supposedly hidden deep below the hilltop but had never believed them. Many stories passed down through the years of the giant beasts that once lived on the land. No one living had ever witnessed one of them, though, so the Patricks ignored the warnings as mere rumors and started building anyway.

After the groundwork for the construction of the families' new home began, many believed that perhaps the explosions while excavating, or the constant noise from the equipment moving about, had awakened the long-sleeping dragons. At any rate, shortly after the construction work began, there were multiple sightings of the creatures reported in and around the area.

Those sightings caused immediate problems for the Patricks. Several of the worker's family members reported their loved ones never returned home after working at the Manor. After that, fear for their lives prompted many laborers to leave the job site and refuse to return.

The Patricks were still in denial about the presence of dragons and continued to discount the reports. They had to pour even more money into their project to keep construction work going. Construction work continued after that but with fewer workers and a much slower pace. As the completion of the enormous undertaking began to take shape, the owners were anxious to start decorating their new residence. They began moving their furniture and other personal items inside the Manor.

On one of those scheduled delivery days, the couple brought their children to see their new home. They had a son, who was about five years old, and a daughter, around seven. The way Protecus heard the story about the children was gruesome. They were allowed to run and play freely within the confines of the stone fence which surrounded the entire Manor. The children were in plain sight while they played, so their parents felt safe, allowing them to run around on the hillside. Suddenly the little girl began incessantly screaming and running around in circles. Everyone came rushing out to see what was causing all of her distress. The little boy was gone. He had disappeared.

The little girl was hysterical, and between bouts of crying and screaming, she kept repeating the exact words: The giant bird took him; the giant bird took him.

The parents began frantically searching for their son and called all their workers to help. Everyone thought the boy probably left the confines of the yard and fell off the cliff. They searched the entire beach area below the Manor until after dark but never found the little boy.

A search and rescue mission began that night that lasted for several weeks, to no avail. No one ever saw the little boy after that. They never located his body, not even a shred of clothing. After that tragedy, the boys' mother was so distraught she refused to return to the Manor. The couple abandoned the construction project, and no one ever returned to the site. The building remained unfinished. The owners never retrieved their furniture or any of their personal effects. Everything slowly became reclaimed by nature after that. When Protecus happened upon the property, that was the state he found it in.

Protecus had never seen a real dragon, nor did he wish to. The tales were scary enough. So, he approached the area most resembling what he had seen in his dream with great trepidation. He shivered just thinking of that horrible story about the little boy. He could hear the old storyteller's voice in his head saying, *No one ventures there anymore because anyone who dared to go there vanished and was never seen again.*

Protecus was not a brave man by any measure, and his conscience was speaking to him at that moment, almost yelling, saying, stop, don't do this. You have no backbone, and who will take care of the baby if you get killed?

Who indeed? Certainly not Devant. The only thing that you could depend on her for was to eat and sleep. For that effort, you could always count on her.

Protecus knew that Miranda would see to the baby's care. He could count on her but was still hesitant, as fear almost overtook him. Protecus considered placing the sword in the tall weeds near the cave entrance. Then he could leave quickly while he still had his head on top of his body. That seemed like a plausible solution, but then Protecus remembered his dream and how vital the sword was. While dreaming, the voice he heard had been emphatic about where the sword should be placed. Protecus was to put it *inside* the lair.

Protecus took a deep breath and tried to bolster his inner strength, which genuinely didn't exist, and then he forced himself onward. He slowly dismounted and then tethered his donkey to a nearby bush. He then got down on his hands and knees and began pulling out the weeds and underbrush that had grown over the area he was shown to be the entrance to the cave. All the while, inwardly, Protecus hoped the opening wasn't there. True to his dream, though, he found a small gap behind the briars and underbrush. It was the entrance he had seen in his dream. Once again, Protecus hesitated as fear of the unknown crept back into his thoughts.

"Surely," he said aloud, "No dragon could fit through this small space. Besides, if any still existed, surely I would have seen one by now." He reasoned that he should be able to quietly slip inside, hide the sword, then get out again without being detected by anything that might be alive inside. Somehow having a plan made him feel somewhat better about what he was about to do.

Protecus slowly stood up after clearing enough debris from the entranceway to enter. He looked at the opening once more, then, satisfied that he could fit through the small space, returned to where he had tethered his donkey. He retrieved the pouch from the animal's side that held the sword and strapped it to his back. He had to creep on his hands and knees to get through the small opening, which yielded no more than a dark, narrow tunnel on the other side. As his eyes adjusted to the darkness, he slowly began to creep his way through. Protecus could hear strange noises around him within the dank and dusky tunnel. There were squeals and hisses, all of which seemed to intensify as he continued along the dark, narrow passageway, which didn't help to calm his fears. The entire area seemed infested with rather large crawling things that were happily gnawing on every exposed part of him. He was thankful he couldn't see what was in the tunnel with him, for he would have abandoned his task completely.

As he inched along, little by little, he was finally able to see a small amount of light, indicating, hopefully, that he was nearing the end of his plight.

At the end of the tunnel, he slowly climbed into the opening. There was very little light to see, so Protecus cautiously advanced into the cave. As his eyes slowly adjusted to the dimness within the cave, he found himself in awe of his surroundings. The cave's interior was immense, completely belittling its size from the outside. As he continued surveying his surroundings, a bright light beam slowly streamed down from an opening high above. When it hit Protecus directly on the top of his head, it gave the appearance of a heavenly glow explicitly aimed at him. The light was so intense it blinded him for a few seconds with its brightness. Protecus had to close his eyes to readjust to its brightness before he could see well enough to move again. The bright light streamed throughout the cave, allowing him to see more. Unaware that he was shaking with fear, Protecus took a few tentative steps further into the cave. More strange noises emanated from within the area where he was now standing. The echoing around him indicated that the place where he was standing was quite vast.

Protecus then saw something shiny directly in front of him. It was beautiful, almost iridescent, and glowing brightly in the darkness. It appeared to be a large rock, which looked like the best spot for him to place the sword, as he was more than ready to leave this scary place. He withdrew the sword from the pouch on his back and carefully slid it into a crevice underneath the rock. Protecus turned then and was about to go when he heard something new. He looked back at the boulder where he had placed the sword and was astonished to see it move.

A voice resonated within the cave, completely silencing all other noises. It said, "Protecus, you have done well to bring the sword to me as instructed."

The sound seemed to be coming from the big rock where he had placed the sword, which made no sense. The iridescent-looking boulder then moved again, and Protecus froze in his tracks, afraid to breathe. He quickly realized it wasn't a rock at all but a giant foot. The light then hit upon the creature, and Protecus could see that it was immense. It was a dragon, brilliant pearl white in color with silver iridescent shapes dotting its enormous body. Large horns protruded from its head which glittered as it turned. When the light hit the emblems embedded there, they glowed. Beautiful images that twinkled like the stars in the heavens were embellished all about the enormous dragon's body. Their brilliance appeared to be intensified by the darkness. Each star-like appearance was more vivid than the one before it. As the creature turned to face Protecus, he realized how truly immense the beast was.

“I am Adolla,” the dragon said, “and I will guard the sword until it is time to return it to my master. Bringing the sword to me is not the only reason I had you seek me out.” Adolla was now facing Protecus with her giant wings tucked neatly at her sides. She was striking. She quickly sensed the terror emanating from Protecus.

“Do not fear me, Protecus, for I will not harm you. We chose you for this deed because of your knowledge and love for this world. It is not your fault your discovery was destroyed. It would have worked, and I would not have to be here now, but alas, that was not to be.”

Protecus was unable to move and realized that he was holding his breath. When he began to breathe again, and the oxygen started to return to his brain, the reality of what she said hit him. His experiment would have worked had it not been sabotaged. A smile upturned the corners of his mouth until he realized where he was now standing again.

He wasn’t dreaming. He was wide awake, and this enormous dragon was speaking to him. She even knew his name!

“The infant entrusted to you this morning is a little girl, and her name is Babrea`, which means brilliant ray of light. She is the gift that you were to receive from your dream. You are to be her tutor. You are to nurture her mind as she grows to adulthood. Guide and teach her in the ways of man. You and you alone are to direct her and provide her with the knowledge she will need in the coming months.”

Protecus had been in a state of shock until that moment. He then tried to pull himself together. When he finally collected his thoughts enough to speak, he asked, “Of all the people in the world, why me? I’ve never raised a child before, and this is such a harsh place now.

It's not safe to raise a child here. Food is scarce, and I don't know where I will ever find milk for her."

Adolla inhaled slowly, then, as she released her icy breath, it enveloped Protecus with its chill.

"A man of pure heart was needed to direct Babrea` on her pathway to adulthood. You are the chosen one, Protecus. She will soon direct her own destiny, and when that day arrives, she will be ready because of the guidance you gave her. Soon your world will no longer be able to sustain itself. When that day comes, Babrea` must be ready. She must grow strong of heart, as well as mind and body. When the time arrives, she will face many difficult choices. For now, you only need to allow her to grow. Do not shelter her. She must learn all there is to know, both good and evil. Give her freedom, and fear not for her safety. She is small now, but she has a protector that will be with her always. He will guard her against all that would try to harm her until she is strong enough to care for herself. Everything that is needed, he will provide for her."

Protecus was now more confused than ever but also fearful. He feared that he would fail the mission that was before him. What if he should not succeed at what sounded like a crucial assignment?

Adolla knew his thoughts and reassured him, "Do not fear what you do not understand, Protecus. You will not fail. Babrea` will only require your guidance and direction. Even as small as she is now, she can summon any help she may require with only a thought. She can see to all her other needs. Remember this one important thing, though. You must keep the pendant that arrived around Babrea's neck safe. Keep it hidden from all eyes until the time comes when it is needed."

Protecus didn't understand, so he timidly asked one last question, not wanting to anger the great dragon. "How will I know when the time comes to give her pendant back to her?"

Adolla said, “It will call to her when the time is right. For the time being, I will remain here until my master summons me. You must now leave this place and never return here, for I am not the only creature that dwells here.”

With that statement, Adolla slowly turned away from Protecus and once again appeared like an iridescent stone. There was a giant rumble, and the entire mountain began to shake. Darkness began to overtake the cave as the opening at the top of the massive cave began to close. The light that had been streaming from above slowly faded away as the cave became shadowed in darkness.

Protecus quickly scrambled toward the area that he had entered in through to escape. Within seconds after exiting the small opening, it, too, began to close. Once it closed completely, it sealed shut in an explosive cloud of rock and dust. Once it closed, there was no sign that an opening had ever existed.

Protecus tried to stand up but immediately fell to the ground on his knees. He realized his legs were unable to support him. The events that had just occurred had shaken him, and he felt overwhelmed by the mass of information he had just received but mystified at the same time.

Adolla had told him the baby girl that arrived at his doorstep was the gift he was to receive from his dream.

His head was spinning as he thought about everything he had just heard. He was still kneeling on the ground in bewilderment when he was shaken back to reality by the sound of a bell ringing. When he looked around, he was amazed to see a cow. A live milk cow was standing just a few feet away from him, and she appeared healthy. She was looking straight at him as if waiting for him to come and get her, which was an unbelievable stroke of luck. He needed milk for the baby and didn’t know what he was going to do. Now, miraculously, his problem was solved, as if by magic. He stood slowly, trying not to scare the animal, and once he had his balance again, he went to his donkey to retrieve a small rope he had tied there. The cow never moved as Protecus eased up on her and tied the rope around her neck. Then he returned to his donkey while leading the cow, climbed back on its back, and began to make his way home.

On his way home, he felt almost numb, thinking about this morning's events. The things Adolla had told him were overwhelming. Still, at the same time, they gave him hope for a possible end to their current tragic situation.

Since the day of The Great Disaster, the sun had begun to dim. Actual daylight now only lasted a few hours each day. A pale dimness seemed to cling to the daylight hours, and nightfall came much earlier, bringing colder temperatures. Twelve-hour days no longer existed. Daylight now averaged about eight hours daily, all of which were dim.

The sun was fading now, so it was later than Protecus thought. It would be dark soon, and with darkness, the scavengers would come out, making his travel home dangerous. Protecus knew that he must hurry. He must have been gone for a long time, much longer than he had intended. Devant would be angry with him for being away for so long, especially for not bringing home any food for her. Hopefully, the cow would please her. Among her many other complaints, she had complained about not having anything to drink but water. Protecus was happy they had water to drink, but mostly he was thankful to be alive.

As Protecus neared home, he immediately noticed two figures standing outside the wall surrounding the Manor. The closer he got to them, he could tell they were young men he didn't know. They were standing beside the broken gates, which had served for years as the primary means of protection for all the residents. Now, one of the gates lay sideways on bent hinges while the other one was on the ground in a pitiful heap. The crumbling, degrading stone wall now looked weaker without its grand steel gates.

Protecus had chosen this place as his refuge after escaping the city because of its remote location. He could tell it had been deserted for a long time, even before The Great Disaster tore everything apart.

Greystone Manor was quite secluded, which afforded it some protection from looters and pillagers, especially in the early days immediately following the disaster. The tall stone wall surrounding the grounds was a bonus, as it afforded even more means of protection. However, the wall now urgently needed repair, as well as the large gates.

The most valuable asset of Greystone was the underground artesian spring. Protecus had discovered it while inspecting the property before moving it. He had stumbled upon the caves below the Manor through a hatchway underneath the Manor. He intended to keep the well a secret, but after Devant moved in, she found the spring while following Protecus on one of his inspection trips. He tried to impress upon her the urgency of keeping their water supply a secret because of its importance. Thankfully she had kept its existence safe.

Protecus had outfitted the spring with his water purification system, which he had designed several years earlier. He had brought the plans with him when he escaped the city. Once he discovered the artesian spring, he knew his system could work here and provide safe drinking water. He built his plan from scratch with parts he salvaged from the surrounding areas, so he had to redesign it somewhat. It also had to be adapted to pump to the well above ground, which was how he provided water to the Manor residents. His water system worked perfectly on the underground spring. To the average person, the water appeared to be coming from a conventional well, which also helped disguise it. They would not have had safe drinking water without Porticus' water purification system.

Through years of diligent work, while Protecus was working at the college, he developed growth additives that could be used on vegetation to intensify development. He could now utilize his knowledge of chemistry to grow plants at an accelerated rate in his hydroponics gardens. The residents now assembled at Greystone would have surely perished without his knowledge of chemistry.

Within the past three years since he first arrived at Greystone, more people struggling to survive, with no food, no water, and no place to go, had wandered into Protecus's care. Many of these individuals were elderly or helpless, and some were disabled. Caring for these people had been a heavy burden for Protecus to bear. Over time, providing for them had become increasingly more challenging, especially with them now numbering seventeen individuals.

These two new strangers, however, appeared to be reasonably fit and much younger than the group that had come to be at Greystone thus far. The tallest boy seemed to be assessing the damaged gates quite intently. As Protecus pondered over these two young fellows' and their intentions, he noticed a beautiful black horse standing near the entrance. His gaze quickly took in the fine young buck carelessly thrown upon the horse's back. Regardless of whatever else these two young men had on their minds, Protecus knew that his people needed that meat. He decided to ask if they would be willing to share some of their venison in exchange for shelter for the night. Protecus hadn't seen real meat in a long time and had almost forgotten how it tasted.

Their recent fare had been mostly roots, berries, and an occasional slow-moving rabbit. Protecus's hunting skills had never been that great, or his eyesight, either. He had misplaced his only pair of glasses many months prior, making seeing off at a distance much more difficult for him.

The oldest lad, who appeared to be no more than seventeen or eighteen, strode purposefully toward Protecus. As he approached, the young man politely held out his hand, which impressed Protecus immensely. He then said, "Good evening, Sir. My name is Seth Parkus." Then he pointed to the boy beside him, saying, "This is my brother Tanus. We couldn't help but notice that your gates are broken. We need a place to rest for a while and thought perhaps we could exchange some carpentry work for a few nights of lodging."

Protecus liked that idea but hoped to sweeten the deal by making his own proposition.

"How about if I feed and water your horse and fill your canteens for a share of that venison?"

Everything was in short supply now, especially water. It was now a higher commodity than money. There were many willing to kill just for a small amount of it. Seth saw Protecus eyeing his recent kill and made him a counteroffer.

"We would be willing to share the entire deer with you and repair your gates if you allow us to stay here for a week. We've been traveling for a long time and need a safe resting place."

Protecus could not pass up such a fantastic offer. That venison was enough to feed his people for several days, and he knew they desperately needed it. The boys seemed trustworthy enough, so he agreed to the bargain. It had been a long time since anyone was willing and capable of helping him with the much-needed repairs around the place. The gates were their only means of protection from whatever lurked outside in the woods after dark. Without them, the wall was almost useless. None of the current residents could assist Protecus in maintaining the property, as they could barely care for themselves. The young men had arrived at a very auspicious time. Protecus knew he couldn't do the repairs alone, and those gates needed repairs as soon as possible. Protecus contemplated his choices for only a second before making his decision. He reached his hand out, saying, "You have a deal. Let's shake it."

Seth reached out for Protecus' extended hand and asked, "Do you also agree to us staying here for a few days?"

Protecus smiled and nodded, saying, "The two of you can stay in the barn for now. We might change our arrangements if you share the meat and fix the gates."

They shook hands on their deal, and then Protecus pointed toward a small building just inside the stone wall, near the entranceway, and said, "That's my smokehouse. We'll cook some of the meat tonight and then put the rest in the smokehouse to preserve it for another day."

Seth smiled and told Protecus, "I'm sorry, but I don't know anything about smoking meat. My father never taught me how to do that. My brother and I have been on the run for a long time. We can usually only eat our fill, and then we have to leave the rest behind. I found that if we stay too long in one place, it becomes dangerous for us. So, we are constantly on the move."

Protecus understood and said, "Well, you're both safe here, son. It isn't much, but it's our home. We've lived here for over three years without incident, and I hope that continues. I have to go now and put away the animals and check on my wife. I'll return after that and teach you how to process that meat. No food goes to waste around here. We preserve what we don't eat and save it for another day." With that, Protecus led the cow and donkey into the makeshift barn he had assembled from spare lumber he had salvaged. After tying the animals for the night, he walked to the kitchen door and quietly entered.

CHAPTER 5
THE MYSTERY

After entering the Manor, Protecus walked straight into the great room. He quickly spotted the small basket on the sofa. It was the one the baby had arrived in earlier that morning. He could see her little hands waving above the brim of it and immediately became alarmed. It appeared that she had been left there unattended. He thought it was odd that she was in the same spot where he had left her earlier. He reached down and touched her on the cheek. She giggled, smiled at him, and then grabbed his finger. As she reached up toward him, the chain around her neck slowly slid across her blanket, which caused the pendant to fall into Protecus' hand. He remembered Adolla telling him about Babrea's chain and necklace and that he was to hide them in a secret place that only he knew. He quietly placed the chain and pendant behind the loose stone in the wall where he had hidden the sword earlier.

After carefully hiding them, he turned his attention back toward the baby. He lifted her in his arms and gazed down at her. She was a beautiful child. She had pale blonde hair that was so light it was almost white. Her eyes were the most striking blue/purple color he had ever seen. They seemed to jump out at him. That prompted Protecus to remember his siblings, whom he lost while working on The Project.

While he was reminiscing about his lost loved ones, Devant entered the room in her usual flurry. She was speaking loudly, as always, demanding that Protecus explain himself to her.

"Where have you been, and what have you been doing, husband? I've been looking for you all over the place."

Oddly, she hadn't said anything about the baby that Protecus held in his arms. Her focus was on the basket that was lying on the sofa.

She purposefully strode toward the basket, thinking it would be full of food for her. When she realized all that was in it was some dirty straw and a dirty old blanket, she angrily turned on Protecus. That's when she seemingly noticed the baby for the first time.

Devant gasped as her eyes came to rest on the infant in her husband's arms, and she immediately began to rant. "Where on Earth did you find that thing? Precisely what we don't need around here is another mouth to feed. I swear, Protecus, you would bring home every stray cat in the world if I allowed it!"

"Devant, this is a baby, not a stray cat," he stated."

"Well, I can see that, you stupid old fool." she shrieked. Then she reached for the baby and almost yanked her out of Protecus's arms.

Devant stared at the baby in her husband's arms, giving her a long, penetrating look. She had never cared for children, especially babies. She said they ate too much and always smelled terrible. This one was different, though. It made her feel really uncomfortable. She didn't know why but didn't like being near it.

She sneered at her husband, then said, "Well, if you're going to keep it, then you're going to be responsible for taking care of it. Otherwise, it will starve. Thanks to you, there are already too many mouths to feed around here. We don't need any more vagrants." Then she unceremoniously whirled and left the room.

As she climbed the stairs, she yelled back at him, "Tell Miranda to bathe it too. It stinks! Then tell her to find something for it to wear other than those filthy rags. She needs to burn those things immediately. There's no telling what vermin are crawling around in them as we speak."

Protecus was speechless. Devant acted as though she was seeing the baby for the first time. He looked at the baby's blonde hair and sparkling blue eyes and wondered what he was missing. He felt like he was experiencing a déjà vu moment because everything that had happened earlier that morning seemed like it had never happened.

Protecus looked down at the striking gold and silver cloth carefully wrapped around the baby and was confused about what Devant saw. Babrea` was not dirty, nor did she smell bad. It was baffling to him. He decided that Devant must be in one of her angry moods and acting accordingly. She was always hateful, but more so since food had become scarce.

It seemed Devant was growing meaner and more insufferable with each passing day. As she climbed the stairs, Protecus remembered the cow. He hurriedly told her the news, thinking she would be excited to have milk for a change. "Oh, I had some luck today foraging. I stumbled upon a cow that seemed to be just wandering around aimlessly. I decided to catch it and bring it home. I thought it was a miracle since I needed milk for the baby. Plus, I know how much you missed having milk."

Devant stopped halfway up the stairs and turned to face Protecus. She shocked him with her next words. Smiling, she said, "Finally, you found some decent meat for me. Hurry up and kill the thing, then fire up the pit. I'm hungry."

She had entirely ignored Protecus's need for milk for the baby.

Devant said, "The faster you get going, the sooner I can eat. It's probably tough as whitleather and will take all night to get tender enough to eat, so get started."

Devant's words totally shocked Protecus. The way that woman thought never ceased to amaze Protecus. He was glad there was venison for her to eat. He knew that his wife was not kidding about killing the cow. She would have no problem slaughtering the cow and then commanding Miranda to cook it, as she had done with his beloved horse, Lady. If Devant were hungry, she would not hesitate to eat just about anything and not give it a second thought.

Even though they needed milk for the baby, Devant would never give that an instant of thought.

Protecus quickly explained, “The cow isn’t for supper, Devant. She’s a milk cow, and we need milk for the baby. You don’t have to worry about food tonight because we have venison for supper.”

“Finally, you killed something worth eating!”

Protecus was hesitant to let Devant know how he came about acquiring the venison in the first place. He knew that she would find out about the boys anyway and be even angrier because he had withheld the information from her, so he plunged forward. As Protecus began to speak, Devant turned and slowly descended the stairs.

“This evening, two young men happened upon our doorstep, and incredibly, they are the ones that killed the venison. Their names are Seth and Tanus, and they will be repairing a few things around here. While they do the repairs, they will be staying here with us. They already have the pit fired up and are cooking the venison. It should be ready any minute now, so I’ll bring some up to you as soon as it’s cooked.”

At that point, Devant was standing directly in front of Protecus. She cocked an eyebrow at him and began to query him about where the two boys had come from and where they intended to go when they left. Protecus knew she didn’t want them to stay. If she had her way, she didn’t want anyone there. Devant was a loner and cared not for having company. At times Protecus felt she didn’t even want him around.

He attempted to explain to her, “I’ve only just met them myself, but they are willing to help me repair the gates out front, and since they were willing to share the meat, I offered for them to stay a few nights. I'll question them more fully in the morning."

Devant snapped at him, "What's wrong with the gates?"

Protecus knew he had told her about the gates being broken, so he was surprised by her question. It appeared everything that had taken place earlier that morning had suddenly disappeared from everyone's memory. It was a mystery that made Protecus wonder if he was the only one that recalled the morning's events.

Devant quickly brought Protecus back to the present, yelling, "PROTECUS! Are you listening to me? You better get those gates fixed and make certain the two new strangers know the rules around here and stay away from my Castle," as she always referred to the Manor. "Make sure they know they are to sleep in the barn, and I expect them to come and meet me first thing in the morning. I will be the one to decide if they can stay or if they must go. Now hurry up, get me something to eat, and bring me some milk when you bring my plate."

Protecus knew that Devant would not be happy having more strangers on the property, and she detested newcomers.

At that second, the baby began to cry from all of Devant's rantings. She shouted, "Protecus, I told you to have Miranda bathe that thing. What is the matter with you? Miranda, get in here!" Devant commanded in her usual harsh manner.

Miranda was never far away for fear of upsetting Devant, so she came in a rush. Devant barked more commands, "Take this thing and give it a bath. It's filthy and probably riddled with fleas or something worse."

Protecus had never cared for the way Devant treated Miranda. She was always demanding and short on temper.

Protecus didn't like Devant calling the baby a thing and spoke before thinking, saying, "Her name is Babrea`."

When Devant gave him an ugly blank stare, Protecus quickly explained, "It's her name, and it means a brilliant ray of light."

Devant didn't care and said as much, "Call it anything you like but get it out of my sight."

Miranda arrived at that moment and retrieved the baby from Protecus's arms.

"Get that thing clean, Miranda, Devant barked. It stinks, and find something for it to wear besides those dirty old rags."

Then she turned to Protecus and reminded him, "I'm still hungry, and that plate of venison you promised me isn't going to cook itself. Hurry up and fetch it, then bring it upstairs."

After that, she proceeded up the stairs to her bedroom. As she flounced upstairs, she shouted back down at Protecus. "You better bring my milk and food before you feed any of those other vagrants squatting on my property!"

Protecus nodded his head, but he was perplexed. Miranda was taking Babrea to bathe her when he left earlier that morning. It was now several hours later, but all of the events from the morning seemed to be repeating themselves. With Devant acting like she was seeing the baby for the first time and not knowing about the broken gates, Protecus was perplexed. It was all so bizarre.

Miranda, too, was acting strangely. She said, "Come with me, you pretty little thing. I'll bath you because it will help you sleep, but you don't stink at all,"

It was as though she was also seeing the baby for the first time. She tickled Babrea` under the chin, and the baby giggled as Miranda walked away. "After your bath, I'll find you something soft and warm to wear from the old trunk in the attic. Although the blanket you're wrapped in is made of the prettiest material that I've ever seen, and most unusual. If it's all right by you, Protecus, I want to make Babrea something to wear from this gorgeous fabric. And if any material is left over, maybe make something for Solarian too."

Protecus was still pondering over the day's events and nodded in approval. There was most definitely some strange time delay or something going on today that he, as a scientist, couldn't quite comprehend. He decided that, for the time being, he would keep quiet about everything. He figured it probably had something to do with Babrea, so it would be best to keep it to himself for now.

Another very peculiar fact was that Devant thought the baby was wearing rags and she was dirty. At the same time, Miranda saw her as clean, the same way Protecus saw her. She had even commented about the cloth wrapped around her as being pretty and unique. Protecus decided there were too many strange and unexplainable events happening today, but he would leave everything be for now. Considering everything that had happened, finding a baby, he had no way to feed and then happening upon a milk cow. Then, meeting a live dragon that spoke to him and even called him by name.

Protecus felt very lucky just being alive. As he pondered over the day's events, with all things considered, the day had turned out pretty good. He had managed not to be eaten and was lucky enough to have a large amount of meat literally delivered to his doorstep. It was enough to feed all of the residents in his care. Yep, things had turned out pretty good.

Protecus and Devant never had children, and they never would. They had never consummated their marriage because Devant believed that sex was a dirty and unnecessary act. She had no intention of getting pregnant and hated the thought of having children. She hated them and never wanted any. After that initial argument, they never discussed sex or children again. Not having sex with Devant was okay with Protecus. He didn't find her desirable in any fashion. He had never understood why he married her in the first place, but that would remain another unanswered question.

He had missed the sound of tiny feet running around the house, though. Children were curious little things and always so full of life. He was amazed at their constant questioning of everything. The only time they were usually quiet was when they were asleep.

Protecus had grown up with two brothers, but after leaving the project, he returned to the family farm to find them both dead. Seeing the family farm ransacked and losing his brothers was difficult enough, but learning his parents were deceased was too much. That meant he now had no living relatives in the world.

He missed his brothers dearly, and now, with no family except Devant, he felt entirely alone. When his brothers were small, he recalled how they always questioned everything, asking why, at least ten times a day. Protecus smiled as he remembered those days.

His reverie was shattered, however, when Devant stepped back downstairs again and began to shriek in her usual manner, "Protecus, why are you still here? I told you I'm hungry. Go and get me something to eat. Now! I've been waiting for my food and milk, and there you are, still in the same place I left you in and as stiff as a tree. Go and get my food!"

With that, she stomped back upstairs, muttering under her breath that he had better hurry up or she would have to take care of it herself.

Protecus knew well what she meant by that as memories of his horse crossed his mind. Devant was hungry then too, and she didn't hesitate to take care of it herself, as she had put it. He figured he'd best hurry and do as she had commanded. She was steadily becoming harder and harder to deal with as time passed. In retrospect, he guessed it was a good thing they never had children. He knew that she would not have been a very nurturing mother. Protecus felt confident, leaving Babrea in Miranda's care. He knew Babrea would be safe as long as she was with Miranda. She was very good with children.

As Protecus made his way out to the barn, he remembered the harsh words Devant said to him on the day she killed his horse. She had brushed his loss off by flippantly saying, "Oh well, that stupid animal was a gift from me in the first place. So, actually, it was half mine anyway, which meant that I could do whatever I wanted to with it. We're married now, you know. So, whatever is yours is mine too. Besides, if you weren't so busy caring for those vagrants that you've let move in here, you would've realized that we didn't have anything to eat, and I refuse to go hungry."

It was best not to dwell on the past because there was no way to go back and change things, anyway. But, if he could, he certainly would.

It was dark as Protecus made his way to the barn, but along the pathway, Solarian ran headlong into him. She quickly excused herself, saying, "Oh, I'm so sorry, Mr. Protecus," and off she flew again. She was obviously in a big hurry.

Solarian had just heard the news about the new baby and wanted to see it. She hoped that her mother would let her help bathe and dress it.

Protecus could hear her as she flew into the kitchen doorway. "Mother, please, please let me help with the baby." She begged.

Miranda had just finished preparing the bathwater for the baby. While attempting to keep Solarian quiet, she said, "Okay, you can help me bathe the baby, but you must calm down. Don't be so noisy."

Miranda knew if Devant were disturbed, she would be upset, so she tried to calm her daughter. Miranda would do anything to protect her.

Miranda remembered all too well when they evacuated from the city. Everything was utter chaos. Death and dying were everywhere, while multiple fires burned out of control all around them. She had to leave her two sons under a pile of rocks. There was no time for a proper burial. It had been three years since that awful day, but Miranda remembered it like it was yesterday. She didn't talk much about it, but Protecus could tell she still grieved her losses.

Protecus sometimes saw Miranda sitting by the window, aimlessly staring into space. He would see her cry over seemingly nothing but never questioned her. Protecus would smile and nod his head, then quietly walk away. Miranda understood that if she needed to talk about it, she was confident he would be there for her if the day ever came. Protecus felt perhaps Miranda and Babrea might genuinely be good for one another.

Miranda was a mother in need of someone to love, and Babrea needed a mother to love her.

Protecus looked into the night sky and knew he was wasting time. He must attend to his chores and get Devant's food. He grabbed a lantern from the barn wall, which he only used for emergencies. Oil was precious and getting harder to find. He located a small stool to sit on while he milked the cow. She stood still for him when he sat down, which was a good sign. He felt that fate, destiny, or possibly a little bit of both, had stepped in and brought this healthy bovine to him. He was sure everything that happened that day was in some way connected.

Protecus decided he wouldn't question fate and accept this much-needed gift. Once he finished milking the cow, Protecus put away the stool. He grabbed the lantern in one hand and the milk bucket in the other and headed toward the pit. As he neared the fire pit, he could hear the two young men talking. Tanus was begging his brother to please not move anymore.

"Seth, I'm tired of moving from place to place all the time. Please ask Mr. Protecus if we can live here. I like this place, and I want to stay. I feel safe here."

Hearing Tanus say that tore at Protecus's heart. He knew how Devant felt about inviting more people to live at the Manor. He feared she would reject the idea of them staying at the Estate. He had to try to convince her to let them stay.

Protecus greeted the boys as he approached. The three of them finished cooking the meat on the pit together. Protecus enjoyed having other male companions around to talk to, especially anyone under the age of eighty.

Once the venison was ready to eat, the pleasant aroma permeated through the air. Many residents came out of their crude little houses, curious to know where the wonderful smells were coming from. Everyone under Protecus's care was either too old or physically unable to hunt for themselves. Protecus tried to provide for them, but that was usually only once a day. They were thankful for anything they received. The residents at Greystone that had drifted into Protecus's care through the years had not been allowed to live inside the main dwelling, Devant's Castle, as she called it.

Devant let everyone know that the Castle was hers and hers alone. The only people she allowed to live inside were Miranda and Solarian, even though there was plenty of room. Devant had declared to Protecus on the day the first survivors arrived, "None of those dirty old people are to set foot inside my Castle."

All of the arrivals had managed to stay away from Devant. They had managed to create some semblance of a domicile within the safety of the Manor walls.

Protecus was beginning to hear the people as they wandered toward his direction. They were mumbling to one another as they crept toward the fire pit. Protecus called them, “Come on out and join in the feast our guests have brought us.”

While Protecus prepared Devants fare, he pointed to two of the little cottages that were the farthest away. He then asked Tanus, “If you don’t mind, would you take a plate of meat and some water to those two cottages. The first is Mr. Hardy’s hut, and the other belongs to Father Samuel. Neither one of them can walk very well.”

Tanus looked in the direction that Protecus was pointing and nodded that he understood. “Sure, Mr. Protecus, I’ll take both of them a plate and water.”

Protecus explained to Seth, “Make certain that as soon as the sun rises in the morning, you come to the main house and meet my wife, Devant. She will be the one that decides if the two of you can stay or have to leave.”

Then Protecus grabbed the lantern once more while precariously balancing the plate of meat and the bucket of milk. He then proceeded toward the main house. On his way, he looked back and saw more residents coming out to meet the newcomers and partake of the abundant feast. He was pleased that for at least one more day, they would all be able to have something to eat. Protecus didn’t know what the next day would bring or if they would even have another day. Making the best of what they had was all they could hope for, at least for now.

Protecus could only hope that Devant would be pleased with the food he prepared for her and the fresh milk they hadn’t enjoyed for several years.

After reaching the main house, he went upstairs to deliver Devant her meal. Devante ate greedily and, surprisingly, appeared to be satisfied with her food for a change and began to eat greedily. While she ate, she began to question Protecus about the cow.

"It's odd to me that you've never been able to find any big game around here before, and these newcomers suddenly appear with some out of the blue. You usually only bring home berries and rotten roots. I can't remember the last time you killed a squirrel or rabbit for us. So, explain to me how in the world you managed to find a living, breathing milk cow?"

Devant knew many predators lurked beyond the stone walls, especially at night, even though she never ventured outside. She couldn't figure out how a passive milk cow had avoided being eaten and somehow survived on the barren ground outside. She wanted to know how Protecus just happened upon it at the very point when he needed it the most.

Protecus had no answers, at least no good ones for her. He wasn't sure how it had all come about himself but told Devant what he thought made the most sense.

"She was roaming around near the road, and I decided to catch her since no one was nearby. I remembered how much you missed having milk, so I slipped a rope around her neck and brought her home."

That was a feeble explanation, and Devant didn't believe a word of it, but for now, she would let it go. She continued her questioning in another line.

"Where did you find those two young men you said killed the deer? Do you honestly expect me to believe they, too, just happened to be wandering around beside the road, like the cow?"

"I didn't find them, Devant. When I came back from foraging, they were here. They were both standing outside the wall. When I saw the venison, I quickly decided to make a deal with them because I knew how much you loved meat. Both of them are strong and willing to help me repair the gates so I can better protect the Manor. They will be an asset here because they are bright, young, and willing to work. I need help around here, not only to repair the gates but also to help defend our home. If something happened to me, you would need protection too."

Devant thought about what Protecus said and realized he had made a valid point. Her safety was the most important thing, after all. She always scolded him anytime a new face showed up at the Manor. For once, what he was saying made sense. She decided to meet the two young men, then determine if they could stay.

"You make certain that both of them come to my Castle first thing in the morning to meet me. I'll be the one to decide if they will be a valuable asset to this place."

"Yes, dear, I'll bring them to meet you at sunrise in the morning," Protecus said, and then he hurriedly excused himself to check on the baby.

Miranda and Solarian were in the kitchen playing with Babrea when Protecus returned downstairs. Babrea was bathed and giggling.

Miranda asked Protecus, "Do you think it would be all right if the baby slept in our room tonight? Solarian wants to share her bed with the baby. Of course, I will be there right beside them, and I'll watch over her carefully. Solarian won't stop begging me to let her help with the baby."

That was an excellent idea. Protecus hadn't considered the sleeping arrangements for Babrea. He had feared she might cry during the night if he put her in their room, and he knew that would upset Devant. Then he would have her peering down his neck and angry all night. He knew Miranda would see to all the baby's needs and ensure that nothing happened to her, so he readily agreed with her suggestion.

Protecus told Solarian, "If she cries during the night, be sure to let your Mom know, so she can help you take care of her."

"Oh, I know all about babies, Mr. Protecus," Solarian said confidently. "I'll let Mom know if I need anything, I promise. Babrea is going to be just fine, and I'm going to love her like a sister. I think she loves me too. I can tell."

Protecus laughed. Solarian was so full of life. She could always make him smile with her quick wit and bravery. Her innocence made her fearless and capable of facing whatever challenge came her way.

Babrea giggled again, and Protecus said, "You know what, Solarian, I think you might be right."

Protecus had sat the bucket of milk on the kitchen table when he went upstairs with Devant's plate, and now he watched as Miranda prepared a makeshift bottle for Babrea. Once she had fashioned the bottle, she sat down with the baby in her arms and began to feed her. Babrea greedily drank, and Protecus was relieved. He was glad Miranda was there. She was a lifesaver.

"Thank you again, Miranda. I don't know what I would have done without you. I know nothing about babies and still don't understand why this one was entrusted to my care. Hopefully, one day soon, I'll understand."

Miranda curiously tilted her head and wanted to ask Protecus what he meant by that odd statement. She was also curious about Babrea and her mysterious appearance but held her questions for the present. She figured that Protecus would explain in due time.

Protecus smiled, saying, "If you need more milk, just let me know. I'll put what's left down in the root cellar."

Then he smiled, grabbed the bucket with the remaining milk inside, then politely excused himself.

It was pretty chilly in the root cellar, especially at night, and there was a large wooden barrel down there where the milk would keep well. Protecus placed the bucket with the milk inside the barrel, then replaced the lid and secured it. He felt confident it would be fine there until morning.

He thought about Babrea as he climbed out of the cellar. She was, indeed, an amazing child. It was still hard for him to believe the day's events.

Babrea was only a baby, yet knowing what oddities had transpired throughout the day, and thinking about what her destiny was to be, was hard for him to conceive. When he returned to the kitchen, Babrea had already drifted asleep. He lifted her from Miranda's arms and carried her to Solarian's bed, where Solarian was already impatiently waiting for the sleeping infant. Protecus kissed her on the forehead and let out a sigh. He was exhausted from the day's adventures and ready to turn in for the night.

After forcing himself to climb the stairs, he grudgingly crawled into bed beside his snoring wife and almost immediately drifted off to sleep.

That night Protecus had another dream, but this time it was different. It wasn't the same as the one that had repeated itself. He saw a vibrant garden, and Babrea stood in the middle. She was grown and sitting atop a splendid black horse. There were hundreds of colorful flowers and a multitude of tall trees surrounding her. The sky was crystal clear, and the air was fresh and clean. Protecus asked Babrea if they were in heaven, and she only smiled and said, "Father, you are home now, where you will remain forever."

It was such a pleasant dream. Protecus slept peacefully that night for the first time in a long time.

CHAPTER 6
PHASE ONE

As soon as Protecus arose the following morning, he dressed and went to check on the baby. She was sleeping soundly, snuggled close beside Solarian in their little bed. Seeing that she was okay, he went down to the cellar, poured himself a large glass of milk, then went upstairs and sat at the kitchen table to drink it. He reminisced while he drank.

Protecus was getting older and acutely aware that he needed younger blood around Greystone. He knew that time, in general, was running out for everyone. Indeed, everyone and everything still living was quickly entering the end of times.

Having been present from the beginning stages of The Project, Protecus knew what the chemicals he engineered could do. He also knew how dangerous they could be if anything went wrong. What was happening now was the result of everything going wrong.

Since he left before the launch was to take place, he wasn't entirely sure how everything had unfolded. However, it wasn't hard to figure out after piecing together this end result.

He knew that the soldiers at the control center were responsible for directing the rocket launches and controlling the timing mechanisms for releasing the nanorobots.

If the radicals targeted the base station, as they had threatened, it meant there was no way to guide the rockets once launched. They would fly aimlessly and deploy at will. Protecus was uncertain how many had launched or where they finally landed. There was an excellent chance some returned to Earth with their cylinders intact and still hadn't released their cargo.

Protecus knew anyone that survived the initial onslaught was now living on the edge, and their time was limited.

Three days before the scheduled launches, the President of the United States made a public announcement. He had intended to reassure the public, belaying all rumors of terrorist threats. During the national broadcast, he stated. “Safeguards are in place, and all of the necessary precautions have been implemented, so there is nothing to fear.”

He had been lied to.

In actuality, there were no safeguards in place. There was no way to test the nanobots without launching them. Nothing remotely resembling them had ever been created. No rocket had ever been launched before carrying such a chemical. Nor had any chemicals like the nanobots ever been developed.

Once the rockets were launched, the base station was the only mechanism designed to control them. After the saboteurs destroyed the station, all control was lost.

At a specific checkpoint after the launch, the control center was to give the ignition system the signal, which would allow the nanorobots to release into the ozone layer. They were then to dispense their payload at a slow, calculated pace to conjoin with the ozone gases. The chemicals were designed to give new life to the depleting ozone.

Ideally, this would renew Earth's protection against the sun's harmful rays. The ozone layers had become dangerously depleted through many years of degradation, giving definitive evidence this would continue.

With no way to control the release of the nanorobots, there would be no way for the rockets to complete their intended mission. The timing mechanisms on the capsules would have no direction.

Protecus was sure everyone at the base station died instantly because some of the gases would have also been released inside the building. The gases were deadly and never intended for human consumption.

Some of the rockets could possibly have reached the Troposphere. There, they would cause even more devastation. Some rockets probably flew toward the sun from its gravitational pull. The sun's extreme heat would then produce a catalytic reaction, prompting the rockets to explode, releasing their capsules. That action would cause even further, long-lasting disparaging effects. A chain reaction of catastrophic events would result, leaving no one to tell the tale.

Millions would die from the initial fallout, and everyone in the affected areas was doomed. All of Earth's inhabitants still living would soon face exposure to one of the deadliest gases man ever created.

Once the toxic gases became fully airborne, many more individuals would quickly perish. When the gases were introduced to a host, the nanorobots would conjoin with the host and slowly become absorbed into the bloodstream. Then it would begin reproducing itself. For all living things, there would be no escape.

The victim would immediately develop uncontrollable spasmodic shakes. Then, their nervous systems would shut down, causing them to experience difficulty breathing as the soft tissue of their lungs began to dissolve. The internal organs would then slowly start to liquefy. Just before death, festering boils would erupt as the nanorobots slowly began to eat their way from the inside out, leaving only skeletal remains and the hair of the victim behind.

Those only slightly exposed could linger on for a few days, only to suffer the same fate. They agonized from extreme pain as they developed grotesque festering boils until their internal organs ceased functioning.

Death was imminent. This horrible catastrophe would later be called The Great Disaster.

Not only would the Earth and its inhabitants feel the effects of this destructive cycle of events, but the entire universe would also. The natural balance of our world is falling apart, but no one will realize to what extent for many years to come.

Our sunlight was changing almost weekly, and Protecus was concerned. Through his careful monitoring since arriving at Greystone, he was confident in his findings. According to his readings, since The Great Disaster, the daylight hours had steadily decreased, albeit minimally at first, but more pronounced as time progressed. Other changes were becoming more evident, too. Subtle changes at first, but with each passing month, there seemed to be more indication that the temperatures were slowly dropping. Protecus had discerned that Earth would soon lapse into darkness with the current rate of decrease in our sunlight. Our time was running out. Without his scientific instruments to accurately calculate, Protecus could only guess when our days would end. His best measurement was now in years, possibly ten at most. His calculations meant there would not be enough time for Babrea to grow to adulthood.

Protecus had prayed for help, so with Babrea's arrival, he fully believed Adolla's predictions for the future. Had he put too much faith into something that no one would live to see? Would humanity survive this final onslaught?

Had he been a fool to put his faith in a dragon? Thinking about the day Babrea arrived, had he dreamed the entire event? Babrea was real. Protecus was sure of that. He wasn't so sure about the rest of what transpired that day.

Dragons did not exist, at least not live ones anyway, nor could they speak. Protecus desperately wanted to believe that Adolla and her message were real.

Had he only convinced himself that he had spoken to her? Now, he was beginning to wonder about everything that had happened that day.

Had Protecus put too much trust in what she had told him? Had he materialized the entire meeting in his mind? How could he have believed that a child would be the savior of the world?

He shook himself. "Stop," he said out loud. As he thought about it more, Protecus knew that to maintain his sanity, he had to believe.

There seemed to be no other hope for them. If believing in Adolla's words and placing faith in Babrea was what he had to do to go forward, then that was what he would do.

"I believe," he whispered the words. Saying them seemed to give Protecus strength. They fortified him. So, he repeated them, louder this time. "I BELIEVE!"

He then smiled. He would stay firm in his belief that everything would work out as foretold to him. He felt empowered, reaffirming his faith. Babrea was their future. He had to believe in her and what he was told. He stood and went out the door. It was time for Seth and Tanus to meet Devant. Another challenge for Protecus to face.

CHAPTER 7
THE MEETING

When Protecus reached the barn, Seth and Tanus were already awake and ready to meet Devant. She was impatiently waiting for them when they arrived back at the Manor. Devant was sitting on the couch in the living room with a broad smile on her face. She completely shocked Protecus with her overwhelming politeness. She seemed to accept the two young men as if they were part of her family, almost doting over them. Protecus had never seen her so invitingly demure, almost polite. He wasn't aware that she possessed this form of kindness. She had indeed never shown this side of herself toward him. Protecus inwardly smiled as he watched her demonstrate this different side.

"So, Seth," she asked softly, almost cooing, "how old are you?"

Seth politely replied, "I'm seventeen years old, ma'am, and my brother, Tanus, is almost seven. We're happy to meet you and appreciate your letting us stay here. I noticed earlier that several things around here, besides the gates, need fixing. The wall around the main building is crumbling in several places, and there are several broken windows that we could board up for you. That big opening upstairs is hazardous, and I imagine drafty as well. My brother and I can fix that right up for you if you would like."

The only response Devant gave was a forced smile. That odd reaction made Seth fear he had overstepped his boundaries, so he excused himself and his brother.

"Well, it was nice to meet you, ma'am. I guess Tanus and I should get to work now. Those gates won't fix themselves. It will probably take a few days to complete the repairs, but we will work quickly and make everything secure again."

They departed to begin the work they had promised to do. Immediately upon their departure, Devant resumed her hateful manner and pompous stance toward Protecus. He knew her new facade wouldn't last long, and he was right.

"You can go too, husband. I don't need you standing around while I'm sitting here starving. I want some of that milk and a large chunk of venison. Hurry up now and fetch it for me." She ordered.

"On your way, you can tell those two young men that as long as they do repair work around here and help me, anytime I ask, they can stay. But only as long as I'm satisfied with their work."

Protecus smiled while nodding his head that he understood. Then he quickly excused himself. He feared if he gave her more time to think about it, she would change her mind about letting the boys stay. Devant was fickle that way.

Protecus knew that Babrea and Solarian would be waking up soon, and they would both be hungry. So, he went to the cellar to get the milk from the night before. It was still good and cold. Miranda was rousing then, so she took the milk from Protecus, poured it into a different container she retrieved from the cupboard, and returned the bucket to Protecus. He took it and headed out the door. He first walked to the gates where Tanus and Seth were already hard at work and asked Seth, "Would you please go to the smokehouse and get some venison for Devant. Then stop by the kitchen and ask Miranda to give you a glass of milk for her, too. You'll like Miranda. She's a lovely person."

"Sure, Mr. Protecus, no problem." Then Seth put down his tools and headed for the smokehouse. Protecus invited Tanus to join him at the barn to watch him milk the cow while Seth was busy. Tanus had never seen a cow before nor watched anyone while they milked one.

So, he enjoyed watching as Protecus taught him the best technique for milking.

Seth made his way to the kitchen, where he quickly located Miranda. She was still feeding the baby her breakfast. They visited for a while, and then Miranda poured the milk for Devant and politely excused himself. "I guess I better take this food up to Ms. Devant. I don't want her to get upset because I delayed her meal."

Miranda softly chuckled, "You're right. You don't ever want to upset Devant. She can rage quickly, and sometimes, her anger lasts for days."

Seth smiled, and Miranda smiled back. "It was nice to meet you," he said. "I hope we run into each other again."

"Oh, I'm sure we will. I usually do all the cooking around here, even though sometimes I have to get creative to stretch whatever I have to cook."

Seth smiled at Miranda's comment. She was like a breath of fresh air, and he enjoyed her sense of humor. He hadn't smiled for a long time. It was hard to relax when everything around you was trying to kill you. Miranda made him feel at ease. He would most definitely make a point to visit with her again.

When Seth delivered Devant's meal, he would have left immediately, but she detained him. She asked him frivolous questions and had him hand her odd things from around her room. When he finally got a word in, he said, "If you don't need anything else, Mrs. Devant, I'll get back to repairing the gates."

Devant agreed, "Yes, we need those gates fixed." Then she brushed him away as if he were a fly.

Once Seth left, Devant quickly finished her food, and when she heard Protecus coming into the house, she began yelling for him. He had just returned from milking the cow, and upon hearing Devant yelling for him, he climbed the stairs. Devant immediately started to bark orders at him.

"You need to make sure those boys understand that they are to do whatever I need them to do, and what I need must always come first, especially that older boy, Seth.

"I've already spoken to them, Devant, and they understand the rules. As soon as the gates are up again, I'm sure they will both have more time to do whatever task you have for them."

Protecus slowly eased out of Devant's earshot. The day was already drawing to an end, and the light was fading fast now. The colder winds were beginning to blow in, so Protecus sought to check on the boys. They were still diligently working on gate repairs, trying hard to finish before nightfall. But Protecus knew the light would be fading fast now, so he pitched in to help them finish the job.

Having the gates back in place was the only sure way of securing the courtyard, which was very important for the safety of the residents. The entire wall was in dire need of repair, but at least having the gates back in place meant a much better means of protection.

Once the gates were secure, Protecus stepped back and smiled as he surveyed the work done on the gates, "You two did a fine job on those old rusty gates. I'm sure we will all feel much safer knowing those iron gates are back up and protecting us again. Thank you both for finishing the job so quickly. The sun will be setting soon, so grab your tools and put them away for the night. Miranda has some venison waiting for you. Go to the kitchen and eat, then get a good night's sleep because we must start fortifying the wall tomorrow. It is in much need of repair."

Seth smiled. He was glad that Protecus approved of their work so far. It meant a lot to him that Protecus was pleased.

Protecus told Seth, "Devant has approved you and your brother staying here as long as you earn your keep.

Try to stay out of her way unless she asks you to do something for her.

You'll have to continue sleeping in the barn, though, because she won't allow anyone else to live in the main house."

Seth nodded that he understood and would abide by Devant's rules. Tanus was thrilled that they could stay. He was bone-weary from moving and glad they had finally found a place they could call home. Tanus hugged Protecus. The young man's emotions moved the older man. It almost brought tears to his eyes.

Protecus hugged Tanus, saying, "I'm happy to have you both here. I think your joining our group will be beneficial to everyone."

Protecus told the boys goodnight. Then returned to the barn to feed the animals the last of the protein pills he had developed as a substitute for the lack of grain. Finding a good food source for the animals had been difficult until recently. Lately, greenery had started to sprout inside the courtyard, something that hadn't happened since Protecus arrived at the Manor. He planted some vegetable seedlings to see if they would take root, and they sprouted like wildfire. After that, he planted even more vegetation in the courtyard grounds, which also reproduced. However, the topsoil outside the stone wall continued to worsen with time. The miraculous changes in the soil seemed to have only happened after Babrea's arrival.

In the past, the only food Protecus could provide was what he could grow in his hydroponics gardens. He had run out of the herbs needed to concoct his protein stimulator for the livestock many weeks earlier. With the changes in the soil in the courtyard, he was now able to grow the necessary herb. The only thing he could attribute this unexpected change to was the arrival of Babrea.

Protecus was glad for the improvements in the soil, but he feared it would be short-lived. Outside the walls, the weather continued to disintegrate. Protecus prayed the changes that Adolla had told him about would arrive soon.

As the days turned to weeks, the two young men became more of a welcome sight around the place. Each day, both boys would go out early in the morning to hunt for food. They always brought back some fare. The residents were becoming quite fond of the newcomers rather quickly.

During the afternoon, Seth and Tanus worked diligently on the stone wall surrounding the Manor. They piled more rocks on top of the existing ones making the wall taller and more substantial. They filled in the broken or missing areas, fortifying it even further. They worked every day until the light faded and darkness descended. After dark, they busied themselves fixing odd, broken things around the Manor. They were always at Devant's beck-and-call and attended to her many demands without hesitation.

The boys were excellent hunters, which relieved Protecus of his foraging responsibilities. He had never been very good at it anyway. Protecus helped Seth preserve the excess meat they killed, so the smokehouse now stayed full all the time.

Once the boys finished the wall, Protecus hoped Devant wouldn't say they had to leave. He liked both of them and wanted them to stay. They had come to know Greystone as their home, and Protecus enjoyed having them there.

Thankfully, Devant seemed to enjoy having them around too. It was apparent that she liked having her every whim catered to daily. She was a fickle person, though.

Protecus didn't want to take any chances, so he decided to do his part to delay their leaving in any way possible. He found more broken things for the boys to repair.

Devant appeared to enjoy having Seth around. She liked having him do her bidding instead of her husband, which was fine by Protecus. Any time away from Devant was good, and he enjoyed every second.

Protecus wasn't sure, but it seemed she was purposefully breaking things so she could call upon Seth to repair them. Protecus chuckled when he noticed her doing this because she was obviously flirting. It was laughable.

Having the boys around to care for Devant's needs freed up time for Protecus to do other things. He had been able to devote more of his energy to working in his laboratory and hydroponics gardens. As time passed, the Manor and the surrounding grounds began to shape up and become a better haven for the extended family. The smokehouse was full, and so was everyone's belly. Babrea was growing and becoming more attached to Miranda and Solarian.

Protecus was finding Tanus more and more in his company. Any odd moment Tanus could find free, he loved joining Protecus in his lab. If Protecus started a new project that Tanus had not seen before, he would quiz him about it. He was like a sponge. He loved learning and quickly absorbed everything that came his way. Protecus enjoyed the question-and-answer sessions between the two of them. He couldn't help but love the boy like a son.

Having more free time allowed Protecus to reminisce about when he first arrived at Greystone. He recalled how run down the old place was, which appeared deserted. It also appeared vacant.

The gates at the entrance were closed, and a sizable bold sign hung above them proudly displaying the name Greystone Manor. Protecus entered the grounds cautiously. After further inspection of the property,

Protecus discovered it was indeed abandoned. He felt this place would work for him and his needs. It was off the beaten track, and the high walls also afforded some protection.

Protecus had just moved into the Manor when Devant's arrived at the front gates. He remembered that day all too well. She rode up on a large wagon with a beautiful black horse pulling it. Walking behind the wagon was Miranda, who Devant quickly said was her maid, and standing alongside Miranda, was Solarian. A priest sat on the wagon's front seat beside Devant, and two other young men were walking behind the wagon.

Protecus's attention was immediately drawn to the horse pulling the wagon. It was a mare, and she was solid black. She reminded him of his horse, Lady, he rode as a small child.

Protecus grew up on a farm with his family, and they had many animals. His favorite was his horse. Protecus's father had given the mare to him for his sixth birthday. She was pitch black and as shiny as a silver dollar. He was so proud of her. She had lived for over thirty years, and when she died, Protecus mourned her death and missed her still.

While Protecus was eying the beautiful mare, he only half heard what Devant was saying to him. She explained that she and her group were tired, thirsty, and needed a place to rest. She told him that her wagon contained several unique things that she required. While Devant explained everything to Protecus, she discreetly directed the two men with her to open the gates. Even though Protecus had not yet given his permission for them to come inside, Devant and her group ceremoniously entered.

Protecus was unaware, but at that instant, a precedent was taking place regarding how things would be from that point forward. As far as Devant was concerned, whatever Devant wanted, Devant got.

Devant quickly noticed Protecus' admiration for her horse and took advantage of that fact.

"If you allow us to stay here, I'll give you the horse. I have no further need of the animal. You can have her as a gift if you let us stay the night."

Protecus agreed to that deal. However, Devant's one-night stay became two, and two turned into far too many.

Protecus was pleased with getting the mare. He named her Lady in memory of his childhood horse. Although, before Protecus knew what was happening, Devant had moved in, and the priest had the two of them married.

Along with her came a vast collection of unusual items, which seemed endless as she began to move everything into the Manor.

Shortly after their marriage, the two men that had accompanied her on that first day had mysteriously disappeared. Protecus had never untangled that mystery. Until this day, he still had not discovered what had happened to them. They had just vanished without a trace.

It seemed that time for Protecus, after Devant's arrival, almost stood still, as he didn't remember much else from those earlier days.

As best Protecus could recall, he no longer existed after Devant entered his life because everything revolved around her and her needs.

CHAPTER 8
BONDING

It had now been seven years since The Great Disaster. Seth and Tanus had been at the Manor for about five years now. The boys were happy to have found the Manor house. They both admired Protecus, especially Tanus, who would soon turn ten. He looked up to the older man immensely and felt close to Protecus. He thought of him as one would their own father.

Tanus was barely four when he lost both parents to The Great Disaster. He couldn't remember them very well because he was too young. Seth had used the skills his father had taught him to get him and his brother out of the city. Seth had managed to provide for them for almost two years on their own, although it had been tough. Since stumbling upon the Manor and meeting Protecus, he had been relieved of a lot of stress. Having a place they could call home and feel safe lifted a considerable burden off Seth's shoulders. Tanus was happy and thriving now that he had a stable environment with Protecus.

Tanus had never learned to read or write. He never had the opportunity to attend school, and Seth had never thought to teach him. The two of them had been far too busy struggling to survive. Seth was pleased his brother spent all his spare time with Protecus. It was evident that Tanus loved being alongside him while he worked in his laboratory. Seeing the two of them bonding prompted Seth to let Protecus know that his brother had never learned to read or write. That fact had escaped Protecus too. Once Seth had made him aware of it, Protecus felt he had neglected Tanus too. It should have been evident due to his age when he arrived at the Manor. Protecus decided to amend his mistake. He told Seth, "I'm sorry. I should have known. Would it be okay if I teach him?"

Seth had a great deal of respect for Protecus and knew that Tanus could learn much from him. Protecus was wise, well-read, and patient, as well. "I would be thrilled for you to teach him. I think he will learn faster from you than me anyway. He respects you."

Once Protecus began teaching Tanus, it was apparent he was enjoying learning. Protecus told him stories of the world and how things were before everything fell apart. Tanus was fascinated to hear about the wondrous bridges and tall shiny buildings that once stood so impressively. He could sit for hours and listen to Protecus describe the plush green grass and splendidly tall and graceful trees that had once billowed and swayed in the soft breezes. Tanus was too young to remember anything from before the day of The Great Disaster. Thankfully, that day had somehow become erased from his memory, which was a blessing in disguise.

Protecus had many books, some with pictures showing the wondrous things he spoke. Tanus would sit for hours and look through them. He had no memory of trees or flowers but loved looking at all the beautiful colors.

Protecus enjoyed spending time with Tanus because of his inquisitive mind. It pleased Seth to see his brother happy again. He hadn't seen him smile in a very long time. It was good that Tanus was forming a bond with Protecus because he was very impressionable at this point in his life.

Most reading materials had either been destroyed or burned for firewood after The Great Disaster. Books of any kind were hard to find, especially educational books. Having been a scientist, Protecus knew the importance of preserving knowledge, so he made a consorted effort to save as many of his books as possible. Luckily, he had managed to protect his precious science books while evacuating. Protecus was glad he had taken the risk involved because he could now use those books to teach Tanus reading and writing skills.

Most repair work needed at the Manor was taken care of. Tanus could now spend his time learning. Seth could handle any remaining repairs that were required alone. He could also go hunting alone because their smokehouse was now full.

Protecus was at a loss for how Seth could quickly find big game. He had personally never been that fortunate at hunting. He always experienced difficulty in finding anything to eat. Even berries were sparse. He had only seen a few rabbits and an odd squirrel a time or two, but nothing more substantial. Of course, Seth was much younger and had excellent eyesight, unlike Protecus.

Though Seth had never mentioned it to Protecus, he, too, was amazed at how simple hunting was in this area. Everywhere he and Tanus had traveled before, hunting was difficult. There were very few small animals and next to none of the larger ones. Finding deer while hunting became almost impossible. However, in this particular area, livestock was bountiful. Until arriving at the Manor, he and Tanus had survived mainly on rabbits and squirrels when they could find them. Occasionally, they would stumble upon a grocery store that hadn't been completely ransacked. They would confiscate anything left that was edible.

Seth had taught Tanus how to hunt and scavenge at a very early age, but game was sparse. The nice buck Seth killed the day of their arrival had been bagged just outside the stone wall here at the Manor. That magnificent creature appeared to be waiting for them. Since arriving at the Manor, multiple types of wild game seemed to almost jump out onto the trail before them. All wildlife appeared to be more abundant in this area. It felt like the animals knew they were hunting for them and waited to be caught. Seth was proud that he could provide food for not only his brother and himself but all of the other lost folks in Protecus's care. It gave him a feeling of self-worth again and made him feel he was doing his part in this most challenging time.

CHAPTER 9
MEMORIES

Tanus didn't remember much from those early days, just after the world fell apart. But Seth did. His memories of that terrible day would stay with him for the rest of his life. He remembered well the deafening initial explosions that left him unable to hear for several minutes. Smoke filled the air, and it was so thick that it enveloped everything and everyone for days.

The President declared the day of the launch a national holiday. That Monday morning, there was to be no school for Seth and no work for his dad. The event was to be televised, and the national government wanted everyone to be able to view them.

Seth's mother, Laurel, had decided to make them a special breakfast. Her husband, Paul, loved omelets, and so did the boys, so that is what she prepared for them that morning. Once she had everything ready, Seth's mother called them to the table to eat. They all gathered around the breakfast table to enjoy a leisurely breakfast. Seth recalled the sun was shining brightly through their breakfast room window that morning. His dad brought a small television into the breakfast room for them to watch the launch while they ate. Tanus had climbed into his playpen to play with his toys. His mother kept them in there to keep the floor organized. Tanus was too old for the playpen but loved climbing into it to play with his toys. He would put a blanket across the top of his playpen and pretend it was a fort. Many times, while playing, he would fall asleep there.

Seth quickly gobbled up his omelet because it was his favorite food. His mother noticed how fast he finished his plate and commented, "Oh my, aren't you the hungry one this morning! That's good, son. Would you like another omelet?

"Sure thing, Mom, I love omelets."

Laurel returned to the kitchen to make Seth a second omelet, and on her way to the kitchen, she checked on Tanus. He had played himself down and was fast asleep on the playpen floor. Knowing Tanus was content, she smiled, rounded the corner, and vanished behind the kitchen wall. The instant she disappeared behind the wall, the entire world felt like it had ceased rotating. It felt as though the whole house shook.

Seth remembered feeling that everything was moving in slow motion. He recalled hearing a deafeningly loud whistling sound, followed by a horrific explosion. For several seconds following that explosion, Seth couldn't hear anything except a loud ringing sound in his ears. He couldn't see anything because there was thick smoke everywhere. Seth tried to move but was unable because something weighty was on top of him. He immediately began yelling out for his Mom and dad but received no response. He pushed against the object that was pinning him down and was finally able to get free. Seth then began searching frantically for his parents. He found his father buried underneath several pieces of broken lumber and shattered glass. Seth called his name but received no response. He desperately tried to free his father but could only remove a small section of the rubble. Paul was unable to move and barely able to breathe. When he was finally able to speak, he was scarcely audible.

Paul told his son, "Don't move anything." He could see a sizeable broken section of the ceiling precariously dangling just above him. He could tell that it was ready to fall at any moment. Paul knew that if Seth moved anything else, he would dislodge the wreckage, causing it to fall on top of both of them.

Paul felt intense pain in his chest area. He could see multiple shards of wood protruding from his chest and realized there was no way Seth was going to be able to save him. Paul's lungs were punctured, and he knew he was bleeding internally. Paul was dying.

With his last breath, Paul instructed his son, "Go find your little brother and mother and get them out of this house. It's going to collapse soon. Once you're outside, you can call for emergency help for me."

Seth hesitated to leave his father's side but did as he was instructed. He quickly found his mother. After pulling her into his arms, she softly uttered, "Son, you must be brave now. Go and find your little brother and take care of him. I love you both more than anything in the world." Then she closed her eyes and was gone forever.

Seth held his mother's lifeless body in his arms for several minutes. He was unsure how long he sat on the floor with tears streaming down his face when more deafening explosions resounded nearby. That sound immediately shook Seth and prompted him to move. He lay his mother's lifeless body down, then crawled back to his father's side.

When he was finally able to dig his way back to his father, Seth grabbed his dad's hand and instantly knew he was gone. He didn't know how much time had elapsed while holding his father's hand when he began to hear his little brother crying. Seth inched through the rubble surrounding the area where the crying was coming from until he finally spotted the playpen. Seth knew his brother, Tanus, was in the playpen when the explosions began. It was half-buried and partially crushed from the weight, but it had somehow managed to save his brother's life. After digging it out from under the rubble, he pulled Tanus out. He was terrified, wet, and dirty but physically appeared alright. Seth wrapped his arms tightly around his baby brother, attempting to comfort him. He sat in the middle of the rubble and rocked Tanus until he stopped crying. As Seth consoled

Tanus, he began to hear a loud siren. He realized it was the city alert, warning all residents of impending danger.

Once the reality of their situation finally struck him, Seth realized that they were in danger and all alone in the world. He stood up, still holding Tanus in his arms, and walked to a gaping hole in the wall of their home that had once been a large picture window. Broken glass lay everywhere.

As Seth looked out at their neighborhood where he had lived all his life, he was horrified at what he saw. As far as he could see, nothing had been left untouched by the devastation. Fires were burning everywhere. To Seth, it looked as though the entire world was ablaze. He felt like he was in the middle of a horrible nightmare and unable to wake up.

Tanus began to whimper and complain of being hungry, which jolted Seth from his lethargic state. He slowly made his way to the kitchen. Then cautiously worked his way through the broken glass and shattered boards of what remained of the family dining area. Only a short while earlier, he and his family had been enjoying a meal in that room, and everything had been normal.

Seth tried to decide what to do next when he heard people screaming outside. He knew he must get them out of their crumbling home and away from the city as soon as possible. Tanus was still whimpering, so Seth knew he had to act. He began to look through the rubble for his camping equipment. There was a backpack with a small tent inside that his mother always stored in the kitchen pantry. After locating it, Seth sat Tanus down to retrieve it, and then he dug for some food for his brother, along with all of the bottled water he could stuff inside the backpack. Seth tried hard to remember everything his father had taught him about survival. His father had taught him to hunt and fish, as well as how to build a fire and set up a camp. Seth remembered where his father's gun was, so he picked his brother up and maneuvered his way to his parent's bedroom to retrieve it and the shells for it. Seth then carried Tanus into his bedroom and located the hunting knife he had received from his father for his birthday the year before. Seth then rummaged through the rubble until he found his fishing equipment and his bow and arrows buried under a large pile of debris in his bedroom.

Seth then bundled his baby brother in warmer clothing and worked his way out of the remnants of their home. After exiting outside, Seth continued walking forward in a trance. He hadn't noticed, but their house had now begun to burn. Their entire neighborhood had started to burn as well. Seth slowly maneuvered down the street until he cleared the burning buildings. Then, he put his brother down, grabbed his little hand, and led Tanus away from the devastation.

Seth didn't know where they were going but knew they had to escape the city as quickly as possible. He was young to have to take on the responsibility of a child, but they had no other family members. There was no one that he could turn to, but he knew he had to get them someplace safe.

Seth couldn't remember much else of those early days except walking for what seemed like forever and being afraid to stop in any one place for too long. He remembered hiding if they heard gunshots because there were lots of looters. Seth had witnessed people being killed for something as menial as a piece of bread.

Tanus was a bright child, so he quickly learned how to survive with his brother's coaching. Seth taught Tanus all he knew about hunting and fishing like his father had taught him.

Seth soon found out, however, that he was not as wise as he needed to be, and if he and Tanus were going to survive, they both had to learn very quickly.

CHAPTER 10
TIME PASSAGE

Once Protecus began teaching Tanus to read and write, Miranda took notice. She realized that Solarian needed that training as well. Miranda had been remiss in Solarian's education, but Protecus could help rectify that situation.

Miranda hadn't finished high school, so she knew she didn't have the skills required to teach Solarian, but Protecus did. Miranda decided to ask him if it would be alright for Solarian, now nine, to attend his instruction classes. Protecus agreed that Solarian should join them and Babrea as well.

Babrea was five years old now and eager to learn about everything. She absorbed knowledge quickly and loved being with the other children. She would jump at any opportunity she had to be near them. Protecus was impressed with her ability to learn and anxious to teach her. Babrea was very enthusiastic about learning. It seemed the more she learned, the more she wanted to know. She adored Protecus and loved being with him. She followed him everywhere. Soon she was in his every footstep and no longer tagging after Solarian and Tanus. She questioned all things and always seemed to remember what he told her. It was fascinating how quickly her grasp of knowledge grew. She hungered for it.

As time passed, Babrea was thriving, and their home was getting a much-needed facelift. There was plenty of food to eat, and everyone was happier except Devant. The more comfortable and pleasant her surroundings seemed, the more unpleasant she became. Protecus knew this was the calm before the storm, and storm Devant was about to drop her furor.

Protecus had many things on his mind, but worrying over Devant's happiness was the least of his worries. The sunlight had continued to fade, and temperatures were steadily dropping. The daylight hours had now dwindled to about ten per day.

Seth had to curtail his hunting trips with the days shortening and temperatures dropping. Shorter hunting trips meant less meat, so their well-stocked smokehouse would suffer soon. Protecus had a few of his growth chemicals left, but they, too, were beginning to play out. With his precious supply dwindling, he worried that he would no longer be able to grow the vegetables needed to feed the Manor residents. His herbs needed to concoct his unique growth hormone would no longer grow in the courtyard, and the artificial sunlight in the lab was insufficient for them to thrive. Once the chemical mixture was gone, Protecus couldn't make more.

These were just a few of the worries that troubled Protecus. He had kept this information to himself because he knew there was nothing anyone could do to change them. The diminished sunlight would be the same all over the world. Protecus knew their time left on earth was running out.

Protecus must remind Seth to hunt only during the lightest part of the day for his safety.

"Seth, be sure to return home before sunset. You need to limit your hunting area to a radius no further than an hour's walk from the Manor from now on."

Seth didn't understand why Protecus advised him to limit his hunting, especially with them now in greater need of food than before. Seth wanted to question the reasoning behind Protecus's request but deferred to the older man's request as instructed.

Protecus didn't mean to frighten Seth, but it was vital that he did not venture too far from the protection of the high walls. So, he explained, "Lately, there have been more scavengers in our area. They're probably having difficulty finding food, so they're becoming much braver. I believe it's wise of us to be cautious."

Protecus had heard many new animal noises in the late afternoon, moving closer to Greystone after dark. He saw the shadow of an enormous bird pass above him when he was out searching for herbs the night before. Protecus couldn't see well, so he was uncertain what it actually was, but he heard wings flapping. He was sure of that much. The creature seemed to be stalking him, and it was pretty large

Seth had also started to worry about the lessening of the big game around the Manor lately. He kept it to himself but was aware of the increased scavengers around their immediate area.

Seth had started worrying that something might happen to him while on one of his hunting expeditions. He was Tanus's only living relative, so if something happened to him, Tanus would be alone to fend for himself. Seth knew Protecus accepted them as a part of the family there, but Devant was unpredictable. He decided to air his thoughts with Protecus and discuss the matter further.

The following afternoon after another unproductive hunt, Seth told Protecus, "My brother worships you like a father, Protecus, and he looks up to you. Tanus thinks he's all grown up and can care for himself, but you and I know better. I know you love him like a son, but I'm afraid that if anything ever happened to me, Devant would not want to be responsible for him and ask him to leave.

I'd rest much easier knowing that you would see after my brother if anything did happen."

It honored Protecus that Seth trusted him to take care of his brother. "Seth, you know you can count on me. I will protect and care for Tanus as if he were my own. If he needs anything and it's within my power to give it to him, I will see that he gets it. Don't worry about Devant. I would never put her wishes ahead of your brother's safety. Now that it is settled, I want to repeat how important it is for you to be careful on your hunting trips. I don't want you to take any unnecessary chances."

Seth had hesitated to say anything, but after considering it further, he changed his mind. Protecus had so many responsibilities already, and Seth hated worrying him any further but was led to bring it up.

He needed to discuss something else with Protecus and felt that now was as good a time as any.

"Protecus, there is something else that I need to discuss with you. I think it's important because many people live here, and I think they may all be at risk. Today, after I finished hunting and was heading home, a huge shadow passed over me. I looked up, but it was gone. I wouldn't have bothered you with this, but that's the second time I've seen it. The shadow was large, and it made me feel very uncomfortable. I think it was stalking me and may have followed me home today."

Protecus believed it was most likely the same creature he had seen, and Seth was probably right about the creature stalking him. There were other predators skulking in the area that Protecus hadn't seen before, and with Seth reporting seeing the flying creature, Protecus was very concerned.

"There was another incident that happened close to dark when I was on my way home a few days ago. I heard several low-pitched growls. It sounded like three or four different animals were trailing me. I never saw them, only heard them, but they came quite close. I thought they were after the horse, so I pushed him into a gallop and hurried back. They couldn't keep up with me after that, but they weren't that far from here when I outran them."

Protecus explained to Seth, “The lack of game lately has drawn the predators closer to us. We’ll likely see more of them moving into our area as time passes.”

Seth feared that Protecus was right. These new predators had changed their area of hunting. The game was becoming less prevalent further away but still abundant close to home, so it made sense.

Protecus reaffirmed his wishes to Seth, saying, “We still have a good supply of food stored, so don’t take chances on your hunting trips.”

CHAPTER 11
THE CHILDREN

When Protecus woke the following day, his first thought was of the children. What would become of them if something happened to him? Seth had voiced his worries about Tanus, but what if something also happened to Protecus?

He was getting up in age, which was another concern. If he were no longer around, what would happen to the children? It was his responsibility to raise Babrea and tutor her. Devant had never cared for children or anyone else except herself. She definitely couldn't be counted on to be a parent figure. Protecus knew that he could count on Miranda. She would always love and care for both children equally.

Even though Seth was young, he was very wise for his age. Since sharing his fears about the future with Protecus, he now felt led to share with Seth his worries, especially regarding Devant. Protecus thought that it was also wise to include Miranda in the discussion.

Protecus went to find Miranda first thing because he felt they needed to discuss this as soon as possible. Miranda had just prepared breakfast for the children, and they were at the table eating when Protecus found her.

He softly asked her, "Miranda, can you stop outside with me for a few minutes? I have something important to discuss with you?"

"Sure, Protecus, just give me a few minutes." She finished what she was doing and then followed Protecus outside. He was anxious to talk to her, so as soon as Miranda closed the door, he began to tell her what was troubling him.

"Miranda, I need to talk to you about something that I can no longer put off. It's an important matter concerning the children. I'm sure you know about Devant's mood swings and how easily she can rage."

Miranda was surprised at Protecus's statement. He caught her off-guard with his openness. Protecus seldom spoke to Miranda and had never said anything negative about his wife. She nodded in agreement because she was very aware of Devant's temper. Miranda had never said anything before, but since Protecus had brought it up, she felt relieved to discuss it with him.

They both sat down as Protecus continued to explain further. "Devant has never cared for children. In truth, she has never really cared for anyone except herself."

"Well, actually, Protecus, I've known about Devant's true feelings regarding the children for a long time. I've never spoken to you about it before, but since you brought it up, perhaps it's time to let you know how we first met. We were destitute when Devant found Solarian and me in the city. We were out of food and had just drunk the last of our water. I was weak from hunger and afraid I would pass out any minute and leave Solarian alone. Devant appeared out of nowhere, offering to help us, which I accepted because I had to do something to save my daughter. We would have most likely starved or, even worse, had she not saved us, but I felt from the beginning that she had an ulterior motive for helping us. I can't explain it to you. I just had a feeling. When she found us, she had two men with her and ordered them to help us into her wagon. The men gave us food and water and led the horse out of the city. It felt like we were heading here from the onset. She lied to you when she told you I was her maid. I had never met her before. Protecus, please don't misunderstand. I've never regretted being here. I'm glad we found you. You openly accepted us into your home, and I can't thank you enough for that. I have never understood how we ended up here. It was like she knew you were here from the start and purposefully headed straight for you. I don't know what happened to those two men that arrived with us. They seemed to have just disappeared. I needed you to know because I didn't want you to think that I have any loyalty toward Devant. I take care of you and the children because I love all of you, not because Devant commands me to, and I will continue as long as I live. Have no fear of that."

"I appreciate your honesty, Miranda, and I'm glad you shared this information with me. I wondered how Devant stumbled upon this place because it is very secluded. I never could figure out how you two ended up together. Devant is a difficult person to get along with, so I feel blessed to have you and Solarian. She and Babrea are good company for one another. The thing I mainly wanted to discuss with you, though, is something that I have already spoken with Seth about. He knows my concerns, but I wanted you aware as well. I trust both of you and have no hesitation when I say I could easily entrust Babrea's care, and well-being, to the two of you. You both needed to know that I don't trust Devant with the children. She can never be depended upon, especially when it comes to Babrea. I know how much you love her, but if anything should happen to me, you both must assert your will more forcibly upon Devant. That is the only way that you will be able to protect the children. Both of you must ensure that Devant understands you are in charge of the children and she is to have no say in their care. She has always had a mean streak, which I'm glad you're aware of, but Seth has seen her exhibit her spite firsthand. Devant is a bitter woman, almost cruel, and she has shown that side of her on more than one occasion. Seth has assured me that he will support you with any decisions the two of you make regarding the children or their welfare. So, rest easy knowing he has your back."

Miranda was very much aware that when the children were excessively loud while playing, Devant would become livid. Devant frequently expressed anger toward all three children but more actively toward Babrea.

Babrea always trailed after Tanus and Solarian and had done so since she was old enough to walk. Wherever the older children were, that was where you could always find Babrea. They had witnessed Devant's wrath and knew to stay away from her as much as possible. It gave Miranda hope knowing that Protecus knew Devant's sadistic nature.

"You can count on me, Protecus. I will do whatever is necessary to protect the children. It may appear that I don't have a backbone, but I assure you, when it comes to the safety of the children, I can be a tiger." She smiled as she spoke those last words.

Protecus smiled, "I'm glad we had this conversation, Miranda. Worrying over Babrea's future has weighed heavily on my heart for some time now. Especially lately. I love her as if she was my own child, and knowing Seth is willing to step up if necessary will help me to rest easier at night. I can't express how much that means to me. I truly appreciate both of you more than you will ever know."

Miranda smiled and said, "I can't tell you how much it means to me to have your complete trust in me, Protecus, and I promise to carry out your wishes."

"Thanks, Miranda, I truly appreciate that. If Devant gives you an unusual request concerning Babrea to keep the peace, agree with her, then do what you know is best. There is no sense in raising her ire when it isn't necessary. If Devant voices a complaint about anything, let me handle it. Some things are better left alone if you know what I mean."

Miranda nodded in agreement, silently indicating that she understood what he was saying.

Miranda returned to the kitchen to make sure the children had finished their breakfast, and then she sent them out into the courtyard to play.

CHAPTER 12
BUMBLE

Later that day, the three children played hide and seek and scampered all over the courtyard. Tanus could always find Babrea because she was once again talking to herself. It seemed that she did that quite a bit lately, especially lately. Babrea's behavior puzzled Tanus, but he never told anyone. He would merely walk away and leave her alone while continuing to play with Solarian, as that was what Babrea seemed to prefer.

Babrea, however, was not talking to herself. She had a friend that followed her every move. It was a baby dragon. On one of the days when Devant had been exceedingly hateful to Babrea, more so than usual, Babrea wished for someone she could talk to about Protecus's spiteful wife. Devant had always been cold and biting towards Babrea, but on that day in particular, she had severely scolded Babrea after innocently calling Devant mother.

Devant shouted at Babrea, "I'm not your mother, you little brat. You don't have a mother, and you don't have a father, either. Protecus isn't your father. Your family didn't want you, so they deserted you. Nobody wanted you, so they dumped you on our doorstep. They threw you away like a sack of trash and then left you for dead when you were just an infant, so they must have hated you."

Hearing those cutting words upset Babrea more than any other hateful things Devant had ever said to her. She began to cry uncontrollably, and her tears materialized her first miracle. A baby dragon formed from her teardrops. Babrea had wished for someone to love her. Without realizing it, a baby dragon appeared before her. He stumbled and fell when he tried to stand up in the small room. He accidentally knocked several things over when he tried to break his fall with his tail.

Babrea heard the noise, and when she looked around the room, she saw him for the first time. She immediately stopped crying.

“Well, aren’t you a bumbly little thing, she said to the baby dragon.”

“I guess I am.” He said to her.

“Oh, my goodness, you can talk!”

“Now that you have made me physical, I can talk to you. You are the only one that can hear me, though, and no one else can see me except you.”

Babrea giggled and smiled, “So, can I keep you?”

“I’ve been with you since you arrived, but you had to summon me to make me physical. I’m here now and will stay with you as long as you need me. You can talk to me anytime because I will always be near.”

“So, what do I call you? Do you have a name?”

“You can choose what you wish to call me.” With that, the little dragon spun around the room. As he turned, his tail hit a small table, and it fell to the floor.

Babrea said, “Oh no! There you go again, Bumbling around and knocking things down.”

Then she began to giggle. Suddenly she stopped laughing and smiled, “That’s it! I know what your name will be. You are going to be Bumble. Do you like it?”

“If you like it, I love it! He said. Bumble, it shall be.”

After that day, anytime Devant spouted hurtful things aimed at Babrea, Bumble was by her side to cheer her up. It infuriated Devant that Babrea would giggle whenever she scolded her. Eventually, she lost her desire to hurt the child and completely ignored her. If Devant became frustrated, she would wave her hands in the air babbling something unintelligible, and walk away.

Bumble could always cheer Babrea up, no matter what horrible things Devant did or said to her. He explained to Babrea why Devant was so cutting with her words.

“Devant feels threatened by your presence, so she will always treat you as she currently does. She doesn’t know why she feels intimidated by you, but she will soon figure it out. You have an important purpose for being here, and when she figures out what that purpose is, she will try to stop you. She can’t have her plans for the future interfered with, and soon she will figure out that you have the power to destroy her plans. She would have stopped you when you first arrived, but Adolla was able to turn back time. That action allowed Protecus the opportunity to hide your pendant. Devant needs that jewel to increase her power. She hasn’t figured out why you are here, but she’s uncomfortable around you. She thinks that if she can drive you away from the safety of the Manor and kill you. She’s wrong, though. Devant knows there is something special about you, and she cannot allow you to complete what you are here for. She has been unable to destroy you physically, so she continues to fling verbal abuse at you to make you feel unwanted. I have told you this to make you aware of the truth. Now that you know, you will no longer fear her, for she cannot harm you. You are special and destined for greater things.”

Babrea was very intelligent, far beyond her years in many ways, so what Bumble told her didn’t frighten her. It fortified her. She now knew that she didn’t require Devant’s love, and no matter what hateful and abusive things she spat at her, it wouldn’t matter anymore. She had Bumble to give her strength and Protecus to give her knowledge. Miranda and Solarian loved her, and Tanus and Seth loved her too. Bumble would be by her side, day and night, making her feel safe and happy. Even though he was clumsy, with his big feet, horns, gangly tail, and wings, she knew he was there for her. Bumble was awkward, always knocking things over or bumping into something. That didn’t matter, though, because he would always be there for her. She was loved, and that was all that mattered.

A few weeks after Bumble's arrival, Tanus and Babrea were playing together near the gates in the courtyard when he noticed her talking to herself again. This time was different, though, because as she spoke, she walked toward the iron gates that led outside. As she neared them, they slowly began to open. Seth had always told Tanus that he should never go outside those gates because it was dangerous out there. Tanus watched as Babrea continued talking to herself while steadily walking outside. He was frightened, but he didn't know what to do.

Bumble had opened the gates for Babrea, though Tanus could not see him. As Babrea proceeded outside, Tanus called her several times, "Come back, Babrea, we're not supposed to go out there. It's not safe. We'll get into trouble. Come back!"

Babrea turned to face him and softly said, "Don't worry, Tanus, I'll be fine." Then the large gates slowly closed behind her, and she disappeared from his sight.

Fearful that something terrible would happen to her and he would get blamed, Tanus ran to find an adult. Devant was the first person he came upon, so he quickly caught up with her and told her what had happened.

"Babrea went outside the gates, and then she disappeared. We're not supposed to go outside."

Devant stopped and turned on Tanus like a viper, sneering at him. Then she sharply snapped at him, saying, "I don't care what that silly child does, and as far as I'm concerned, she can disappear forever. I could care less about what happens to her."

Devant continued on her way, shouting back at Tanus over her shoulder, "Go away, you little brat. Go play or something, and don't bother me again."

Tanus didn't understand. He was confused. He had never liked Babrea's mother because she was a mean person. But he was afraid of her too, so he didn't bother her anymore. He decided to tell someone else because he was fearful that something was going to happen to Babrea. He quickly went in search of his brother. Seth would know what to do.

Babrea followed Bumble as he led her farther away from the protected area. She was deep in thought as she walked. All that she could think about was her father. She loved Protecus very much, but lately, he had seemed overly sad, and she wanted to do something to cheer him up. His laboratory and books were the only things that seemed to make him happy, and Protecus was always working in the lab. She remembered one of the books he taught her from when she was younger. Inside it, there was a picture of some beautiful colorful things. Father had called them flowers. He had said that he missed having them around.

As Bumble drifted further from the Manor, steadily leading Babrea away, she had more time to think. She thought about how much her father would love having some of those colorful flowers, and before she realized it, she was saying those words out loud.

Bumble heard her and readily agreed, "Giving your Father flowers would indeed make him happy. But if you want to give him something living, you must create it. You will need something to help you begin. For this to happen, you need a proposer of color and a special place where things can grow, for they cannot flourish in the current soil. Bumble then began to run and told Babrea she should run with him. He explained that he would find her a place where she could create. Bumble then suddenly stopped running.

Beside where he stopped were two rocks lying on the ground, one small and another slightly larger. Surrounding them was nothingness, only dry soil coupled with dead and dying weeds. Bumble jumped on top of the smallest rock and then stepped onto the larger one. He then told Babrea, "Climb up on the boulder beside me."

Once she was beside him, he told her, "Now close your eyes and clear your mind completely. You must think of nothing but those beautiful flowers you saw in that book and visualize them in front of you."

Babrea then closed her eyes and pictured the book before her, as Bumble said. She visualized her father turning the pages, and she could hear him telling her the story of a time when many beautiful colors covered the Earth. Then she remembered how colorful they were, and as she began to see the flowers in her mind. She knew if her father could hold them in his hands, they would make him smile again. The colors began to come to life in front of her. They looked so real that she could almost smell their sweet fragrance. As Babrea thought more of those beautiful colors and delicious smells, she began to hum to herself. While she hummed, she began to spin around. As she turned, she rose onto the tips of her toes like a ballerina, with both arms outstretched. She giggled with happiness as she spun. When she finally stopped spinning and opened her eyes, a new baby dragon stood beside her. He stretched and yawned, and when he opened his eyes, Babrea reached out to pet him. He placed his nose against her hand to nuzzle it, and when she touched the tip of his nose, he opened his clawed paw to reveal a small bunch of brightly colored flowers. Babrea reached out and lightly touched the flowers, and when she did, they began to float about. As they floated higher, they spread out around her in a sea of color. Then the flowers started to drift to the ground. Once they touched the ground, they sprouted and spread out in a wave of color. There were so many different varieties of flowers, all with striking colors abounding. They spread out as far as the eye could see in a marvelous profusion of greens, purples, yellows, and blues.

Babrea was so excited. She turned to her newest baby dragon and told him, “I am going to call you Nese because you helped me create this perfect nest where my Father’s special place will be.”

The baby nodded his pointy head and said, “I like my name. Thank you! I’m glad you like the special place we have made for your father.”

Babrea looked around and said, “Father will love this place. I know he will. I must bring him to see all of these beautiful things.” As she spoke, she reached down and picked some flowers to take home to her father, but the instant she pulled them from the ground, the progression of color ceased. It was as if she had shouted at them_to stop, and they heard her and immediately obeyed. Babrea hadn’t noticed the cessation as she picked her bouquet. Her thoughts were only of her father and how happy he would be with this surprise gift. Babrea was so excited and couldn’t wait to show the flowers to Protecus.

Babrea turned to Bumble and said, “I want to go back home now so that I can give my father this lovely gift of flowers.”

She started to leave but thought about Nese. She knew that she couldn’t take him with her too. It was hard enough keeping Bumble from unintentionally destroying everything around him. She knew that two dragons would be impossible to watch over.

Babrea told Nese,” You stay here and take care of my father’s garden, and I’ll come back to see you very soon.” Nese nodded his head that he understood.

Babrea was then ready to go but suddenly remembered she didn’t know the way back home. Bumble sensed her dilemma and said, “Don’t worry, I’ll show you the way home.”

As Bumble led the way for her, a trail of tiny stones appeared behind him, forming a path for Babrea` to follow. She followed the trail as quickly as her little legs would carry her. When Bumble stopped, a beautiful translucent waterfall appeared before him. It seemed to fall from the sky, with no real beginning. Bumble swept his wings forward and then backward, which prompted the waterfall to part. In the opening he created, Babrea could see the two rocks she remembered climbing onto when she entered. Bumble told her to step onto the rocks.

Before exiting, Babrea looked back at the beautiful garden she and Nese had created and saw Nese standing there. When she stepped onto the rock, Nese, and the entire field of color, slowly began to disappear as the translucent waterfall started to close.

With a mighty rumble, all the grandeur disappeared, and only a solid wall of rock appeared in its place. There was no sign of the waterfall. The beautiful field of flowers had disappeared behind the waterfall. The entire garden was gone, and all that remained visible was dust and a pile of rocks.

Babrea followed Bumble's trail until she was close enough to see the Manor off in the distance. She knew her way home from that point and began to run toward it. She could hardly contain her excitement as she rushed past Bumble. She couldn't wait to give her father his present.

Babrea arrived at the gates out of breath. She was slightly ahead of Bumble, so she had to wait for him to open the gates.

"Come on, Bumble, hurry."

Once Bumble opened the gates, she rushed inside. She immediately saw Tanus and Solarian playing and hid for a few seconds. She didn't want anyone else to see her surprise for her father before he did. When Solarian and Tanis finally ran off in a different direction to play, Babrea proceeded into the Manor.

Straight up the stairs, she flew as she headed toward her father's laboratory. Devant, however, was on the stairs and, upon seeing Babrea running, immediately began to scold her. "I've told you repeatedly, never run inside my Castle. You almost tripped me, you stupid little girl. What are you hiding behind your back? Let me see what is in your hand!"

Devant almost spat the words as she spoke them. Babrea then desperately tried to slip around Devant while keeping her flowers hidden. She didn't want Devant to see them before her father because they were a present only for him. Devant wouldn't allow her to pass, though. When Babrea continued to hide her hands behind her back, Devant repeated her demand, "I said, let me see what you're hiding behind your back!"

Babrea continued to hide her present, telling Devant, "These are a gift for my father. I'm sure they will make him smile."

Devant then grabbed Babrea by the shoulders and squeezed them painfully hard. Once again, she demanded, "Show me what you have in your hands right now!" Then she forcibly pulled Babrea's arm from behind her back so she could see what was in her hand.

As Devant peered down at Babrea's outstretched hand, she laughed. All she saw in the child's hand was a bunch of dead weeds. Devant responded sarcastically, saying, "Oh yes, Protecus will love those. What an appropriate gift. A handful of dried-up weeds for an old swiveled-up man."

Then Devant laughed even louder as she viciously knocked them from Babrea's hand onto the steps. "I've told you at least a thousand times you are to never bring weeds into my Castle. Those awful things stink, and I've told you before, Protecus is not your father, and you better stop calling him that."

After Devant finished scolding the child, she stomped off, muttering something to herself. Babrea knew what she held in her hand was not weeds, but she didn't want Devant to see the lovely flowers. They were not for her, so Babrea made them appear as weeds in her eyes.

Babrea smiled as she carefully picked the flowers up from the steps, then gleefully ran to the top of the stairs to her father's laboratory. She was so excited she could hardly contain herself. She couldn't wait to show Protecus what she had created for him. She burst into the lab and found him sitting on his broken stool, bent over his desk, totally engrossed in one of his books. Babrea quickly ran to Protecus to show him what she had made.

Protecus was so immersed in his reading material when Babrea rushed in that she took him by surprise. He turned too quickly on the wobbly stool he was sitting on, and one of the cracked legs gave way, and he crashed to the floor.

Babrea immediately dropped her flowers and rushed to her father's side. She feared he might be injured.

"Father, Father. Are you all right?"

"I'm fine, little one, don't fret. What is all the fuss about?"

Babrea looked down at the broken stool, saying, "Father, you need a new stool. I'll wish for one for you." Looking around his thrown-together laboratory, she noticed his desk was also broken and said, "You need a new desk too, so I'll wish for that as well."

Protecus only half heard what Babrea was saying because he had just spotted the beautiful flowers lying on the floor beside him. They were remarkable. He hadn't seen anything of color in so long that he had almost forgotten how beautiful it could be. These flowers were a most unusual shade of purple and yellow, and they were a species he couldn't readily identify. The colors were more vibrant than anything he had ever seen before. He reached out for one of them while asking Babrea, "Where did you find these beautiful things?"

Babrea giggled and said, "Oh, Father, I didn't find them. I wished for them. Then Nese came to me, and with his help, I made them. They are a present for you only. Do you like them? I saw them in one of the books you showed me before, and I remembered how much you loved them. I wanted to make you happy and make you smile again.

Babrea pulled the book from the shelf where she had seen the beautiful flowers, then showed her father. She explained to him, "I've made several pretty flowers like these, and I want you to see all of them."

Babrea eagerly pulled on his arm, insisting he get up from the floor and come with her. Protecus was still in awe of the flowers scattered around him but stood at her insistence. She urged him forward by pulling on his arm, so he complied and went with her. As they walked toward the stairs, he questioned her about who Nese was.

"Who did you say helped you to grow these flowers, Babrea?"

Babrea was so excited to show her father her beautiful garden all that she could say was, "One of my new friends helped me."

Protecus wanted to know more about this new friend Babrea had referred to. She was apparently too excited about something she wanted to show him, so she couldn't stop long enough to explain. Protecus decided to wait and question her about her new friend later. Babrea was almost dragging Protecus along as she continued toward the front door.

Protecus was so preoccupied thinking about what he had just seen and how it was even possible. He was only vaguely aware of what Devant was saying to him as he passed her on their way. She said something to him about several people being out in the courtyard with a cart full of lumber. With Babrea steadily pulling him along, he wasn't sure what Devant was saying.

As Babrea and Protecus rounded the doorway, Babrea quickly headed toward the main gates. They were closed for protection at all times. However, as they got closer to them, they opened seemingly automatically.

That was when Protecus noticed the cart in the courtyard Devant had mentioned earlier. It was full of lumber, and lots of people were bustling about. Protecus would've stopped and questioned them, but Babrea was insistent he came with her and continued pulling him toward the open gates.

Protecus told Babrea, Sweetheart, you know you're not supposed to ever leave the courtyard."

Protecus was always cautious any time he left the protection of the wall. He couldn't see as well as he once could, and it was becoming more dangerous outside. He hesitated before scolding her because he remembered what the dragon had told him many years before. He recalled Adolla telling him that Babrea had a protector and nothing could harm her. Protecus remembered he was to allow Babrea freedom to do what she needed. Protecus thought this could be one of those essential steps she needed to take, so he decided to give her the space she needed.

After exiting through the gates, Bumble quickly took the lead showing Babrea the way. Protecus hadn't been outside the courtyard wall for a long time, so he was shocked at the degradation he was now witnessing. The soil was almost dust because the land was so severely dehydrated. Brown weeds were the only plants that marked the ground. The air was thin and hard to breathe. Everything appeared grey and lifeless. The Manor grounds must have some type of preservation that the outside world did not have.

The source of that protection must have something to do with Babrea. That was the only thing that made sense.

Babrea could see Bumble was getting ahead of them, so she tried to rush Protecus along a little faster.

"Come on, father. We must hurry. The darkness will be drawing near soon." She spoke with such maturity as she assumed responsibility for the situation. "I want you to see all there is, but we must go quickly!"

As they walked faster, they drifted further away from the protection of the stone wall. Protecus began to lose sight of the Manor and became somewhat alarmed. With his failing eyesight, he felt very uncomfortable entering into unfamiliar territory. Though he had been outside the gates many times before, everything seemed different to him now, almost foreign. The ground was so dry it crunched as he walked on it. The sky had an unusual hue to it. Everything had a greyish-purple haze to it.

Babrea could sense Protecus's alarm and smiled as she reassured him, "Don't worry, Father, Bumble knows the way. He will lead us safely to the garden and then back home."

As they continued onward, Protecus began to pay more attention to what Babrea was saying to him and less about his surroundings. He was fascinated by the tale Babrea was spinning. She was very animated when she described the flowers to him, "They are stunning, and there are so many of them. I can't wait for you to see them. They're everywhere, and I know you'll love them."

Bumble suddenly stopped, and then he told Babrea to do the same. She raised her hand and whispered to her father, "Bumble wants us to stop here."

Protecus could not see or hear anyone speaking to Babrea, but he did as she instructed and waited to see what she wanted him to do next.

"We must wait for Bumble to open the gateway for us," Babrea explained as she stood quietly.

Protecus's curiosity got the best of him, so he had to ask, "Who is Bumble?" Babrea giggled and said, "Bumble isn't a person, Father; he's my friend and protector."

Protecus surveyed the area where they were standing but still saw no one near them. Once again, he was confused by what Babrea was saying to him.

Bumble was busy checking out the area while intently sniffing the air. When he was sure there was no danger nearby and it was safe for Babrea and her father to enter, he signaled her to come forward. He then jumped up on the large boulder and waited for them to climb onto the small one beside him.

Babrea climbed up, then extended her little hand toward Protecus, indicating he was to join her. "Come stand beside me, Father. It's safe for you to join me.

Protecus methodically did as she instructed and stepped onto the boulder beside her. As soon as he was atop the rock, he heard a loud rumbling sound like flowing water. Shortly afterward, the waterfall became visible. It was the most beautiful waterfall he had ever seen. It appeared translucent as it glittered upwards from the ground instead of downwards, as water usually did.

Bumble then opened his wings, and the water parted. Babrea then led Protecus through the center of the glittering waterfall. As they walked through, the rumbling sound seemed to intensify, but once they were on the other side, Protecus realized he was completely dry. What he had thought was water wasn't water at all. It only looked and sounded like water.

Once Bumble joined them, he turned to face the waterfall, and it slowly once again. Then the sparkling scene they had just passed through seemed to disappear into the ground leaving only a stone wall in its place. Protecus watched as the stunning novelty he had just walked through faded away. Now there was no sign that water had ever been present. What had been beautiful falling water was now a solid wall of stone. Protecus was still wondering about everything that just happened when Babrea pointed, saying, “Look, Father, at all the lovely colors. I hope you like it.”

When Protecus finally saw what Babrea had been so desperately trying to describe to him, he was in awe.

Before him, as far as the eye could see, the most incredible field of color lay. Protecus hadn’t witnessed this type of beauty in a long time.

Flowers were everywhere, all manners of flowers, many of which Protecus had never seen before. The wondrous sight brought tears to his eyes. He was overwhelmed by what he saw and sat on a nearby boulder to collect his thoughts.

Being a scientist, Protecus knew that what lay before him was a complete improbability. There wasn’t enough sunlight or nutrition in the soil for these lovely things to be alive, let alone thrive in numbers, yet there they were. Thousands of colorful flowers were living and growing. Above him, the sky appeared the brightest blue. It was evident no catastrophe had ever touched this beautiful place.

“Babrea, how long have you known about this place?” She giggled and said, “Father, I just made this garden for you this morning.”

Protecus marveled at what Babrea was saying. As he took in everything around him, he could only stare. He was unable to speak as realization finally struck him. Babrea told him she had made this special place, meaning she had physically exhibited her ability.

Babrea was six years old now, and Protecus knew what she had done was nothing less than a miracle. He was proud of her, but at the same time, he knew what she had done must be kept secret, at least for now. No one could know her abilities until he better understood what she could do himself. Some might try to take her from her home and exploit her capabilities. The first thought that came to his mind was Devant. She detested the child and had done so since her arrival. What if Babrea's secret was already out? If Devant already knew about this place, it could be disastrous. Protecus had to find out If anyone else knew about Babrea's abilities. So, he asked her, "Babrea, does anyone else know about this garden besides us?"

"No, the only people that know about your garden are Bumble, Nese, you, and me. I made it just for you. Bumble will keep it hidden from all those you don't want to enter. Nese helped me to create everything. He lives here, so he will guard it for us. I wanted to give you something beautiful that would make you happy. Does the garden make you happy, Father?"

"Oh, yes, sweetheart, this place is perfect and the best present I've ever received from anyone. I can't thank you enough for creating it for me. We must keep it secret from those that would want to abuse it. Who are Bumble and Nese that you keep referring to?"

Protecus asked as he looked around the garden, "I don't see anyone. Are they here now? I want to meet them."

Babrea let out another little giggle and said, "Bumble is my protector, and Nese brings things to life. He is the one that helped me to create this place and all of the beautiful colors for the pretty flowers. They are my friends, and they're here right now, but you can't see them because they are only visible to me."

Protecus understood that Babrea needed her friends and was thankful they would remain a secret. The fact that he was unable to see them was something that he would have to accept. He recalled Adolla telling him many years earlier that Babrea had a protector. Protecus felt reassured that her protector was someone she could trust. He was still concerned about Devant, though. He knew Babrea had brought the flowers inside the Manor, and he feared she might have passed Devant when she was on her way to the lab. So, he questioned her about what had happened earlier.

"Sweetheart, you said the only ones that knew about this garden were me, you, and your two friends, but no one else. Is that right?"

"No one else knows about your garden, Father. You don't have to worry about Devant. She doesn't know anything. She caught me running up the stairs to your lab and was angry with me. She wanted to see what was in my hand, but I didn't allow her to see. I wanted you to be first, so I hid their beauty from her by making them look like weeds. I took away their loveliness and sweet smell so Devant could not enjoy them. I made them look ugly too. She got even angrier when she saw them as weeds and scolded me for bringing them into her Castle. She said that I better never do that again, then she slapped my hand and made me drop them."

Protecus could only shake his head in disbelief. He had never understood why Devant hated children so much and treated them with disdain. She had always been hateful towards them, especially Babrea. It was time for him to have that long-needed discussion with her about how she handled the children. Protecus was glad Devant was unaware of the garden or Babrea's unique abilities.

Protecus thought for a minute, then told Babrea, "Devant can never know about our garden, and she must never see the flowers. This place has to remain our secret, and we won't show it to anyone else or tell anybody how to get here. Okay?"

"Of course, Father, this is your garden, and if you want it to remain our secret, then it shall."

Then Babrea asked Bumble, "Do you understand what Father just told us?"

Bumble nodded his pointy head that he understood. He was the only one that knew how to get here, and Babrea knew their secret was safe with him. He was her protector and would never allow anything to harm her. Nese would also keep her secret because he lived in the garden and would never leave it unless Babrea told him to.

Babrea began to yawn as her hectic day was starting to catch up with her. She crawled up onto her Father's lap and curled into a ball. Then in her innocent way, she softly asked, "Father, why does Devant hate me so much?"

Protecus was speechless upon hearing Babrea's question. He knew Devant's true feelings but hadn't realized the child knew them. Even at her young age, she seemed keenly aware of his wife's hatred for her. Devant seemed to enjoy being hateful at every opportunity she could get.

Protecus's silence made Babrea question him further about what had happened earlier that week. "Devant said that you weren't my real father and that I was to stop calling you that. She said my birth parents abandoned me when I was born because they didn't want me. She told me that no one ever loved me, and that's why they left me on your doorstep like an unwanted sack of garbage."

Protecus couldn't believe the cruel lengths Devant had gone to hurt Babrea. He couldn't understand why Devant felt it necessary to belittle Babrea. He attributed her behavior to jealousy, which was the only explanation he could think of for her malice. Protecus had always done everything Devant had asked and did his best to care for her. He knew this time she had gone too far. It was time to have that long talk with her about this matter in much greater detail. Devant must soften her demeanor with the children, regardless of her feelings toward them. For the time being, he had to try to explain this mess to Babrea in a way that made sense.

"Babrea, you are an extraordinary child and have been since birth. I've always considered you my gift and have loved you like my own. You are more special to me than anything else in this world. In every possible way that matters, I am your father, and I always will be."

As Protecus spoke, he reached down and kissed her on the forehead. Hearing him say those words made Babrea very happy. She jumped off Protecus' lap and began to run around in circles, giggling as she turned. As she did this, another miracle began to unfold, and this time, right before Protecus's eyes.

More flowers blossomed around her tiny feet as she danced in circles. Babrea then started to run across the field, and as she ran, more of the blooming flowers began to pop up. Like flowing water, they trailed behind her as she ran. The further she went, the more blossoms spread out around her.

Protecus could feel his heart swell with pride as she ran, not only because of all the beauty she was creating but because he had never seen her so animated. Bumble flew behind her as she ran, and she shouted back at him, "Did you hear him, Bumble? Did you? Father does love me!"

Babrea was unaware of what was happening around her. She was far too excited with what Protecus had said to her.

Protecus was amazed at what he was witnessing. When Babrea would come to a stop, so would the procession of flowers.

Babrea appeared to be speaking to someone as she ran, but Protecus couldn't see who she was speaking to or hear what she was saying. All he could tell was that she was talking to something or someone other than him.

Protecus truly believed in miracles, recalling the day he spoke to Adolla. He realized now that he had actually talked with a dragon, and somehow, she knew him because she had called him by name. Protecus had spoken back to her and lived to breathe another day. He now believed that anything was possible.

After Babrea had made a full circle, Bumble stopped and sniffed the air. Then he told her, “It’s time for us to return home.”

Babrea immediately stopped running and returned to her father’s side. The instant she stopped moving forward, the color ceased to spread any farther. She told Protecus, “Bumble said that it’s time for us to return home so we can rest.”

Bumble knew that even though the sun was shining brightly inside the garden, it was getting dark outside. Babrea had a long day, and she now needed to rest. It was not safe to be out after dark. Protecus was unaware it was getting dark out, but he agreed that Babrea needed to rest. She had been a very busy little girl. Protecus agreed, “Your friend is right. It is probably later than we realize and time to return home.”

Protecus knew that predators now lurked everywhere, especially after dark. They would be hunting for food, and he and Babrea were probably on the menu. Then she told her father, “Bumble said he would bring us back tomorrow.”

Bumble then led the way back to the stone wall, and as soon as he spread his wings, the iridescent waterfall began to appear again. Babrea grabbed Protecus’s hand and would have walked through the water, but no opening appeared. Bumble told her to wait, so she did as he instructed. Then she watched him raise his nose into the air. He could smell something that was all too familiar to him. It was the strong scent of evil, and it lingered in the air. All animals knew that smell well, for nothing else was like it.

Something was lurking outside the garden perimeter, and it was still close by. Bumble could see nothing, but whatever was out there was utterly evil, so he waited before opening the gateway to the garden until he could no longer smell the overpowering odor. After the stench was no longer apparent, Bumble spread his wings and opened the rock wall. The translucent waterfall then appeared again. Bumble walked through the waterfall, stood on the boulder, and stomped his foot, breaking the largest of the rocks into several sections. As the pieces fell downwards, they formed a staggered set of steps. Bumble knew it was difficult for Babrea and her father to maneuver down the rocks, so he made a stairway, making it easier for them to step down.

Once outside the garden, Bumble spread his wings, and the waterfall again appeared as a solid rock wall. Bumble scanned the perimeter again, checking to ensure the area was safe, then slowly began leading them back to the Manor.

On the trip back, Bumble continued to check the area but couldn't detect any movement. He threatened whatever might be present with a low reverberating growl. He was letting any presence that might still be in the area know that he was aware of their existence and was warning them to stay clear.

While Protecus followed Babrea home, he sensed the presence of something with them, even though he couldn't see or hear anything. With Babrea's assurance that she had an ever-present protector, Protecus had faith that she was safe. He reluctantly accepted her explanation that whatever was protecting her was something only she could hear and see.

Protecus was concerned about the odd smell that permeated the area after leaving the garden. It was pretty odiferous and left a bitter taste in his mouth. Thankfully it was beginning to dissipate somewhat as they got closer to the Manor.

Bumble quickly led Babrea and Protecus home as he knew nightfall was descending, making travel unsafe. Oddly, within the garden walls, the sun was shining brightly.

When Protecus and Babrea arrived home, they ran into Devant at the doorway.

"Well, there you are, husband. I've been so busy instructing these little people since their arrival that I lost track of time. After they showed up this morning with their tools and lumber unannounced, I was angry with you. They said you had invited them to come here. I don't remember you mentioning anything about them to me. When I tried to locate you to find out what was happening, I couldn't find you anywhere. They told me they were carpenters and you hired them to build me some new furniture. I couldn't turn them away when they told me they were working for free. They said they would build me anything I wanted if I allowed them to park their wagons inside the courtyard for a few days. Their horses were tired, and they needed rest. My Castle needed a perk-me-up, so I allowed them to stay. As long as they do as promised, they can stay. I'm pleased with their work so far. Look at the new sofa they built for me, isn't it lovely? They are fast too."

Devant was in a most pleasant mood, which surprised Protecus. Her behavior, though odd, was welcome. He was relieved that he didn't have to deal with her dark temperament at the moment because he was too exhausted.

While Devant cooed over her new sofa, Miranda came into the room and softly told Protecus. "I've fixed something for the two of you to eat. I figured you would be hungry when you returned because you'd been gone all day. Is everything alright?"

Protecus smiled and said, "Nothing to worry over Miranda, but thank you for saving us a bite to eat. I'm starving, and I'm sure Babrea is too. She is exhausted too, so as soon as she eats, would you please see that she's bathed and then put to bed?"

With a more than eventful day behind him, Protecus was feeling the day's stress catching up with him. He was so enthralled with everything that happened he had forgotten they hadn't eaten since early morning.

While Protecus was contemplating the day's events, Babrea stretched and yawned.

Miranda smiled, "Don't worry, Protecus, I'll take care of the little one. Come with me, Sweetheart," she said as she led Babrea to the kitchen."

Protecus wasn't far behind her.

While they ate, Miranda inquired, "I don't know what was happening here today. When those little people showed up early this morning, Devant immediately allowed them in, which I found unusual. She never invites anyone into her Castle. When they arrived here, they were prepared to work. They had their tools, and they even brought lumber. They immediately got busy and worked amazingly fast, and they haven't stopped all day or ask for a single thing. They even brought their own food and water."

Protecus pondered over all that Miranda had said. It seemed that everyone believed Protecus was the one who invited them, but he had no idea who they were or where they came from. Protecus was too exhausted to think straight.

Everyone seemed happy with their work, so Protecus would let them continue. That seemed the best way to handle things, for the time being, anyway.

"I'll keep an eye on them, Miranda, but they don't appear to be a threat. In fact, quite the opposite. With Devant hovering over their every move, I don't think we need to worry about their intentions. I have to tell you, though, I had nothing to do with them being here, and I don't know any of them. I'll talk to them tomorrow, but in the meantime, I need to talk to Seth and Tanus. Do you happen to know where they are?"

"Yes, they've been working alongside the carpenters all day. Seth said it was incredible how fast those little people worked. He was impressed with their work, and they worked like a team together. They had Devant's sofa finished in only a few hours. Seth said he was learning so much from them but was hard-pressed to keep up with them."

Knowing that Seth was okay with the new arrivals made Protecus relax a bit more about the new guests. With Miranda in charge of Babrea and knowing Seth was monitoring the new arrival, Protecus felt more at ease to retire for the night and lay his weary body down.

His belly was full, and he was exhausted. Protecus bid Miranda and the girl's goodnight and turned to leave. As he walked out the door, Babrea grabbed his arm and whispered, "Father, I'm happy you love your presents? I will make you more things when we wake up."

Miranda looked at him with a questioning stare. Protecus was too tired to answer questions at that moment. He just wanted to go to bed.

He waited for Miranda to bathe Babrea, then carried her to bed. Protecus kissed Babrea on the top of her head and tucked the covers under her chin. He then said, "I love you, little one. We'll talk more in the morning, but now it's time for rest. I'll see you in the morning."

Protecus then watched as she closed her eyes. He smiled and then headed toward the stairs. Devant stopped him as he was about to head upstairs, saying, "Did you see my new sofa? Look at the beautiful fabric and the fine wood," she rattled on while caressing the wood. "I have them working on my new bed now," she said, excitedly giddy. "They work so fast they will probably finish it by morning."

"Well, I'm glad you're happy, Devant, but I'm exhausted, so I'm going to bed. If you want to stay up and supervise the workers all night, that's fine with me. I'll see you in the morning."

Devant had to make a final parting jibe, "You know, Protecus, when these little people first arrived this morning, I was very unhappy with you. You hadn't consulted with me before inviting them here, and you know I don't like strangers loitering up the property. When the group leader told me they were here to build new furniture for me, I figured I would give them a chance to prove their worth. I let them build me a new bench for the kitchen, and when they did such a good job on that, I had them make me a new sofa. They finished that so quickly that I decided to have them build me a new bed. I told them they could stay here as long as they continued working for me. They had to park their wagons in the far corner of the courtyard and sleep in their wagons. They can't dawdle in the courtyard. They have been doing a great job so far. They brought food and water and said they would keep to themselves and not bother me. After seeing their work, I understand why you invited them here. I can't wait to see my new bed when it's finished. They are already asking what I want them to build for me next. I intend to have them build me lots of new furniture. Their leader said that if I let them park in the courtyard, they would make me anything I wanted at no charge. So, I readily agreed to their terms."

Devant had never been this animated before. She was not one to like strangers, so Protecus found it odd that she had taken to these new little people so quickly. The entire group was all little. None of them appeared to be more than four feet tall.

Protecus was too tired to correct Devant's assumptions. He would allow her to believe he had invited the caravan of little people to the Manor. He felt that as long as Miranda felt comfortable having them around, he was okay with them too.

Protecus told Devant, "I'm going to bed. You can stay down here and supervise as long as you want. I'll see you in the morning."

Once Protecus disappeared at the top of the stairs, the carpenters ceased hammering and sawing. It was as if they had received a verbal command to stop. However, there had been no such order given. They collected their tools without saying a single word to one another. Then they left the Manor, heading straight for their wagons in unison. They said nothing to no one. Devant was left standing alone in the middle of the living room, staring at the walls. She appeared to be about to speak but said nothing, simply dropping her arms and falling silent. Then she turned and climbed the stairs to bed.

As Protecus slowly drifted to sleep that night, he thought about everything Adolla had told him. She said he was to nurture Babrea and give her complete freedom to do what she needed. He remembered the words Adolla had used when she said that. She had told him that Babrea was a special gift.

Protecus had come to love that little girl as if she were his own. She was the child that he had always wanted. He then recalled the rest of what the dragon had said. Babrea was to give light and life back to the entire world.

Protecus knew from the start that she had a much higher purpose. Adolla had told him that when Babrea arrived. Protecus still thought of Babrea as just a little girl, and he couldn't help but worry about her.

He decided that first thing in the morning, he would concentrate on furthering her education more vigorously. Babrea needed complete access to all of the knowledge that Protecus could provide, and he intended to give it to her. If Babrea was to take on a monumental task, then Protecus would do all he could to help her reach her destiny.

CHAPTER 13
THE CREATION

Early the following day, Protecus awoke to the sound of hammering. He instantly remembered the carpenters that had shown up the day before and assumed that Devant had put them back to work on some project she deemed essential. He inwardly smiled as he thought she had someone new to nag, so perhaps he could now have a respite. He dressed and went downstairs to check on Babrea. She was politely waiting for Miranda to serve breakfast when Protecus walked in.

"Father," she asked excitedly, "Have you seen your newest surprise yet?"

Protecus was unaware of what she was talking about, so he didn't answer her immediately. He turned his head sideways and looked at her with a queering look. She persisted with her, questioning, "Have you been in your lab this morning?"

"No, sweetheart. I just woke up. I slept a little late this morning after our long day yesterday. I'm surprised you're up so early."

"I feel completely rested now, Father, and I'm anxious to start our day. You need to go upstairs and look at what is up there first. There is a surprise waiting for you there."

"May I eat first?"

"Yes, we can eat together, and then I want you to come with me upstairs to your lab. I want you to see the new present I have for you there."

They finished their breakfast, and the second Protecus laid his fork down, Babrea jumped up from her chair and began pulling at his arm.

"Come on, I want you to see, hurry…. hurry."

Protecus stood and then climbed the stairs to his laboratory. On the walk upstairs, he wondered what had caused Babrea to be so excited. She could hardly contain her enthusiasm. As soon as Protecus rounded the door to his lab, he saw, standing in his laboratory, a brand-new worktable, long and sleek, and in front of it was a shiny new chair. They were both so beautiful even a king would have been proud to have them.

A big smile crossed Protecus's face. Babrea could see he was happy with his surprise. He took a seat in the chair. It was perfect, as was the desk. Sitting in his new chair, Protecus marveled at the quality and wondered how the carpenters had created such beautiful pieces so quickly.

Protecus remembered Babrea saying she was going to wish for him a new chair and a new desk. Now, before him, stood this beautiful pair. Protecus had never seen such craftsmanship in his entire life. The carving was grand, and the wood was superb. His chair was so comfortable he could probably sleep in it, especially considering Devant snored all night. It was odd how, seemingly out of the blue, these new little people had shown up and coincidentally brought their tools and lumber as well. Where did they ever find such beautiful wood? As a matter of fact, where did they find lumber at all? No large healthy trees grew near the Manor. Definitely not enough to build the type of furniture they were producing. Protecus had never seen wood like this before. He realized that he had just witnessed another miracle. Babrea was still very young and such a tiny little thing, so it was hard to believe, but somehow she was responsible for all this. She was such an amazing child. He wondered, at that moment, how this new day would unfold.

"Thank you so much for my new gifts, sweetheart. They're perfect and exactly what I needed. I will enjoy using them."

Protecus remembered planning a renewed effort toward Babrea's education today. He intended to start by explaining their need for food. He would then show her pictures of vegetation so she could see what they most needed for survival. However, at that instant, Babrea had other ideas. She became extremely animated and began jumping up and down.

"You must come with me now. I have more things to show you today."

Babrea grabbed Protecus by the hand and began to pull him toward the stairs once more. He knew better than to protest because she was far too excited. When they arrived at the bottom of the steps, he was amazed at the construction work downstairs. There were several pieces of beautiful wood scattered about and even more new strangers scurrying around. Everyone was busy sawing or carrying hammers and nails for their next building project. They were all small in stature, and upon closer inspection, they all appeared to be older men as every one of them sported healthy beards. They all wore hats with strange feathers and were continually bustling around. Protecus made his way through the living room as he tried to avoid the scattered objects. He had to be careful not to run into anyone along the way because there were people everywhere.

Devant entered the room at that moment in her usual extravagant manner. She immediately started snapping orders to first one person and then another. She then spotted Protecus, who quickly caught the brunt of her demands. "Get out of the way, you old fool. Can't you see that people are working here!"

Protecus took that as his cue to leave. Devant was on one of her rampages, so this was a good time to exit, especially since the children would wake soon and be hungry. He decided to milk the cow now because the children would want breakfast as soon as they awoke, and, of course, Devant was always hungry.

A lot of production was going on outside in the courtyard as well. Little people were everywhere, carrying lumber, sawing wood, and lots of hammering was going on. It was apparent he was not needed there.

On his way to the barn, a small, rather portly older man with a long white beard and a funny little crumpled hat stopped Protecus. He introduced himself to Protecus, "I'm Carver, the eldest of our clan, and I am the leader as well. If you find fault with any of our work, please report it to me. It is my greatest desire to meet your approval. Once we finish building the furniture your wife requested, we plan to fortify the stone wall surrounding the grounds. It needs to be much stronger than it is now. The small huts that your residents are currently living in require upgrading. The entire group needs far more substantial living quarters than they currently live in. It is unsafe for them to be in those makeshift tents and huts. They will need much greater protection for what is about to come."

Protecus gave Carver a second look when he said that. It was as if Carver knew something horrible was about to happen, but that was all the information the little man seemed to want to share at the moment. Carver smiled, tipped his hat, and off he went, whistling as he walked away.

Protecus was aware of the substandard housing the Manor residents lived in. He knew they needed better living quarters, but he was surprised that Devant would allow that construction work to occur.

As Protecus looked around the grounds, it was apparent that Carver, and his fellow workers, had already begun work on cottages for the residents. The workers had already finished several of them. Protecus knew he could not pay these men for their hard work and excellent materials. Protecus appreciated all of the beautiful things they created, but the livestock was the only thing he owned of value. The donkey wasn't worth much, and Protecus desperately needed to keep the cow for the children. He knew their work and materials were worth far more than the donkey. Protecus decided to offer all he had. He would find Carver the next day and tell him of his offering.

After Protecus finished his chores, he grabbed some venison from the smokehouse and returned to the house. Seth stopped him on his way to give Protecus some eggs.

"Where on earth did you get these?"

Seth shrugged and said, "Well, a couple of days ago, a group of chickens just showed up in the courtyard. Miranda said that since they decided to stay, I should build them a pen, so I did. Then Miranda suggested that I build nests for them to lay their eggs in, and she showed me how to build them. When I finished building them, the chickens laid in them. Since they were obliging enough to fill the nests I built for them, I'd collect the eggs they so graciously laid for us."

Protecus laughed and smiled, then accepted the eggs Seth was handing him, saying, "Come up to the house later and eat breakfast with us. Miranda will cook these eggs for everyone." Protecus smiled as he walked the rocky path back to the kitchen with the venison, milk, and eggs.

Tanus, Solarian, and Babrea were awake and running around the kitchen, playing hide and seek, when Protecus entered. Immediately after spotting Protecus, all three of them became very excited.

Miranda took the eggs and cooked them on the wood stove. Once the children ate, she fixed something for Protecus. Seth entered the kitchen just as Protecus finished his meal, so Miranda fed him next. Protecus would have visited with Seth for a while, but he knew Devant would be hungry and soon start barking demands. Protecus didn't desire to feel her wrath. She expected him to always wait on her, and he usually did rather than meet her ire. However, this morning, he asked Miranda if she would please deliver Devant's food to her. Protecus had other plans this morning.

At that moment, Babrea asked, "Father, can we go for our walk today?"

Protecus knew what Babrea was asking of him. She wanted to return to the garden again. Protecus wanted to go back, too, but he felt it was more important to do a little bookwork first. He told Babrea, "Let's have class this morning, and then we can go for a walk afterward."

The children loved going to class. That was the only real entertainment they had all day, so when they heard Protecus say the word, class, they could hardly wait to go upstairs and get started. Protecus let both of them come with him, then set Tanus and Solarian busy planting seeds in one of his hydroponics gardens. Then he turned his full attention to Babrea.

Today he intended to devote his primary attention to Babrea and her studies. He first retrieved one of his planting books on vegetation from the bookshelves, then sat her down to explain how important growing food was to them.

"In the books, I'm going to show you today, there are no pictures of trees or flowers, which are beautiful and necessary. However, vegetation is also important, and that is what I'm planning to show you. We must eat to survive, so. Therefore, we need food to eat. The vegetables in these books cannot grow in the soil outside anymore, but they can survive in the garden you created. We need them to grow to provide food for all the residents. I'll show you pictures of what we need to grow in our garden."

As Protecus pointed out the vegetables needed for their survival, Babrea laid her hands down on the book and said, "I thought you loved flowers and trees, Father."

Her statement moved Protecus because it was so innocent and sincere. "Yes, sweetheart, I love flowers and trees very much, and they are necessary. Right now, to survive, we need vegetables. Our meat supply is starting to run low, and if we don't find another food source soon, we will not be able to survive."

"Father, why is it so hard for vegetables and trees to grow outside the Manor wall anymore?"

Protecus must explain to Babrea something he didn't quite understand himself.

"Well, Sweetheart, a horrible accident happened, which everyone has called The Great Disaster. Before that happened, abundant vegetation grew from the ground everywhere. The soil had the right nutrition to grow beautiful things, and everything was plentiful. Since the disaster, our soil can no longer produce the necessary nutrients required to bring forth life."

Babrea took the book from Protecus and began to turn the pages. She was amazed at the bright colors and different shapes of the objects inside. Many colorful pictures sprang before her eyes as she flipped through the pages with vigor. There were large red ripe tomatoes, bright yellow corn, and vibrant green beans. After studying the pages, Babrea's curiosity peaked. She asked. "What caused the horrible accident, Father?"

Protecus thought about her question for a moment and decided he needed to let her know more about the world before it all fell apart.

"We were careless with our world and didn't respect it enough. We didn't love what we had enough."

"Did we hate our gift?"

"No, hate is an ugly word, Sweetheart. Once you allow that to enter our hearts, there is no longer room for love and sharing. Hate isn't what caused all of this devastation. It was all a terrible mistake, made by many people trying to do good things, but our efforts backfired."

"I understand, Father. Love and sharing are good things that we need more of."

"Yes, they are very good things. They are probably the two most important things in the entire world. Without sharing, there can be no love."

"That sounds like a good idea to me. I want to be loved, so I'll share with everyone."

Protecus felt he was making progress with Babrea's understanding of their needs. He showed her one of the small tomatoes he had produced in his hydroponics garden. When Babrea touched the plant, it instantly grew in size and brightened in color.

Protecus quickly grabbed the tomato and hid it from the other children. He didn't want anyone to see what Babrea had done. He was amazed, but this was what he was hoping would happen. He now knew that she could do much more than blooming flowers.

Protecus felt if she could see and understand what they needed for their survival, she could provide it for them. Babrea quickly became absorbed in what she was doing, so she had no idea Protecus was attempting to keep her abilities a secret. After touching the first tomato, Babrea touched another one, which immediately became larger and brighter in color. They were the most beautiful tomatoes Protecus had ever seen, so vibrant and plump.

He hurriedly ushered the other two children out of the lab and off to the kitchen. Protecus told them that class was over for the morning and they should go into the courtyard to play. He didn't want them to see what Babrea had created and then accidentally report it to Devant. For now, he needed Babrea's abilities to remain a secret.

Babrea was about to touch more of the small vegetables when Protecus stilled her hand. It was magnificent that she could do this impressive thing, but he needed to hide these extraordinary things. Protecus was pleased, but at the same time, he needed to explain why it was essential that no one else knew where the impressive vegetation came from.

"Babrea, the ability you have, which allows you to touch things and they grow, is a miracle. For now, though, we must keep it a secret between the two of us. Do you understand why we must not let anyone else know?"

Babrea was excited that she could make her father happy, but at the same time, she understood what a secret was. She giggled and whispered to him, "Father, it's not the touch of my hand that causes the miracle to happen. I ask these things to live and thrive, and they do it for me."

Once again, Protecus was surprised by her explanation of the miracles she could perform. He was excited about her new ability, but at the same time, it was essential to keep her secret. Protecus grabbed a pouch from the shelf and put all the newly enhanced vegetation inside. Then he placed the bag on the shelf.

His excitement was broken by Babrea, however, when Bumble sensed his brother, Nese, calling out to them. Bumble then told Babrea that it was time for them to return to the garden.

"Bumble said that Nese needs us to return to the garden, and we need to go now."

Protecus understood and silently slipped the two of them downstairs, then out the back kitchen door. He desperately wanted to avoid being seen by anyone, especially Devant. She would ask far too many questions, and he was not ready to offer any explanations, not right now, and possibly not ever. Thankfully, Devant was absorbed with being a construction boss and too busy ordering the little people around to notice Protecus and Babrea leaving. It seemed that she didn't have time to bother with Protecus anymore.

After exiting, Babrea grabbed her father's hand and told him, "We must go quickly. Bumble will lead the way. He's the only one that can open the gateway."

Babrea allowed Bumble to lead the way while she followed with her father in tow.

When they entered the garden today, Protecus stopped short. The day before, everything had been beautiful and in abundance. However, today all the beauty had all withered and died. Everything lay lifeless on the ground. Protecus immediately feared that because of Babrea's youth, she could only make things alive for a short while. That would not be helpful if they were to grow enough food for all the residents in Protecus's care.

Babrea began speaking to something which Protecus could not see. She was talking to Nese.

She asked Nese. "What do you need me to do?"

Then Babrea nodded that she understood what he wanted her to do. Next, she stood up on her toes like a ballerina and began to hum as she spun. When she finally stopped spinning, she spoke again to something Protecus could neither hear nor see.

Protecus stood still, not wanting to distract her from what she was doing. When Babrea came to a complete stop, she called out to her father, "Come here and stand beside me, Father. I have something to share with you. Nese told me that the flowers are dying because they need water to live, and they can't find any. He said I had to ask for water, and when I asked for water, I got another little friend I named Otul. He will bring pure water from deep beneath the ground so the flowers can live again."

Protecus saw no one with them, so he asked Babrea, "Where is Otul, Sweetheart?"

Babrea giggled and said, "He's standing beside you, Father, but you can't see him. You won't be able to see any of my friends. No one can see them except me."

She was right. Protecus could see no one.

At that moment, Otul snorted, and Protecus immediately felt the warmth of his breath as it touched his arm. He startled Protecus, causing him to jump and Babrea to giggle again.

"Don't be afraid, Father. Otul won't hurt you. He is just curious. None of my baby dragons will ever hurt you."

Dragons! Oh my, thought Protecus. Her protector was a dragon! Initially, he was stunned, but it made sense as he thought about it. Adolla was a dragon. Why wouldn't the protector Adolla choose to watch over Babrea be a dragon, a baby one, no less? And, of course, all of her helpers were dragons as well.

"How many baby dragons are there with us, Babrea?"

"I have three baby dragons so far, Father. Bumble is my protector, and he is always with me. Nese helps me grow things because he can see what I see and knows what I want. I wished for my garden to grow again, and Otul came to help me. He can help me bring the necessary nutrients to flourish greenery. Otul needs to see, taste, and feel what I need him to help me with, and then he can grow it. Can Bumble have one of the tomatoes I touched in the lab this morning? If Otul can image it, he will have a picture of what I need his help to create.

"I'm the only one who knows where the vegetable bag is. I must go alone because I have to sneak in and out without being seen."

"Father, Bumble has lived in the bedroom with Solarian and me since I first arrived, and no one has ever known he was there. He is invisible to everyone except me, remember?"

"Yes, I remember that. Bumble can go with me so he can show me the way back. I'll also bring the planters book. There are many pictures of food in it, which might also be helpful."

Babrea explained all of the information she had shared with Protecus. Then Bumble told her he would go with Protecus and wait for him to get the food. He would then show Protecus the way back to the secret garden.

Protecus was uncomfortable leaving Babrea in the garden alone. She reassured him that her dragons would not let anything happen to her.

At that moment, Otul snorted on Protecus again, reinforcing what Babrea said. Bumble then nudged Protecus from behind, prompting him to move forward, further emphasizing the need for them to go now.

"We won't be gone long, Sweetheart, so don't leave the garden until I return for any reason, alright?"

"Father, I'm not going anywhere. I have too much work to do here. I'll be safe, though, so don't worry.

As Protecus turned to leave, Bumble once again nudged him from behind, prodding him to move along. Protecus began to walk in the direction Bumble was pushing him, and soon he heard the waterfall. It began to appear before him again and started to open simultaneously. It was a beautiful sight, as were all of Babrea's creations. As Protecus exited through the waterfall, he saw clawed footprints appear before him as Bumble showed him where he was to go. Protecus realized that Bumble was indeed there, showing him the way, even though he was still invisible. As he led the way out of the garden, one footprint at a time, Protecus peered over his shoulder. Looking behind him, he saw no evidence that footsteps had ever been present. They disappeared as he passed.

Protecus was confident that Babrea would be safe in his absence. He felt sure her dragons would guard and protect her through any danger.

Protecus continued to follow Bumble's footsteps until the Manor was in sight. He could then easily find his way, so Protecus hurried home. As he entered the Manor, Protecus tried to stay hidden as best he could. He didn't wish to run into Devant with all her probing questions. Most of all, Protecus didn't want Devant to know what he was doing.

Protecus slipped quietly into his laboratory and grabbed his planter's guidebook. Then he got the bag of vegetables and quietly crept back down the stairs and out the back door, once again without being seen. Then he returned to where he left Bumble, but Protecus saw no sign of the trail, and there were no visible footprints for him to follow. Seeing no evidence of the path he had arrived on led Protecus to panic. He had no way of getting back to Babrea without Bumble's help. He needed Bumble to show him the way. Protecus called Bumble to try to get his attention.

"Bumble, where are you? I need you!"

Just as Protecus was beginning to lose hope, the baby dragon gave him another nudge from behind. Bumble's footprints began to reappear on the ground showing Protecus the way. He followed them, and soon, he was at the waterfall that led to the garden. Bumble opened the iridescent waterfall, and then Protecus could see Babrea again.

Babrea was in the middle of the garden, surrounded by a beautiful field of flowers, humming and spinning like a top. When she stopped, she started speaking to something. She then knelt on the ground, and after touching the grass, a tree grew beside her.

The tree grew taller and broader even after Babrea started to walk away. As soon as she saw her father, she ran toward him, and as she ran, another tree sprang up, then another. Many trees started to rise from the ground all over the place. Soon there were many fully grown trees in the field.

When Babrea reached her father's side, she said, "Nese told me that he could only help with greenery that humans couldn't eat, like flowers, grass, and trees. I needed another helper to assist me in growing the necessary things to eat. So, I summoned another baby dragon, and Rutus came to me. He will help me make lots of delicious food for us all.

Protecus was amazed at all of the ever-changing scenery around him. Things were popping up so quickly now you could almost hear the creations as they sprouted.

"Babrea, you have created a veritable garden of loveliness." Babrea liked that Protecus was happy. Then she asked, "Can we call it a garden?"

"You can call it whatever you like, Sweetheart."

It was a beautiful garden, lush, vibrant, and still spreading out in size and color. Protecus watched in wonder as the beauty continued to spread out. Then he asked, "How far have the trees and the grass spread?"

Babrea looked across the lush green field and said, "As far as I can see, Father."

Protecus hoped the world could share in this loveliness, but he was uncertain. Since the area surrounding the Manor was still in waste, Protecus feared that only Babrea's garden area could live again. He would have to accept that was possibly all they could expect to receive.

Protecus shared his worries with Babrea, "When I left to get the book and the vegetables, I lost my way. I couldn't find Bumble and feared I wouldn't be able to find my way back to you. The trail Bumble left disappeared, so I couldn't return to you without Bumble to show me the way. I was afraid I would never be able to find you again."

Babrea tried to assure Protecus. She said, "Father, anytime you want to return to your garden, all you need to do is think about the little wooden bench in the middle of the garden."

Babrea pointed to the largest tree in the garden. Underneath it sat a lovely white bench. She said, "You only need to wish you were sitting on that bench, and you will be there."

When Protecus looked at the bench, he could have sworn that he saw Carver sitting there for a moment, but then he was gone.

Babrea explained, "That bench is your doorway to me, and you will always have access to it. If we are ever separated from this day forward, you can always speak to me just as you are now. I will always hear you, no matter where I am. So, you need never fear losing touch with me. I will always be with you. My protector always watches over me, so I never fear for my safety. He told me I will grow in strength as I age, and soon nothing can harm me."

Protecus felt reassured by Babrea's words and all that she had shared with him. He remembered Adolla telling him about her protector and that she would come to no harm. She was still young but so wise for her age. She was much brighter than an average child her age. He knew she was unique in many ways and recognized that he would have to trust her decision-making.

Protecus would have to learn to let Babrea go and allow her to grow as Adolla had instructed, but it would be hard. He had never raised a child before and wanted nothing more than to protect her. He was beginning to realize that protecting Babrea was something he couldn't always do. She was becoming stronger daily, almost by the hour, and he must allow those changes to occur. For her life to move forward, Protecus must not hold Babrea back.

"Bumble can sense love and hate, Father. He knows that you love me and you would never harm me. That is why he created a special opening for you into the garden. It is just for you so that you can always be with me, and I with you."

Rutus came to Babrea and told her he needed the vegetables to help her make more of them. Protecus pulled a ripe red tomato from his bag and held it out for Babrea.

"No," she said, "You hold it. Extend your hand with one of the tomatoes in your palm."

Protecus did as instructed, and it disappeared within seconds after placing the tomato in his hand. Rutus had eaten it.

After the tomato vanished, Rutus unfolded his claws and showed the seeds to Babrea. She passed her hand over them, and Rutus let them slowly fall to the ground as she did. As the seeds touched the ground, many small tomato plants began sprouting. Within mere seconds they grew into lush, full-grown, producing plants. Juicy red ripe tomatoes started to spring forth by the dozens.

Babrea then showed Rutus the planter's book, and as she turned the pages for him to see the vegetables, she explained how the plants felt as she held them in her hands. Babrea then told Rutus that she wanted all of the plants in the book to grow in her father's garden. As soon as Babrea finished explaining everything to Rutus, acres, and acres of corn, potatoes, and beans began to appear. The sprouts developed fully in mere minutes and began to bear their plentiful bounty. As Babrea and Rutus advanced further into the garden, so did the vegetation. Like flowing water, the colorful vegetables spread throughout the entire area. When Nese joined them, the flowers and trees spread even further as they walked. The bluest of skies spread out above them as they moved forward.

Protecus could only marvel at the sight before him. He was shocked and amazed as he watched the progression of beauty continue to spread. Everything in the planter's book began to come to an abundance of life. The garden was full now, lush and thriving.

Protecus was enthralled with the work that Babrea and her baby dragons had done in one day. He hadn't realized how late it was getting, though. Protecus was beginning to feel exhaustion setting in and figured that Babrea was feeling the same way. It had been another long day for both of them.

Protecus sat on the bench under the big tree to collect his thoughts. He knew it was time to return to the Manor but waited for Babrea to say the word. She had done so much to help them. Protecus knew they must return to the Manor before nightfall. They needed the protection the walls afforded after dark. When Babrea finally paused in her work and looked his way, he signaled for her to come to him.

Once Babrea was beside him on the bench, he told her, “I’m very proud of all you accomplished today. The food will save our people from going hungry. The garden is a beautiful place to enjoy but also useful. It’s getting late, and we must return to the Manor before nightfall. We need to eat, clean up, and rest so we can return tomorrow. I’m sure you’re worn out too.”

“I’m not tired, Father,” Babrea said as she yawned and slowly crawled beside Protecus. It was apparent to him that she was exhausted.

Protecus wrapped his arms around Babrea and lifted his little girl up to carry her home.

Bumble began to leave footprints for Protecus to follow once more as he led the way out. Protecus spoke to Babrea as he walked, “We can return tomorrow. At sunrise in the morning, we can come back here. We will bring the donkey tomorrow and fill the baskets to the top with all the food we can carry.”

Bumble was walking much slower than usual, and as he drew nearer to the waterfall, he began to sniff the air as he had before. He smelled something that shouldn’t be there. Protecus noticed that the footprints had suddenly stopped, so he also stopped. Then he softly asked, “Babrea is anything wrong?”

Bumble told Babrea that as soon as the doorway to the garden opened, they should step out quickly so he could seal the opening to prevent anything from entering inside. Once they exited, they should be still and quiet and stay next to the entrance.

Babrea explained everything to her father as Bumble had instructed. While still holding Babrea, Protecus stepped through the waterfall. Bumble quickly closed the opening and sealed it.

The baby dragon continued to feel the presence of something pure evil. Once the garden opening was closed, Bumble growled, and his eyes started to glow a fiery red.

Protecus knew something was wrong when he heard growling noises near where he and Babrea were standing. The growling sounds seemed to be coming from all around them at once, indicating that there was possibly more than one creature stalking them.

Protecus had no weapons, so he continued to remain frozen in place as Babrea had instructed him to do. Bumble told them they would be alright if they stood still and didn't move. Then a hideous creature Protecus had never seen before appeared in front of them and began to circle them. It was snarling viciously and had a multitude of long dripping fangs. It looked like a part wolf and part bear, with long stringy black hair covering its entire body, even its face. The creature was walking on all four legs like a dog, but then it reared up on its hind legs, and Protecus knew it was preparing to attack. It gave out a loud howl, then charged straight toward them. Protecus held onto Babrea as tightly as he could, struggling to shield her as much as he could. Protecus feared they were both doomed.

Protecus continued to hear lots of snarling sounds, and the gnashing of teeth resounded many times, which seemed to go on forever. Then, suddenly, the noises subsided. Protecus slowly opened his eyes. He realized that they were no longer on the path but back within the safety of the Manor walls. He didn't know how they had gotten there, but Babrea was safe and fast asleep in his arms. Protecus silently thanked Bumble because he knew the little dragon had saved their lives.

Protecus carried Babrea to bed. After quietly laying her down beside the now-sleeping Solarian, he heard a loud commotion in the kitchen. As he softly closed the bedroom door, he came face to face with a panic-stricken Seth. Tanus was standing beside him and appeared to be in shock. They both had a look of terror on their faces. Seth was frantically attempting to explain the horror he had just witnessed to Miranda. His voice was trembling as he tried to explain what had just happened. "A huge bird-like creature just flew down and grabbed the donkey. Then it flew away with it. I didn't have time to react because it happened so fast. It just grabbed the donkey and flew away with him."

Protecus couldn't believe what he was hearing. Though he was exhausted, he reacted quickly. He began handing out instructions to everyone. Seth already had his bow and arrows on his back, so Protecus asked Seth, "Please go upstairs and get my bow and arrows." Then he turned to Miranda and told her, "You and Tanus should go into the bedroom with the girls and close the door. Don't come out until one of us tells you everything is safe again."

Miranda nodded her head that she understood Protecus's instructions. She moved fast. She didn't want the girls to awaken to all the commotion and become frightened.

Protecus waited for Seth to return with his weapons, and as soon as he did, they both cautiously headed outside.

Protecus instructed Seth, "Please, go from house to house and tell everyone to stay inside their cottages because that creature might return. Try not to alarm anyone. Tell them that we saw a pack of wolves outside the wall earlier, and to be safe, they should all stay inside until daylight, and it's safe again."

Seth left to warn everyone as Protecus instructed him. The story of the wolves seemed plausible enough, and the people readily agreed they would stay inside until it was safe.

Seth and Protecus were armed with their homemade bows and arrows. Seth had his hunting knife and pulled it out as they neared the barn. He was still visibly shaken.

As they walked, Protecus tried to calm Seth by talking to him about what had happened earlier. Protecus listened while Seth told him about the creature.

"It looked like an evil horse with birdlike wings. It was big. I started throwing things at it when it swooped down and grabbed the cow. The cow was too heavy for the creature to lift, so it let her go. I didn't have any weapons with me then. The creature stared at me with hideous red eyes that looked like dancing fire. It was a bright green color with birdlike wings. When I started yelling, it looked in my direction, and its eyes shot straight in my direction. It had massive claws and a devil's tail. I thought I was next when it looked at me with those fiery red eyes. I truly feared for my life, but something distracted it. Something from the high tower in the Manor caught its attention. When I looked up there, I saw someone, and it looked like Devant. It looked like she was waving at that creature."

Protecus was confused, "Seth, there's no way anyone could be in that tower. We've never repaired the stairs up there, so no one can climb that high."

Seth only knew that whatever distracted the creature had made it turn away from him and gave him enough time to get out of the reach of its thrashing tail.

"Well, I'm thankful that something drew its attention away from me. Otherwise, I'd probably be dead. When I jumped out of the creature's way, I fell against the cow and caused her to stumble sideways. Then the red-eyed demon flung its tail at the cow, but it missed her. It struck your horse, though, and I'm so sorry, Protecus, but Lady is dead. She dropped to the ground the instant the demon's tail touched her. Its tail must have been poisonous. It stared at me with its fiery eyes, then turned, grabbed the donkey, and disappeared into the night."

Seth was still shaking as he spoke of the creature. He begged Protecus to forgive him for not protecting the Manor better while he was away. "I'm so sorry I couldn't stop the monster from killing Lady and taking the donkey. Perhaps I could have saved them if I had had a weapon."

Protecus reassured Seth, "You did everything right, son. Staying safe and out of the creature's reach was all you could have done. That creature would have killed you if you had gotten in its path. It knows there is more meat here, though, so I'm afraid it will return. Hopefully, it's full for now and won't return tonight. The best thing we can do now is to put the cow inside the barn and close the doors."

It seemed more than luck that just that morning, Carver had told Protecus that the residents needed better protection from what was to come. He didn't quite understand Carver's comment then, but now, what was to come had made itself visible.

Seth put the cow in the barn and closed the doors. Then he caught up with Protecus as he checked the main gates. After ensuring the gates were secured, Protecus thanked Seth again for the great job he and Tanus did to repair the gates. Then both of them walked the perimeter of the wall. As they walked around the courtyard, they remained silent. Protecus knew they needed to fortify their perimeter wall, but this was not the time to discuss that issue. He also thought it better not to tell Seth about the dog-like creatures that tried to kill him and Babrea earlier, at least not yet.

Protecus reaffirmed with Seth the need for him to curtail his hunting trips. “I think you need to stop going on hunting expeditions, at least for now. Let’s give that animal some space. Maybe once it realizes there aren’t any easy pickings around here, it will leave our area for good.”

Seth was worried that the smokehouse would run out of food if he didn't continue hunting. He expressed his fears to Protecus, who quickly reassured him.

“By late afternoon tomorrow, we will have plenty of food. A bountiful harvest is coming, and there will be more food than we will ever need.”

Seth smiled, thinking Protecus was trying to comfort him by reassuring him.

Protecus continued, “First thing in the morning, get Carver to help you build a more secure area for the cow.”

Seth nodded in agreement, saying, “That won’t be a problem, sir. Carver said he would help me work on anything we needed. At least we have plenty of lumber leftover from the building they’ve been doing for Devant lately.”

Protecus looked at the night sky and saw no dark shadows overhead. He would have to bury his horse tomorrow morning, and he didn’t look forward to that task. He would miss the mare a lot. With both her and the donkey dead, Protecus didn’t know how he would transport the vegetables home. He was too tired to think of a plan tonight.

Protecus decided that Seth and Tanus should sleep in the Manor from now on for their safety. For tonight, the boys should make a pallet in the room where the girls were sleeping. Protecus would find a bedroom for them the next day, regardless of what Devant had to say about it. It wasn’t safe for them to sleep in the barn anymore.

None of them would get a minute of restful sleep anyway because they would worry that the creature might return. Tonight, would most definitely be a night to keep a watchful eye on the sky outside their windows. Protecus would be holding vigil for anything moving in the black night sky.

CHAPTER 14
THE ORB

At dawn the next morning, when Protecus woke, his first thought was what lay ahead. He had to bury Lady.

Protecus quietly slipped out of bed, trying not to wake Devant. He then grabbed his clothes and silently dressed.

When he bent over to put on his shoes, he placed his head in his hands, trying to collect his thoughts.

Babrea touched him on the arm at that moment which snapped him back to reality. She was already awake and ready to go. She had a big smile on her face and began pulling on his arm, signaling that she wanted him to hurry up.

"Father, it's time for us to go," Babrea whispered.

Protecus quietly ushered Babrea into the hallway and downstairs to the kitchen, saying, "Let's grab a bit to eat first."

Then Babrea said, "I've already finished my breakfast Father, and Miranda has fixed something for you to eat later."

Protecus didn't know how to explain to Babrea that they would have to delay their trip this morning because he had to bury his horse. Babrea loved Lady.

While Protecus contemplated explaining their loss to Babrea, Seth and Tanus entered the kitchen. They were both covered in dirt and carrying shovels. Without saying a word, Protecus figured out the boys had buried Lady for him. He silently thanked the boys with a slow nod, letting them know he appreciated what they had done. He was glad they had taken care of everything. He didn't relish having to put away a second beloved animal.

Seth told Protecus, "Now that is done, I'm going to take care of that other matter we discussed. Carver said that he and his men could help me today."

Babrea was insistent that Protecus leave with her. Seth had barely finished his sentence when she said, "Father, we need to hurry. We have so much to do."

Miranda gave Protecus an endearing look. Seth told her about losing the donkey and the horse and that he and Tanus would bury her for Protecus. She knew how much Protecus loved that horse and mourned her loss. She had other questions about what happened the night before but decided not to discuss them before Babrea. There was no reason to alarm the child.

Having lost both the donkey and the horse, Protecus didn't know how they would convey the fresh vegetables from the garden to the Manor. He also didn't know how to explain to Babrea what had happened to the animals. He decided to tell her that they had just run away.

Just as he was about to explain everything to Babrea, she saved him the effort involved in trying to make up a believable story.

She said, "I'm sorry you lost another Lady, Father. I know how much you loved your horse and will miss her."

Protecus wasn't aware that Babrea knew about the loss of the horse but was glad he didn't have to explain what had happened since she somehow already knew.

"Yes, I'll miss Lady," he said. "She was a good horse. But most of all, she would have helped us bring the vegetables back to the family. Now we'll have to hand-carry them to the Manor, which will take much more time."

"Don't worry, Father, everything will be okay, but we need to go for now."

Protecus grabbed two baskets as he headed for the door. Once outside, Babrea grabbed hold of his hand. They silently exited together.

Babrea led the way as they followed Bumble back to the garden. On the way there, Babrea questioned her father more about sharing. Protecus had explained what sharing was to Babrea, and it had sounded special. She wanted to know more about it.

Protecus gave her some examples of sharing, and she liked the idea. She knew that she could share by contributing something to the residents.

Babrea also questioned him about his horse from his childhood, the first one he had named Lady.

"She was a beautiful mare and very smart. She was solid black, with only a small white patch on her forehead that formed an almost perfect star. She had white socks on both back legs, and her tail was so long it touched the ground. She always made me feel proud when I rode her because she walked with such pride."

Protecus was still talking when Bumble arrived at the entrance to the garden. Bumble opened the rock wall and revealed the hidden waterfall. Protecus once again was awestruck by its beauty.

While he slept, Rutus, Otul, and Nese had been very busy. There were now lots of fruit trees, and all of them were full of colorful fruit, brilliant in color, some of which Protecus had never seen before. Babrea ran through picking the bountiful fruit, and Protecus could see how happy she was.

As she gathered the fruit, she continued to talk to her baby dragons.

"Ram is my newest baby dragon, and I want you to meet him, Father. He's standing beside you right now and wants to touch you so he can get to know you. Hold out your hand for him to smell you. Don't be afraid because he will not hurt you."

Protecus held his hand out as Babrea instructed, and he immediately felt something brush across the top of it, making him jump.

Babrea giggled and then pointed, “Look at what Ram and I have made just for you.”

Protecus looked where Babrea was pointing and saw a beautiful black horse that looked just like Lady standing just a few feet away from him. He couldn’t help but smile. Babrea grabbed his hand and led him toward the horse. She handed Protecus the rope tied around the mare’s neck and asked, “Does she look how you remember?”

Protecus reached out his hand and touched the beautiful animal. When he brushed the mare with his hand, she moved. She was as real as he was. He couldn’t believe his eyes.

“Babrea, where did you find this horse?” He asked her.

Babrea said, “I didn’t find her, Father. I told you Ram helped me, and we made her for you because I knew how much you loved the one you had as a child. Since that creature killed our other horse, you said we needed help to carry the food and fruit. I knew how much you missed your childhood horse, so I thought that you would love having another one just like her. She can pull our wagon for us, just like you said.”

Protecus petted the animal. She was beautiful, all black, with the same mark on her forehead as his childhood horse. She also had two white socks, just like Lady. He led the mare to a grassy area where she could eat until they gathered the food and fruit and were ready to leave.

Babrea asked Protecus, “Will you name her Lady too?

“No, even though she looks like Lady, I think it’s time for a change, don’t you agree? I will name this one Beauty because she’s beautiful.”

Hearing that her Father loved his new gift made Babrea smile. She was happy her father loved his new horse.

Protecus then turned his full attention to the harvest. He began to pick the fruit and ate some as he gathered it. Protecus had never eaten such delicious fruit. It was sweet and juicy and the best he had ever tasted. He ate until he was full. Then he walked over to where the mare was grazing and gave her a ripe red apple. She nickered for him to give her more. “That’s all for now, girl. I’ll give you another one later.”

Then Protecus began to pick the vegetables. There were large full ears of corn, and plump green beans, which were all plentiful. The potatoes had grown so large they were breaking free from the soil, so they didn’t require digging. He picked them up from the dark, fertile ground and put them in his basket.

Protecus quickly filled both the baskets he had brought with him. Everything was exceptional. The garden had only begun to form last night, but everything was already fully ripened and ready to eat. It was almost unbelievable.

As Protecus neared the end of one of the rows of corn, to his amazement, there stood a shiny new wagon. It had mysteriously appeared, complete with a harness. He couldn’t help but smile.

He put his baskets down, which were now quite heavy with food and fruit, and went to retrieve Beauty. After harnessing her to the wagon, Protecus started putting the fruit and vegetables he had gathered into the wagon. He returned several more times after that with his baskets overflowing with fruit and vegetables. Protecus gathered food until he was utterly exhausted.

Bumble told Babrea it was getting late and time for them to return to the safety of the Manor. She told her father, “It’s time for us to return home. It will be dark soon, and we must be behind the stone walls.”

Protecus agreed it was getting late, and he didn't want to run into any of those snarling dog creatures again. He put Babrea on the wagon seat and climbed up beside her. Then Babrea told Bumble to lead the way. Beauty nodded and nickered like she understood some secret signal given to her, and then she followed Bumble as he led the way to her new home.

This time, they arrived back at the Manor without any incident. Thankfully, nothing tried to eat them or jump on them. Protecus was relieved. He felt they had suffered enough drama the night before to last them two lifetimes.

Seth came out to meet them as they pulled up. He was amazed at the abundant bounty of fruits and vegetables they had. He tilted his head with an inquiring look on his face.

"Where on Earth did you find all this food, horse, and wagon?"

Protecus just smiled, leaving Seth to surmise it must have all come from the same miraculous place.

Seth figured that one day when Protecus was ready to share his wondrous tales of surprise with him, he would. Protecus knew that Seth had questions, but he was glad he didn't have to answer them, at least not right then. Protecus was tired from his morning of gathering food and fruit, plus the excitement from the day before, coupled with the sleepless night he had suffered through, had all but drained him.

Babrea broke the silence, "Seth, we are going to share all this delicious food and fruit with everyone."

Seth smiled at her, "How nice of you, Babrea. I'm sure it will be appreciated. Thank you."

"You are so very welcome. I want to share it with everyone, even Devant, if she wants some."

Then off she ran with her little basket, knocking on every cottage door until she had given everyone something. She enjoyed seeing the smiles on everyone's faces as she scurried about. It made her feel good inside.

While Babrea was busy giving away food, Seth, and Protecus unharnessed the horse. Then they put Beauty and the cow away in the new covered area that Seth and Carver had built.

Protecus bragged about what a great job they had done, "This is very nice, Seth. I'm amazed at how fast the two of you put this together."

"I know what you mean. Carver works so fast that I can hardly keep up with him. He and all of his workers are tireless. Once they start a job, they don't stop until it is finished. What I can't figure out, though, is where the lumber is coming from."

There were many strange things around the Manor lately that Seth didn't understand, but for now, he was thankful for what they had.

However, one thing extremely bothered him, and he felt he needed to discuss it with Protecus. Tanus was troubled enough by it to tell Seth, and he thought it important enough to require his telling Protecus.

"Protecus, Tanus told me that he saw Babrea talking to herself, which she has done more than once. He has seen her wander alone outside the Manor walls on several occasions. With the sighting of that creature, I felt it advisable to tell you about it. Tanus said he told Devant about Babrea's leaving the grounds alone because he knew she shouldn't be doing that. He said Devant lashed out at him and told him she didn't care what happened to the little girl. Devant told him that as far as she was concerned, Babrea could disappear forever, and she wouldn't care. Then she told him never to bother her again with details about that silly little child."

Devant's attitude toward Babrea had always alarmed Protecus, so the information Seth shared didn't surprise him. Devant had never cared for anyone except herself and made no secret of that. What did bother him, though, was that she seemed to be wishing harm upon the little girl. Protecus had always felt Devant's viciousness, but lately, she seemed more inclined toward genuine evil.

Protecus assured Seth, "I'll talk with her about it first thing in the morning. She is a harsh woman, and few things matter to her, but she had no reason to speak to Tanus that way. He did the right thing. I'll tell him to speak to me when he has concerns about Babrea and to steer clear of Devant as much as possible."

He tried to explain to Seth, "Babrea isn't crazy. She is exceptional. However, you and Tanus don't have to worry about her safety because she has a protector. He watches over her at all times."

Seth was amazed by that statement but continued to hold his questions. He knew the day would come when Protecus would be willing to share more with him, so he would save all his questions for then.

Most of the Manor people were very old, so it was difficult for them to hunt for food. They were thankful for anything they received and blessed Babrea as she happily distributed fruit and vegetables to all the residents.

Once she had finished gifting everyone, Babrea went to the kitchen, where she found Miranda eating with Tanus and Solarian.

Babrea had saved some of the unique fruit, especially for them, and was excited to give it to them. At that moment, Protecus and Seth brought in a couple of big baskets of vegetables from the wagon.

Miranda couldn't believe her eyes. Protecus had grown some lovely vegetables in his hydroponics garden before. Still, these were much more vibrant in color and massive in size.

"Oh, my Protecus, how did you grow these lovely vegetables? They are gorgeous. The fruit Babrea brought to us is beautiful. I'm sure it will be divine if it tastes as good as it looks. I'll fix a big pot of vegetable stew with all these lovely vegetables tomorrow. It will be a welcome change to have fresh vegetables. You and Babrea must be hungry. I made soup for everyone today, and I've already taken some to Devant. I've kept it warm for you. Have a seat, and I'll fix you a bowl."

As Miranda fixed bowls for Protecus and Babrea, she joyfully asked, "Seth would you like me to fix you a bowl as well?"

Protecus smiled a mischievous little smile and decided to allow Miranda to believe he had grown the baskets of food. It was easier to let her think that than it would be to try explaining Babrea's magical touch. He simply said, "Eat all you want because there is plenty more where this came from."

Hearing all the commotion and laughter downstairs, Devant decided to find out what the noise was. She walked downstairs to the kitchen, and the entire group became silent as she entered. They appeared to be having a party but hadn't invited her.

Once Protecus saw Devant, he quickly explained, "I know how you hate parties, so I hadn't called you downstairs."

Protecus was right, Devant detested parties, but she didn't like that she wasn't informed there was fresh fruit to eat. She grabbed a large tomato and asked, "Is this thing real? Where on Earth did it come from?"

She knew that Protecus had never grown anything so substantial in his entire life and wanted an explanation.

Protecus had to quickly give Devant a plausible answer, so he said, "I grew it with a new formula that I've been experimenting with. I'm very pleased with the outcome."

Devant turned her head sideways and gave him a curious look. She didn't believe him for one minute. She intended to check out what he was saying for herself. She slipped the tomato into her pocket and said, “I’m going to my room and intend to take a nap, so keep it quiet down here.”

Devant knew where Protecus grew the plants in his little indoor garden, so she headed straight to his laboratory. She wanted to see for herself what was going on there. Once inside his lab, Devant compared the tomatoes growing there to the one she had retrieved from the kitchen. There was no comparison. She knew that Protecus was lying to her. He hadn’t produced this or any of the other vegetables she saw in the kitchen.

Devant knew that Babrea had something to do with all of this. She thought that over for a few minutes, then left the lab. She climbed even higher in the Manor, all the way to the tower. Once she reached the point where the stairs stopped, she ascended in midair until she rose to the highest level. There, a mysterious figure was waiting for her.

Red glowing eyes shot in Devant’s direction as the figure hovered outside the tower. Devant then spoke to the dark creature, calling it by name.

“Talon, I have not forgiven your failed attempt to fulfill my commands, but I have a new mission for you. You must not fail me this time, or the consequences will be dire.”

Devant whispered something to the creature. Then with a nod of his grotesque head, it signaled it had understood. Fire seemed to shoot from its eyes as it turned and flew from the broken tower window into the black night sky.

Devant then let out a sinister laugh as she floated back onto the lower part of the tower. She then calmly walked the rest of the way down the stairs to her bedroom. She smiled to herself because she was most pleased with her new plan.

Everyone had eaten their fill, then it was time for bed. Since the incident with the flying monster, Protecus had assigned Seth and Tanus a room inside the Manor. The barn was no longer safe for them as the creature had already attacked there once and could easily return. Protecus didn't want to tempt fate.

Thankfully, no one had seen the beast since the first encounter, but Protecus still wanted to be cautious.

As the boys were about to head off to their room for the night, Seth told Miranda good night with a smile and a wink, and Protecus kissed Babrea good night. Both girls followed Miranda to their room. Miranda told the girls to dress for bed and she would return to tuck them in. She then stopped Protecus as he was about to climb the stairs and asked if she could speak to him outside.

Protecus joined her outside the back door, and Miranda said, "Protecus, I know you're exhausted, but I need to speak to you about something."

"Sure, Miranda. What's bothering you?"

"I've seen Babrea talking to herself before, but lately, she has been doing it a lot more. I don't believe it's cause for alarm because most kids have make-believe friends they often talk to. I only mention it because it feels like something is in the room with us when she talks to her friend. I don't ever see anything. It's more like I sense something is there. I'm sure this sounds crazy, but I felt I had to tell you about it, if for no other reason than for her safety."

Through the years, Devant had almost driven Miranda insane, so she knew what was happening with Babrea could very well be in her mind. However, it had bothered her for some time, so she felt she needed to share her concerns with Protecus. Miranda wanted him to be aware so that he could help watch for any possible problem that might arise.

Protecus knew what Miranda was talking about, and he knew what presence she was describing. It wasn't an imaginary friend. Bumble was always with Babrea, and his presence was getting harder to conceal as he grew.

With Miranda's concern and awareness, Protecus felt led to tell her more about Babrea and her abilities. He decided it was time to share Babrea's history with Miranda.

"Miranda, I will share with you what happened just before Babrea arrived. I think it's time you knew, and it might help you better understand what's going on. Before her arrival, I had a recurring dream about a unique gift that I would receive, which was vivid. In it, a voice told me I was to receive an exceptional gift, and I was to teach and nurture it because it would change the world. I clung to that dream, hoping it would come true one day. Then, Babrea came to us. The morning I found her, she was wrapped in a blanket, tucked inside a basket, and left outside the big iron gates. Since her arrival, I've known she was special, but I believe she has developed a magical touch as she's grown. I can't explain how she does the things she does, but for the time being, we must keep her abilities a secret. Please, tell no one what I have shared with you, especially Devant."

"I understand, Protecus, and I promise you that her secret is safe with me. I've thought for a long time that Babrea was different. I haven't told anyone about this before now, especially Devant, nor will I. I love that little girl as much as if she were my child, and I would never put her in harm's way. I've never understood Devant's treatment of her. Rest assured, Protecus, that I will do everything within my power to keep all of the children safe."

"Thank you for your help, Miranda. I knew I could count on you. Babrea is indeed an exceptional little girl. She craves our love and affection, and she deserves it."

When they ended their conversation, they walked back inside the Manor. Protecus bid Miranda goodnight and drug his weary body upstairs. As he climbed the long stairway to his room, he thought he saw a large shadow pass outside the balcony above him. The balcony was now only a shabbily covered, gaping hole. It had originally been a large set of glass doors leading onto a deck that extended beyond the walls and was probably beautiful at one time. However, those glass doors had long since broken and fallen onto the jagged rocks below.

The balcony was now derelict and unsafe, as many boards were rotten, and some had fallen into the sea. Seth had covered the opening with the materials available to keep out the cold wind and prevent anyone from falling out. However, it was still a very unsafe place to be.

Protecus climbed the remaining steps toward the balcony area. That opening had always alarmed him. He decided that first thing in the morning, he would ask Seth to please have Carver cover it with something more permanent.

If that flying creature got hungry again and returned, it could easily break through that temporary covering and get inside the Manor. That would be horrific.

While Protecus stood there thinking about the opening for a couple more minutes, he felt a cold chill run up his spine. He wasn't sure if it was just the cold he felt or something far more menacing. Protecus hesitated there a little longer until the ominous feeling left him. Then he shrugged his shoulders, thinking it was only in his mind, and went to bed.

An ominous wind passed over the balcony again after Protecus walked away. Or was it something much more sinister?

CHAPTER 15
THE BALCONY

Dawn, the next day felt much warmer to Protecus when he woke. Even the sun seemed somewhat brighter. He thought it could be wishful thinking, but it made him smile.

Devant was still snoring, as usual, so Protecus quietly rolled over to get out of bed. He almost stepped on Babrea when he placed his feet on the floor. She was sitting cross-legged beside his bed. She smiled when he looked down at her and whispered, “It’s time for us to go now.”

Protecus slipped out of bed and quickly dressed, trying not to wake Devant. Then he and Babrea headed down to the barn to harness the horse.

Seth was two steps ahead of them, though. Babrea had already awakened him and asked him to hitch Beauty to the wagon so they could return to the garden. Seth didn't question either of them about the garden Babrea referred to. He was just happy they had plenty of food to eat.

Protecus thanked Seth for harnessing the horse and having everything ready to go. Then he remembered the shabby board over the balcony opening upstairs.

Protecus told Seth, “I was up near the balcony last night and noticed how thin that board is over the opening. If you and Carver could find the time to replace that board and maybe fortify the area, I would feel much safer. I was near that opening last night, and I think I heard that creature flying around up there. It would be easy for that thing to get in through that opening.”

“I’d forgotten about that opening. You’re right, Protecus. That would be an easy way for that creature to get inside the Manor. If we close it off, though, it will be hard to see up there because that opening is the only means of light for the third floor."

"There's no reason for anyone to go up there anyway, Seth. That floor is unfinished and should be blocked off. See if Carver can figure out how to seal off that entire area. With those cliffs below and nothing to cover the jagged rocks below, it's no longer a safe place. It was probably beautiful when first built, but it's dangerous now."

Seth agreed and assured Protecus, "We'll take care of it, Mr. Protecus, don't worry."

Protecus lifted Babrea onto the wagon seat and climbed up on the bench beside her, saying, "Thanks, Seth. We'll return with another wagon load of fresh fruits and vegetables before dark." And off they went.

Bumble began to lead the way, and Beauty obediently followed him down the path to the waterfall. Once they were inside the garden, Protecus lifted Babrea to the ground. She became very animated and began to spin almost immediately. Then she told Protecus, "I have a new baby dragon, and his name is Rana. Come and meet him, Father. He has come to the garden to bring us lots of fresh air so that everything can breathe and grow better."

When Babrea introduced Protecus to her new baby Dragon, he was so close to Protecus that he could hear it breathe. It was a little disconcerting, but Protecus knew that Babrea's dragons were here to protect and help her. He no longer feared any of them.

Protecus began picking the fruits and vegetables, and Babrea helped him. After a while, she asked him if she could pick some flowers for her sister.

"Are you referring to Solarian as your sister?"

"Yes, Father, Solarian is my sister, and Seth and Tanus are my brothers."

Protecus was glad Babrea had bonded with the others, and she felt they were all family. Then she said something that caused Protecus to take pause. She asked if she could also pick flowers for her mother if they had time.

"If you want to give Devant flowers, it's all right by me, Sweetheart, but she won't appreciate them. Then she'll probably end up throwing them away."

"Oh, Father, I wasn't referring to Devant. I meant Miranda. She is my mother. Devant is your wife, but she's not my mother."

Protecus wasn't surprised that Babrea had no love for Devant. Still, in the same breath, he completely understood why she felt that Miranda was her mother.

"Devant told me to never call her mother, so I don't. Miranda saw me crying one day and asked me what was wrong. I told her what Devant had said to me, and she told me I could call her mother if I wanted to. Miranda said it would make her very happy, so I did, and it made me happy too. I've called her mother ever since that day."

Protecus could see that Miranda had loved Babrea from the first day of her arrival. She had never shown any partiality between the children from the beginning. She loved and treated all of them the same.

Protecus was glad that Babrea felt close to Miranda and thought of her as family. She needed a family, and it seemed she had created one of her very own.

Once Babrea had finished picking her flowers, Bumble said it was time for them to return to the Manor. Bumble led the way back, with Beauty following close behind him.

Upon their return, Protecus couldn't help but notice the excellent job Carver and his helpers had done building the cottages for the residents. They had already finished seven of them and were busily at work on the last one. They were very comfortable, sturdy-looking buildings and precisely what was needed for the cold nights that were to come. They would also help protect the people from whatever might try to swoop down from the sky in the middle of the night.

Babrea had finished passing out food to all the residents and told Protecus, "I'm going to take the flowers to Mother now. Solarian will love her flowers too."

As Babrea ran toward the kitchen, she shouted, "Mother, come see what lovely flowers I've picked for you."

Miranda smiled as she took the flowers. She hadn't seen flowers in such a very long time. She thanked Babrea as she hugged her and gave her a long, loving kiss on the cheek. "These are beautiful, Sweetheart, thank you. I'll put them in water so they can live."

Miranda grabbed an old jug and went to the well for water. Babrea headed off in search of Solarian and Tanus so that she could give them their flowers too.

Devant had witnessed the display of affection between Miranda and Babrea and felt immediate anger. She expected Miranda's loyalty because she owed Devant for her livelihood. Devant didn't care for children and resented Babrea most of all. She was consuming Miranda's time and attention from doing what Devant needed her to do.

When Devant heard Babrea calling Miranda mother, it made her blood curdle. Devant hated children. They always had filthy little hands, and she couldn't stand them touching her with them. They perpetually smelt bad, reeking of sweat and dirty shoes.

Devant had no desire to be anyone's mother. However, she was an extremely jealous person and didn't like not being the center of attention. She knew Babrea had already turned the residents against her, and now she was stealing Miranda's attention too.

Babrea had become a nuisance. She was a thorn in Devant's side. Devant had been suspicious of Babrea since her arrival. She was always running around, smiling, happy, and full of presents. Where was she getting all of the flowers from anyway? That large colorful fruit should not be able to grow anywhere, yet there it was. Nothing of beauty should be living now, but since Babrea arrived, things seemed to be thriving again. Babrea was interfering with Devant's plans, and she didn't like her plans being fouled up.

All of Devants attempts to get rid of Babrea, thus far, had been thwarted. It was time to speed up her plans. It was time for Babrea to disappear, like everyone else that got in Devant's way. That little snip of a girl could not be allowed to destroy her well-laid plans.

Devant waited for Miranda and Babrea to leave the kitchen. Then she silently slipped down the steps and into the root cellar, where she knew Protecus stored the extra milk to keep it fresh. She poured most of the milk out of the barrel, leaving only enough for one serving. Then she poured the contents of a flask she had concealed inside her pocket into the wooden barrel. After replacing the top back on the barrel, a peculiar smile crossed her face as she climbed the steps. Devant checked to ensure no one was in the kitchen, then she slipped back upstairs without ever being seen.

Miranda and Babrea had gone to the well to get water for the flowers. When they returned, there was no sign of Devant or evidence of her ever being in the kitchen.

Miranda finished preparing food for the children then she went to the cellar to get some milk for them to drink. Since there was only enough for one, Miranda decided to give it to Babrea since she was the youngest. Miranda made a mental note to herself to let Protecus know they needed more milk.

After the children finished supper, Miranda fixed a bath for Babrea and Solarian. Once they finished bathing, they dressed for bed, and Miranda tucked them both in.

Protecus came in as Babrea was nodding off to sleep and kissed his daughter goodnight. When he slipped out of the room, he passed Tanus in the hallway heading to the bedroom he shared with Seth. Protecus told him goodnight, too, then went to the kitchen to grab a bite to eat.

While Miranda fixed Protecus a plate, she remembered they were out of milk and told him. He finished eating and then went to the barn to milk the cow.

While Protecus was at the barn, Miranda slipped outside the kitchen door. Seth was quietly waiting for her there. Though Miranda was ten years older than Seth, he had led a hard life. His age belittled his experience. They had become attracted to one another through their years together. They had now reached a point where they felt they should make their relationship known. Thus far, they had kept their feelings private, but Seth was proud of Miranda and wanted to shout his feelings for her from the rooftops.

Seth wanted to go for a walk around the courtyard, but Miranda, ever vigilant, didn't want to venture where she couldn't keep an eye on the doorway. She needed to know the children were safe.

After a short while, Protecus returned with the fresh milk and smiled, saying goodnight as he passed Miranda and Seth on the porch.

They planned to tell everyone about their relationship, but after the incident with the flying creature, everything had been so hectic they hadn't gotten around to it. They agreed to make their announcement the following day.

Protecus took the bucket of milk down to the seller to put it in the barrel. He noticed a spot where it looked like some of the milk had leaked onto the floor, so we checked the container to ensure it wasn't leaking. The barrel seemed fine, and he found no leaks, so he refilled sound. He knew that sound could only be one thing. The demon-flying creature had returned.

Protecus could hear the creature's wings flapping above him, and his heart sank. He knew that he could not make it back to safety in time.

Protecus looked down at Babrea, still fast asleep in his arms, and realized that awful flying creature had come for her.

Thankfully, something else was in the sky that night. One minute the screeching creature was hovering just above him and closing in. Then the noise seemed to descend downward, and suddenly there was silence.

Somehow, Protecus managed to make it the rest of the way back to the safety of the Manor. He sighed a long sigh of relief as he stood almost frozen for several seconds. Once he finally collected himself, he looked down at Babrea, and unbelievably, she was still sleeping.

Bumble exhaled, and Protecus felt his breath on the back of his neck. Bumble was letting Protecus know that he had been there all along. The little dragon had never left Babrea. Bumble had been watching over her the entire time.

Protecus slowly carried Babrea to her bed, tucked her in again, and waited to ensure she was alright.

Bumble was uncertain, but he now knew who Babrea's enemies were. He had seen someone lift her from her warm bed and set her out on that precarious perch, but he hadn't seen their face. Once the dark-cloaked figure lay the baby down on the loosened boards, the wind blew the hood off, and Bumble could see the face. It was Devant.

Bumble could see her clearly in the moonlight, even though she was trying to hide her identity with the hooded cloak. He waited and watched while Devant summoned her flying creature, which she called Talon. She instructed it to carry her back home then Talen was to return for Babrea.

Devant said, “Take that child far out to sea and drop her. Let the four winds take her. I cannot allow her to reach maturity. She is an obstacle to my plans for this planet.”

While Babrea lay, appearing helpless, waiting to be cast into the sea and forever lost, Bumble waited. He knew that Talon would return soon, and when he did, that evil demon would die once and for all.

Protecus had appeared before the creature's return, though. Bumble stayed the course and watched for the beast to return.

However, when Protecus walked onto that precarious bridge, Bumble couldn’t allow Babrea’s father to fall. He was human and would die if he fell onto the rocks below.

Bumble telepathed for help because he knew he couldn’t save Protecus alone.

A mysterious icy vapor appeared in the night sky that enveloped the flying creature, turning it into a frozen mass in midair. The foul thing fell to the ground immediately, and as it hit the jagged rocks below broke into a million pieces like glass.

Once Bumble knew Babrea was alright, he watched Protecus leave with her. Bumble telepathed to Adolla, thanking her for her help. She answered back on an icy vapor.

“You’re welcome, little one.”

Babrea continued to sleep deeply, almost as if she were drugged. Protecus put Babrea to bed, then bowed and lovingly kissed her goodnight. She never made a sound. Bumble then nestled down on the floor beside her, ever vigilant in his protection.

Protecus stood beside Babrea, staring down at her when Seth and Miranda came rushing in from outside. They had heard the screeching sound outside the Manor and went looking for Protecus to warn him.

They found him in Babrea's bedroom when they returned inside. Seth immediately sensed Protecus's distress. The events of the horrific night had finally caught up with him. When he stood to go to the kitchen, he almost fell. Seth caught Protecus and steadied him, then walked with him to the kitchen bench. Seth was concerned about Protecus. At that moment, he seemed extraordinarily frail and vulnerable.

"When Miranda and I heard the creature tonight, we came to tell you."

"I saw it, Seth. Babrea and I were almost its meal."

"Oh my God, what happened. Are you both alright?"

"The boards were loose on the opening upstairs, and somehow, Babrea was at the end of the balcony. She was sound asleep. There's no reason she should have been out there. She couldn't have gone out there by herself. Someone must have carried her there. When I got to her, she was asleep and never woke. She acts like she's been drugged."

"Well, the important thing is that she is alright."

Seth was confused. "I don't understand, though. Carver and I worked together on that opening, and we sealed it off completely, just as you asked. We placed new boards tightly together across the opening, then nailed them firmly into place. We sealed that part of the stairway completely before we finished. Nothing could get in or out because we used lots of nails and drove them securely, ensuring the area was safe. I checked every board myself."

Miranda said, "Protecus, I checked that Babrea was asleep before I went outside. I was only a few feet away at the back door. No one entered the Manor from outside after I put the girls to bed."

Protecus realized someone from inside the Manor must have moved Babrea onto the rickety balcony. He knew those nails hadn't moved by themselves. Only one person was despicable enough to have done all of that. It had to have been Devant.

Protecus shared his thoughts with Seth and Miranda, and they both agreed with him. Miranda knew Devant hated the little girl, but it was hard to believe she had actually tried to murder her.

Seth couldn't comprehend anyone having that much hate in them. He knew Devant hated children, but she had gone too far this time.

Protecus told Seth, "I'm going upstairs right now and confront her."

Seth insisted on coming along. Miranda said she would stay downstairs with the children. Protecus almost tripped several times as he climbed the stairs. He was much weaker than he realized from the night's events. Seth steadied him, and "I'll help you, Father" slipped out his mouth.

Seth didn't realize he said them, but Protecus heard him, which renewed his energy to do what he had to.

When Protecus reached the top of the stairs, he headed straight for his bedroom. He then burst into the room, ready to confront Devant. However, all he found was an empty room. Devant was nowhere around.

Protecus was glad, in a way, that she wasn't there because he was afraid that he might have strangled her with his bare hands.

He sat down on the side of the bed and placed his head in his hands, then began to sob openly. The day's events had finally caught up with him, and he was exhausted.

Seth was moved beyond words as he watched Protecus. All that he could do was to give him comfort. Seth kneeled in front of Protecus and silently allowed him to release his anguish. When Protecus calmed down, he began to speak.

Protecus had held too many secrets for too long, and now he desperately needed to tell someone. He decided to share with Seth what he had shared with Miranda. He wanted Seth to know what happened on the day of Babrea's arrival. Protecus then shared with Seth what Adolla shared with him on that day.

"I want to share something I know will sound incredible to you, but it's all true. Before Babrea came to us, I had a dream that repeated itself about a unique gift I was supposed to receive. The morning Babrea arrived, I found her outside the Manor gates. I knew that she was the gift I was to receive. In my dream, I was to care for, teach and raise her as my own. The strangest part was when I met her benefactor. Please bear with me while I tell you this part because it's incredible, and you will probably think me mad. I met the voice I heard in my perpetual dream, foretelling of Babrea's coming. It was a great dragon, and she told me her name was Adolla. She lives far beneath this Manor in the caves. Adolla told me the child's name was Babrea, and I was to teach and nurture her. The dragon also said that Babrea was going to change the world.

The story Protecus told Seth was quite astonishing, but it was also plausible. It brought to light many of the strange and unusual things happening around the Manor for the last few years.

The beautiful fruits and bountiful vegetables were a gift from Babrea. Seth knew the barren soil couldn't possibly grow those incredible things. Protecus was a smart man, but there was no way he could have produced such a plentiful supply of food in such a short time. The miracle of the much-needed cow, seemingly appearing out of thin air whenever they needed milk the most, was a real blessing. The horse and wagon arriving at the exact point when they needed it the most was yet another unusual occurrence.

Protecus felt such relief just being able to talk about all that happened. Telling someone what he had held confidentially for so many years gave him comfort.

He also needed to know that someone else shared Babrea's secret besides himself. If anything should ever happen to him, Protecus felt Seth could be trusted to take care of her for as long as he lived.

Seth assured Protecus that Babrea's secret was safe with him, "You don't have to worry about Babrea. I will always be here and care for her with my life if needed."

Protecus relaxed after hearing Seth's declaration. He then told Seth, "Babrea has never been in any real danger. She has a protector that is always with her. He has been with her since the day she first arrived. On those occasions, when you thought that she was talking to herself, she was speaking to her protector."

Protecus then tried to explain to Seth, as best he could, that her protector was a baby dragon. He hoped Seth would understand.

Seth knew what Protecus was saying was bizarre. Many of the things going on around the Manor were beyond rational explanation. Seth believed that miracles were genuinely possible. He and his brother had escaped harm by getting out of the city when everything around them was going up in flames. While Seth was in deep thought, pondering over all that Protecus had shared with him, seemingly out of the blue, Protecus said, "I don't mind it if you call me Father."

That comment caught Seth's attention and brought a big smile to his face.

"I'm honored to have you and Tanus call me Father from now on."

Seth was speechless for a few seconds. He had thought of Protecus as a father figure to Tanus for a long time, but only this very second realized how much he loved Protecus too. Seth smiled again and then bent his head down for a minute.

"If anyone could ever replace my father, it would be you, Protecus."

With that said, they hugged each other, and Protecus gave out a long, tired sigh. Seth realized how tired he must be and offered to help remove his shoes and get into bed. He felt knew that now, Protecus could finally rest. Seth bid Protecus goodnight and quietly closed the door as he left the room.

Protecus slowly drifted off to sleep that night. In the darkness, as lightning lit up the night sky, a dark aura could be seen hovering just outside Protecus's bedroom window. While the winged beast hovered, it listened to Protecus share his long-kept secret about Babrea's history.

Devant now understood why the child had always been able to elude her wrath. Babrea was the one that history had foretold would come. She was the protector of Earth and had once again returned. Devant would now have to come up with a new plan. She would have to think of something that would cause Babrea's loved one's pain and suffering.

It was apparent the child cared for the Manor residents, especially Protecus. He would have to factor into her next scheme for control. Having the upper hand now, by knowing Babrea's secret, Devant felt she was once again in control. Devant had never been patient, and it would be difficult for her to step back now and reassess, but she could do whatever was needed. She just had to wait until the time was right to strike. All that mattered was that, in the end, she came out the winner. As the aura flew away into the darkness, the haunting sound of Devant's evil laugh trailed behind.

Protecus was exhausted and fell asleep the second his head hit the pillow, so he never heard a sound. However, Bumble heard the sadistic laughter outside, and he knew it was the evil one. He knew it would never give up trying to stop Babrea no matter what it took.

CHAPTER 16
SHARING

It had been several months since Devant's disappearance, but no one truly missed her because she was not well-liked by anyone. Since her disappearance, no one had seen her.

Babrea had just turned thirteen and was growing in leaps and bounds. Protecus taught her how to ride a horse. Seth had made her a bow and some arrows and taught her how to use them. She was a fast learner and became proficient at everything she attempted.

All of the Manor residents loved Babrea. She was such a pleasant child to be around.

Daily she would ride to Protecus's garden and spend hours there alone. Babrea liked to go there to think. She would always bring something back for the residents to eat and something for Miranda, along with flowers for their table.

Protecus would make weekly trips to the garden and gather enough food for the week for everyone because the food was bountiful. Babrea would come with him at those times and help him pick food. On those trips, Babrea appeared bemused and seemed a million miles away. When she would seemingly drift off like that, Protecus would see her looking off into space and wonder what she had on her mind. Protecus felt it was best to leave her alone in those instances and allow her to enjoy some private time.

Solarian and Tanus were also growing up and thriving. Solarian was nineteen, and Tanus was twenty. They, too, had formed a fondness for one another, similar to Miranda and Seth's attraction. Miranda was thrilled because she knew Tanus had become a fine young man.

One day Miranda pointed out to Seth that she thought his brother was falling in love with her daughter. That brought a smile to Seth's face. He was happy about that possibility because he felt destiny had brought the four of them together, and their pairing was imminent.

Seth was in love with Miranda and wanted to make her his wife. They had shared a lot in their young lives, so it was only natural that he was attracted to her. Seth had made up his mind to ask Miranda to marry him.

One afternoon, when Seth finally got up the nerve to ask Miranda to marry him, they were alone in the kitchen. Seth took her hands in his and was about to pop the question, but before he could say the words, Tanus flew into the kitchen.

He immediately began scrounging for something to eat, saying, "I'm starving to death. Is there anything around here to eat?"

Tanus hadn't noticed the two holding hands and Miranda gazing lovingly into Seth's eyes. Miranda quickly turned Seth's hands loose and busied herself about the kitchen. Tanus rambled around the kitchen until he finally found something to munch on, but Seth felt the mood was lost by that time. Seth had wanted this momentous occasion to be unique.

Seth smiled and then politely excused himself. Miranda smiled back and then busied herself in the kitchen as Seth walked away.

A few days later, while Miranda was preparing something for all of them to eat, Seth snuck up behind her and put his arms around her. He hadn't noticed Babrea sitting at the kitchen table, peeling potatoes. With his arms wrapped tightly around Miranda's waist, Seth turned her to face him and pulled her close. He kissed her before she could point out that they were not alone. Miranda smiled and tried to make light of the act, but Babrea had already seen the loving display. Miranda playfully pushed Seth away, then ushered him out of her kitchen while lightly teasing him, saying, "Go do something worthwhile. Go chop some firewood for the stove or something."

Babrea immediately noticed the large pile of wood stacked in the kitchen corner. She pointed to it as she told Miranda, "Mother, we have plenty of firewood. Seth doesn't need to chop anymore."

Seth smiled and continued outside, saying, "I have other things I need to be doing, Babrea. I'll see you two later."

Babrea had seen Seth kiss her mother and knew it made Miranda happy. Miranda even giggled. Babrea had never heard her mother laugh out loud before. Miranda was smiling much more lately, and Babrea felt that had to be partly due to Seth's attention.

Devant was no longer around, screaming her commands at everyone throughout the day and night, which could be part of what made Miranda happy too. Babrea didn't understand love, but watching Seth and Miranda together was special. Any of those factors could be the reason for Miranda's happiness. Still, Babrea felt it was more likely due to Seth's attention. Love was a curious thing to Babrea, and she wanted to know more about it.

One day out of the blue, Babrea asked her mother, "What is love?" At that moment, Miranda realized she had never educated her daughters in the ways of love. She knew that Babrea had seen her and Seth together, so she figured it was probably time to address those issues.

Miranda explained to Babrea, "Well, Sweetheart, the best way to explain love is when two people care for each other and want to be together forever. They are in love. Usually, when a couple falls in love, they want to get married, so they become engaged and plan their special day, called a wedding. Does that help you to understand?"

Babrea nodded, “I understand everything so far, but can you tell me more about the special day, the wedding?”

Miranda tried to explain everything the best way she could, “There are lots of different types of ceremonies. But a wedding ceremony is one where a Priest, or a Preacher, joins two people that love each other together in marriage. Your family and all of your friends are invited to join you. There are lots of pretty flowers and decorations everywhere. Then, after the celebration is over, the happy couple goes on their honeymoon. Then the party slowly winds down, and everyone goes home.”

Miranda looked distant as she spoke of those things to Babrea, so she asked her to tell her more.

“Before The Great Disaster, I attended my best friend's wedding. It was a splendid affair, and everyone there was happy. It would be so lovely if, for just one day, we could have a party like that, with everyone joyous and happy. We could all forget, at least for a little while, the bad things happening in our world.”

As Miranda spoke, Babrea reached for her mother’s hands, and while holding them within her own, she said, “Yes, Mother, I can see it too. Please tell me more about your hopes and dreams.”

Miranda closed her eyes and then told Babrea, “I can see a lovely yard filled with big trees, and they’re full of green leaves. Flowers are blooming everywhere in a blanket of colors. I can see a tiny stream surrounding my cottage, with a rock bridge leading to it. The stream is so clear you can see the fish swimming in it. My pretty stone cottage has a red-thatched roof, and yellow ruffled curtains hang in the windows. Outside there are window boxes beneath the windows, and they are full of live flowers.”

Miranda spoke about her house and yard with such vigor that it made Babrea smile. She explained how the stream flowed underneath the little stone bridge that circled her cottage. As Miranda continued to speak, the corners of her mouth upturned into a broad smile, and she became even more animated. Miranda felt as though she were physically touching the wooden rails along the sides of the stone bridge. She could almost hear the water flowing below as she walked across it. As Miranda looked out across from her cottage, she saw in the distance a sweeping lake.

She continued describing to Babrea the vivid scene before her, "I can see a beautiful lake filled with lots of fish for everyone to catch and eat. People are swimming in the lake because the water is clean and warm. Snow-covered mountains are far off in the distance, rising high into the clouds. They are so high they look like they are almost touching the clouds."

Miranda told Babrea, "I remember when I was a young girl, pretending that one day I would marry a handsome man, and we would live on an island in the cottage with a red roof. Willow trees line the edges of the stream, and a white gazebo is next to the bridge. I'll sit under that beautiful gazebo and read or watch the fish swim past. That is where I'll say, I do, to the handsome man I marry."

As Miranda spoke, Babrea envisioned, through her eyes, all that she was describing. Babrea could see the red-roofed cottage, the warm, clear lake, and the lovely gazebo. Off in the distance, she could see the mountaintops looming above everything, with many fluffy white clouds dancing above them in the clear blue sky.

Babrea had never seen mountains or clouds, but Miranda envisioned them so vividly the picture she painted was clear enough for Babrea to see too. She thought about her mother's vision and dreams, and Babrea instantly knew what she would give Miranda as a wedding gift.

Babrea continued questioning Miranda about love, marriage, and sharing, all of which she tried to answer. Babrea asked her about loss and what it felt like to lose someone you loved dearly. Miranda was confused by Babrea's questioning because, as far as she knew, the only loss Babrea had witnessed was Devant, and surely she didn't miss her.

"What loss are you feeling right now, Sweetheart?"

"I need to know what happens when you die."

Miranda then understood. Protecus was getting older, and she knew how much Babrea loved her father. She would miss him terribly and wanted to learn more about what to expect.

"Well, Babrea, when the time comes, and we have to let go of our loved ones, they will go to heaven. It is a wonderful place where all good people go. It's a happy place where we have no more pain and no worries. Our loved ones remain there forever and in our hearts for as long as we live."

Babrea thought about that information for a minute, and then she smiled. Miranda was surprised by what Babrea said next, "That sounds perfect, Mother. That means I will never lose you or my Father because you will be with me always!"

With that, Babrea ran out of the kitchen, leaving Miranda curious with a puzzled look. Miranda hoped that she had explained everything well, and when the time came for Babrea to let her loved ones, she would understand and be able to cope with it.

Protecus was in his laboratory, working, when Babrea suddenly burst into the room. Turning, he smiled at her because he was always happy to see his daughter. He asked her, "What are you so happy about today?"

Babrea questioned Protecus about love and death and if he and all of the Manor residents would join her in heaven when the time came. He reassured her, "All people with a good heart and kind soul will go to heaven when their time comes."

That answer made her happy, but her smile slowly faded. She began to get that far-away look again. The one she got when she would mentally drift to some other place. Then she became very serious, and the expression on her face grew stern. She said, "That time will probably be soon, Father, so it's good that everyone can come with us."

Protecus knew what she was saying had far more meaning than just life and death, but he was perplexed to know what she was trying to tell him. She hugged him, smiled, and said, "I'm glad we will always be together." Then she left the room, leaving Protecus with a million more unanswered questions.

CHAPTER 17
PROTECTION

Babrea wanted her mother to have all the beautiful things she had described in her wish. She wondered if her mother could live in the garden she and her dragons made for her father. She asked Bumble, "My Mother dreams of a beautiful place like the garden we created. Can she live there with Solarian?"

Bumble reminded Babrea, "Your father's garden is also home for the baby dragons. Where would they live if people were allowed to live inside? There are many people in Miranda's care, and I'm sure she would want all of them taken care of as well."

Those were all facts that Babrea hadn't taken into consideration. She thought about those things for a long while. Then she told Bumble, "I'm going to create a new place for my Mother and all the people in her care. I'll have a unique spot just for Mother. It will be her very own special place."

Babrea envisioned the setting Miranda had described to her with the lovely stream and gazebo. Babrea became animated, thinking about the new place she would create for everyone.

Babrea wanted her Father's approval for her new idea, so she went to find him. She could hardly contain her excitement as she thought about everything she planned to create.

Protecus was in his lab, busy working on a new project, when Babrea burst into the room, shouting, "Father, Father, I have an idea that I want to share with you."

"What are you so excited about, Sweetheart?"

"Mother has shared with me her vision of where she wants to live and the place where she wants to get married. I can make her wishes come true, but I will need to create the place that was in her vision. It must be large enough for all the Manor people because she will want to invite them to share in her wedding celebration. I've thought a lot about how I will design it, and I've decided that it needs to be something that can grow with time. It must also be able to protect everyone inside. Most importantly, I want a special place for Mother to live and a perfect spot for her wedding day."

The word, wedding, was the prominent part of Babrea's sentence that Protecus took away from that conversation. Had he heard what Babrea said correctly? How wonderful! He wasn't truly surprised by that information because it made sense to him that Seth and Miranda planned to wed.

Protecus had been aware of their secret meetings for a long time. He could tell there was much more to their relationship than just friendship.

Protecus focused on the rest of what Babrea said then. She said that she planned to create a special place where Miranda and Seth could say their vows to one another. He knew that Babrea could do almost anything, but it still sounded like a lot for one so small to take on.

"Sweetheart, I have always taught you that sharing is good, and what you want to do for Miranda is the kindest of all sharing. I'm sure any gift would make her very happy, but what you're planning sounds like a monumental task. What if we let Miranda and Seth get married in my garden, it's large enough for everyone. Why can't we have the ceremony there?"

"I thought about that, Father, but Bumble reminded me that my dragons live there, and I must keep them a secret for now. Besides, I want my mother and all the Manor people to have a special place just for them. I made your garden especially for you, and I want to make a different place for my mother. I need her present to remain a secret because I want it to be a surprise."

"I know how much you love Miranda, and it's a lovely idea, but are you sure you're ready to take on another undertaking so large? Maybe you should wait a week or so to rest up before you dive into another project so large. You just finished with my garden, and that was a massive undertaking. I'm confident in your abilities, and I'll support you no matter your decision, but perhaps you should rest for a while.

"I'm glad you have confidence in me and my decision-making, Father. Your faith assures me that I should proceed with this project. The special place I plan to create for Mother will be another step I must take as I grow toward fulfilling my destiny. I plan to call upon my dragons to assist me with my plans, and now that I have your support, I know I can do this, and I'm ready."

She kissed Protecus on the cheek and said, "I'm going now to design Mother's special gift, and don't worry, I'll take care of everything."

Protecus knew that Babrea could do almost anything when she set her mind to it. She had already proven her capabilities many times. Knowing that Bumble was always with her reassured Protecus that he would keep her safe from harm.

Protecus knew that Bumble could help Babrea far more than he ever could. What she described sounded like a lot, and Protecus couldn't help but worry about her. He would support her, though, because, as she had said, it was part of her learning process.

Protecus smiled and said, "I trust your judgment, Sweetheart, and I support whatever you decide. Would you like for me to come with you?"

Babrea hugged her father and said, "You're busy with your project, so stay here and finish your work. I'll let you know when I'm done with everything. Then, you can come and see everything and let me know if it all looks the way it should."

Babrea then set off to work on her plans. She had decided what she wanted to create for her mother, and now she had some designing to do.

After leaving Protecus at work in his lab, Babrea exited the Manor gates. She then took a quick look around to ensure no one was looking, then quickly climbed on Bumbles back, and away they flew to the garden.

As Bumble had grown larger, his wings had strengthened. He was now strong enough to carry Babrea. He couldn't fly for long distances, but Babrea was still small and lightweight, so he could easily carry her to the garden with no problem.

Once they arrived at the garden entrance, Babrea climbed down, but Bumble told her to stay quiet and stay where she was. He then hesitated before opening the rock wall to expose the waterfall. He sniffed the air intently, and then he started to growl. He recognized the all too familiar scent of evil. The devil dogs had returned.

It was evident that they would not stop causing problems for Babrea. There was only one way to end their pursuit, and that was to kill them. This time three of them reared their black hairy heads. One of them slowly crept from behind the biggest rock at the entrance to the garden and ran straight toward Babrea. Bumble rammed him with his head before reaching her, temporarily knocking him out. A second one circled behind Bumble while the third creature jumped on top of the big rock in front of him. They were both snarling with fangs dripping like they were rabid as they prepared to attack. The one on top of the big rock leaped first, and Bumble dodged him, causing him to run headlong into a large pile of boulders, breaking his neck. Bumble then grabbed the third one and ripped him apart with his claws. The devil dog that had previously passed out woke up at that time. Bumble quickly swept his tail underneath its feet, slamming it to the ground. Bumble then jumped on top of him, piercing its neck with his claws. It lashed the air as it struggled to free itself but quickly bled out and died.

Babrea was still where Bumble told her to stay. He reassured her that everything was safe again, then opened the waterfall for her to enter.

Protecus continued to work in his lab after Babrea left. Shortly after she departed, though, he had gotten a very uneasy feeling, one that would not leave him. He covered the new project he was working on and walked outside to search for Babrea. Protecus assumed she would work on Miranda's special gift in the courtyard. He searched for her there, but she was nowhere around. He then remembered her saying she wanted it to be a surprise, so the thought struck him that she may have gone to the garden alone.

Protecus quickly bridled Beauty, and after mounting, he let the mare have her head because he knew she would take him to the garden. The horse returned to the waterfall, as Protecus had hoped she would. It was her home away from home, having traveled there many times.

However, as Protecus rode up to where the waterfall opening should be, he was appalled by the ghastly scene before him.

The fight was over when Protecus arrived, but Babrea was nowhere in sight. Scattered all about were the carcasses of several wooly black creatures. Blood and grotesque mangled body parts were littered around the entire area outside the garden. Protecus panicked.

He dismounted and began to call out to Babrea, and when she didn't answer him, he feared the worst.

Suddenly the waterfall opened, and Babrea stood at the entrance. Thankfully, she appeared to be unharmed. Protecus rushed to her side and worriedly asked, "Are you all right, Sweetheart?"

"Yes, Father, I'm fine. Bumble took care of all of those devil dogs, so not to worry."

Protecus was obviously still shaken and just about to ask what had happened when suddenly, the creatures began to dissolve. The dry soil quickly absorbed them, leaving no evidence they ever existed. There was some strange magic at work here, an evil kind of magic.

Those hideous creatures were sent here to kill Babrea. Protecus recognized them. They were the same devil-dog creatures that attacked them when she was just a baby.

Again, Protecus asked Babrea, "Are you sure you're not hurt?"

"Father, I'm fine. You misunderstand. Those things weren't here to kill me. They came to take me away from this place. They were trying to stop me from completing my tasks."

Protecus was still visibly shaken and concerned about Babrea's well-being. Her safety was his primary concern. As anxiety overtook him, he slowly eased onto a small rock next to him to collect his thoughts. Babrea sat down next to him. She instinctively knew that her father was worried, and she needed to try to explain to him what had just happened.

Babrea explained, "The evil one sent those creatures to prevent me from fulfilling my destiny. It knows that if I'm successful with all of my tasks, the new world I am to create will once again flourish and become a beautiful place. The evil one doesn't want that to happen because it desires to be the sole ruler of Earth and have dominion over all things. It must stop me, or that will not happen. The evil one always talks to me, trying to lure me away from my mission. It tells me not to share my gifts with others because sharing is a bad thing. It says my garden should be kept private, and no one should be allowed to partake in its bounty. It continually discourages me from sharing, but I know those ideas are wrong. I know this because you and Mother have taught me that sharing is good, and I believe that to be true. I enjoy sharing and plan to continue doing it until all my tasks are complete."

Hearing Babrea's explanation put Protecus a little more at ease. Bumble told her the perimeter was safe again, and it was time for them to return inside.

"It's safe for us to enter now," then she reached for her father's hand, and Protecus grabbed Beauty's reins. Babrea led them through the waterfall and back into the safety of the garden.

As soon as they were inside, the wall of iridescent water slowly began to close behind them. Protecus wanted to question Babrea further about everything she had just told him, but she had already turned her attention to her project. Protecus tied Beauty to a nearby tree, then sat down again on a rock nearby. He patiently waited to see what Babrea was going to do next.

Babrea walked a few feet from where her father was sitting, closed her eyes, and seemed to go into her trance-like state again. She went up on her toes and began to spin. As Babrea turned faster and faster, she began to hum. Soon several animals appeared at her feet. There were many rabbits, squirrels, and several other small animals.

When Babrea finally stopped spinning, the animals began to scatter about. Then she said, "I have a new baby dragon, Father, and I want you to meet him. His name is Ram. He will help me as I create all the animals and the sea creatures Mother dreamed of."

Babrea was so excited she glowed. Lately, it seemed that she would shine anytime she became extremely animated. It still amazed Protecus to see this miraculous event. He loved to watch her do all of the magical things that she was capable of doing.

Babrea called all her dragons to come to her. After they had all gathered near her, they were excited to know what was about to take place. Babrea explained, “I need your help to create a special place for my mother. I want it to be a surprise, so it has to be created here, in the garden, away from probing eyes. When it's finished, we’ll take it to my mother. For my plan to work, I must create everything inside a bubble so that when we finish, we can fly to its final resting place inside the courtyard. A bubble can expand so all the elements I plan to create will fit inside. I want everything to be perfect for my mother because she is very special to me. Does everyone understand?”

The baby dragons stood still, quietly nodding their heads that they understood. Babrea then began to give them all their assignments.

“Rana, you are to help me create the bubble that everything will go inside.”

Rana began to blow air through his nostrils until a small bubble formed. Once he released it, it hovered just above the ground's surface.

Next, she told Otul, “We must now bring forth water to form a flowing stream. The stream must run down from the top of the mountain to the bottom, where there should be a glistening lake.”

Once Otul finished the outer banks of the lake, he touched the ground with the tendrils that hung from his wings, and water began to spring forth. The water flowed until the lake was full, and then Otul raised his wings, and the water ceased to flow. The water then began to settle within the boundaries of the lake. Many sea creatures could be seen swimming in the lake as soon as the water calmed.

Then Babrea told Nese, “There must be willows dotting the ground in a circle around a small stream.”

The willow trees appeared to hear Babrea as she spoke because they broke ground and began to form flowing branches almost in unison. The willows now stood fully developed as they began to billow their bright green colors in the soft breeze.

A small stream began to flow, slowly wrapping around the willows, forming Miranda's envisioned island. The water was so clear you could count the pebbles on the bottom.

After Babrea finished the stream, she decided she wanted more animals, so she made more appear, larger ones than before. She remembered seeing deer, antelope, and several even larger ones in the books Protecus used to educate her. She also wanted them in her gift to her Mother, so they began to appear.

As more animals began to dart about, hundreds of birds appeared overhead. Many beautiful sounds could be heard inside the bubble.

With each new element Babrea added, the bubble grew to accommodate, becoming more massive by the minute.

Babrea then had Nese help her create more trees and colorful flowers. Rana continued to refresh the air inside the bubble so the plants and animals could breathe. Otul helped Babrea add life to the new stream, filling it with colorful fish and other sea creatures happily swimming around.

Babrea remembered how Miranda had described the white tops of the mountains, and without realizing it, she had created another baby dragon. When it appeared before her, it stretched and yawned, and when he opened his claws, glittering snow fell from them as if he had just come from atop the mountain. Babrea giggled as she touched the snow. It was cold and soft to the touch, then it melted away like air.

"I will name you Tipper," she said, patting her new baby on the head.

Babrea explained to Tipper, "You are to assist me in raising mountains. They are to all adjoin and form a cascade of beauty. "Tipper immediately turned his attention to that task.

Inside the bubble, the mountains started to grow, and so did the bubble. The taller the mountains rose, the higher the bubble floated above the ground. After Babrea finished forming the three beautiful mountains from Miranda's vision, she stopped and looked at them. Babrea was pleased that they looked as she had hoped they would.

Babrea stepped inside the bubble, and all her dragons followed her. She looked around at all they had created thus far and smiled. Miranda's new world was complete.

All that was left to do was to bring the massive bubble to the Manor courtyard for Miranda to see.

Protecus had watched as the grandeur developed before him with his mouth agape. The creations forming before his eyes were miraculous. All he could do was shake his head and smile. He couldn't remember ever seeing such a beautiful collection of color in his entire life.

When Babrea completed her gift, she asked her father, "Is this how the world looked before the air was grey, and the light of life became sad?"

Protecus thought about what Babrea asked, then slowly answered, "I'm not sure, Sweetheart. I don't know how our world looked when it was brand new, but I would like to think it looked exactly like this."

That answer made Babrea smile. Protecus wondered why she had formed the bubble around the small world she had created. He was just about to ask when she revealed everything to him.

Babrea called all her baby dragons to assemble before her. They were excited as they gathered around her. They were all trying hard to listen to what Babrea had to say to them, but they were so excited. They were proud of their new accomplishments.

They were expecting praise for a job well done, which Babrea lovingly gave to each one as she patted them on their heads and thanked them. Then, Babrea explained to them what they were going to do next.

"Soon, we will all be entering the world of humans, a place where you are never to go. You will only have to be there for a short time, so I need you to all be alert, follow my instructions, and remain invisible the entire time."

They understood their instructions. Then Babrea said, "Tipper, Bumble, and Nese, you are to fly to the right side of the bubble, and Otul, Ram, and Rana, you are to fly to the left side. When I signal to you, grab your section of the bubble and fly with it where I instruct you to go."

The dragons all nodded that they understood what they were to do.

Babrea then dropped to her knees, closed her eyes, and softly said, "We will now enter the human world with the gifts you have given us. We will bring forth this bountiful treasure to share with those of pure heart. May what we give freely shine new life once again to the future of humanity. What we are about to share today will one day revitalize this dying world by sharing its renewed energy and abundance with all that live here."

Babrea stood, then turned to Protecus and said, "It's now ready, Father. We can go home."

Babrea climbed on Beauty's back, then Protecus untied the reins and handed them to her.

Babrea instructed the dragons, "Okay, everyone, you will now assume your assigned places."

When all the dragons were in their designated spots, Babrea told them, "Okay, lift now."

As the dragons began to lift, the giant bubble slowly rose higher and higher. The waterfall then reappeared, and Protecus walked through it. Once he was outside the garden, he stopped and waited.

It was a miraculous sight to watch the bubble rise as if it was free floating. As it neared the waterfall, the opening slowly widened to accommodate the immense size of the bubble.

Bumble and his brothers slowly brought the extraordinary gift for Miranda through the waterfall. Once the bubble emerged, Protecus could finally visualize the true beauty of everything. He could see the immenseness of the mountains and the beautiful blue shade of the water as it flowed from the highest peak down into the crystal-clear lake below.

The lake was so clear that Protecus could see fish of all shapes and sizes as they passed overhead. Many sea creatures were swimming around, most he couldn't readily identify. It looked like a gigantic glass-bottomed aquarium. Protecus hadn't fully grasped the gravity of its magnitude until that moment. He was mesmerized by its size.

Forward the dragons flew, towing with them Babrea's incredible creation. After the entire procession was outside the waterfall, Babrea uttered a few soft words, and the giant water gateway closed.

The waterfall slowly disappeared behind the solid stone wall again, leaving no sign that it existed.

Babrea told Protecus, "We will go to the Manor now.

Beauty started walking in the direction the dragons were carrying the bubble. Protecus followed, continuing to look upwards at the expanse above him.

With a mild tremble in his voice, when he was finally able to speak. Protecus asked, "Will the water in the lake stay forever, or will it dry up like everything else outside the courtyard and my garden?"

"That is why I placed the protective bubble around it, Father. That will keep the light of life from ever leaving it." Then she got a curious look on her face and asked, “Why is the light of life so dim in the world outside?”

Protecus thought about his answer for a few seconds. He needed his response to be as defining as he knew how to tell it.

“Well, Sweetheart, we should have been more careful with what we had. When we realized the extent of damage that we had done to our sun, we tried to reverse the destruction. I helped to create a chemical that was supposed to repair the damage. However, it never made it to its intended destination. Some people thought we would do more harm than good by tampering with nature, so they tried to stop the chemicals from being released. They thought they were doing the right thing but inadvertently caused a horrible accident. That accident caused some of the chemicals to explode in our atmosphere, which polluted our air. It also caused our soil to become contaminated and most of our water. A few rockets probably sat idle for years, eventually releasing their cargo. Some leaked, causing even more contamination. Fires caused more deaths, and looters killed many others. Instead of helping humankind, we caused more destruction.”

Babrea said, “You were trying to help and did what you thought was right. If humanity had not destroyed the light of life in the first place, none of this destruction would have happened. Nothing can live without the light of life.”

“Human beings are not perfect, Sweetheart, and we sometimes make terrible mistakes like this. I wish I could go back in time and stop the damage before it began, but I can’t. We never meant to destroy our sun. The Great Disaster was all a horrible mistake.”

Babrea was silent for several minutes. When she finally spoke, what she said was calming to Protecus. “Father, we have lost that time and can never go back. The Great Disaster isn’t what caused the problem in the first place. The destruction of the sun is what caused the problem. History cannot be changed, but we can change the future. That is what I'm here to do. One day soon, all of humankind will be able to enjoy the gift of light again because I will be able to return the light of life to this world."

For a few seconds, Protecus was speechless. He just received a real revelation for the first time since Babrea's arrival. The realization of what Babrea was, had now become evident to him. He knew he had to carefully phrase what he was about to ask. Protecus needed to know the answer but wasn't sure he was ready to hear it.

He softly asked, "Darling, when you speak of the light of life, do you mean the sun in the sky above us?"

She laughed and answered, "Father, I'm not in the sky now. I'm here with you."

Then Babrea got a most perplexed look on her face and asked him, "Is that why everything is dying, and the sky is dim because I'm not shining above?"

Protecus then knew Babrea's real secret. He knew why at times, mainly when she was happy or excited, she glowed. He later recalled the pendant she had worn around her neck and what it had written on it the day of her arrival.

Let there be light.

Babrea had returned to Earth as an infant to grow, learn, and strengthen. She was now beginning to do just that. She was here to revive everything around her as it had been at the beginning of time. Protecus now understood why he was to be her guide. He couldn't help her with her tasks, but he could explain how the destruction had happened. He could also educate and guide her so that she could better understand the changes that had taken place and why.

He told her, "We are all very sorry for our mistakes, but as you say, they are in the past, and we cannot change them. We can do better in the future, and now that you are here with us, we have another chance to correct our mistakes and hopefully never repeat them."

Babrea had many more questions about the world and the condition it was currently in. The Manor was now in sight, though, so she decided to hold off on her questions for now. She looked up at the bubble floating above her and the beautiful clear water inside, glittering like an iridescent rainbow, and it made her smile.

Babrea was pleased with her accomplishment and hoped it would also make Miranda happy. She then told Bumble and his brothers to stop. She wanted to go ahead of them to prepare everyone for what they were about to receive.

Protecus opened the courtyard gates, and Babrea rode Beauty inside. Walking into the courtyard, he saw Miranda rushing toward him, with Seth close behind her. She hugged Protecus while Seth helped Babrea down off the horse.

Unbeknownst to Protecus, he and Babrea had been away from the Manor for several days, and Miranda and Seth were distraught. They didn't know where the two of them were. They had searched the entire Manor and grounds with no luck. They feared something terrible had happened to both of them.

After Miranda explained how long they had been away, Protecus apologized for worrying them. He had no idea they were away for so long. It felt like they had only been away for a few hours, so he was shocked to find out otherwise.

Babrea apologized, "Mother, I'm so sorry that we worried you and Seth, but I've been busy and lost track of time. I was making a special present for you and Seth, and I hope you both like it and are willing to share it."

Babrea then telepathed Bumble that it was time for him and his brothers to lower the giant bubble. As the dragons slowly brought the beautiful, picturesque scene downward, Babrea called all the residents to come outside. She wanted them to see what she had created for them. Once everyone had assembled in the yard, the bubble began to settle to the ground.

Astonishment and amazement best described the look on the faces of every individual who saw the phenomenal sight before them. Everyone was in awe as the massive bubble began to appear. With the baby dragons still invisible, the giant bubble appeared free-floating as it settled onto the ground. It was immense in size and spectacular in color. Once it was completely level with the ground, Babrea signaled to Bumble that it was time to release their cargo and head back to the garden. Bumble then indicated to his brothers that it was time to leave. They all flew back to their Earthly home.

Carver then rode up in his wagon with his entire group pulling their wagons of equipment behind him. He stopped when he reached Babrea. She spoke to him softly, giving him instructions and pointing toward different areas of the bubble. Carver then directed everyone to follow him as they drove their wagons toward the bubble.

As they got nearer, a small stream appeared and slowly widened as the team of horses pulled closer. It looked like the horses were walking on water as Carver led the way inside.

From the watery pathway, a stone bridge slowly began to rise. As the bridge eased into view, the horses continued clip-clopping across it. After the last wagon entered, Babrea asked everyone to wait in the courtyard until she returned. Then she, too, walked across the bridge, which was now completely visible.

When she made it to the other side, she stopped. At first, she appeared to be standing on water, but when she took her next step, grass sprouted with her every step. When she stopped walking, the grass stopped spreading behind her.

Near where she now stood, a bright light appeared just below the water's surface. Once the light neared the surface, it seemed to burst upon the scene. The beam was a bright, pulsating beacon. As the glittering water receded, a red-topped lighthouse rose from beneath the water. As it broke through the water's surface, a stream began to form, encircling the entire lighthouse.

The stream ran to a waterfall that cascaded down to the beach below. All of the water then flowed into the lake. Once the glittering water receded from the lighthouse, the light beacon on the top began to turn.

As Babrea walked further inside the bubble, more bright green grass appeared with each footstep she took.

Then, another red-topped building emerged in the center of the circle.

When it became completely visible, it was evident that it was a red-topped building. It was Miranda's cottage, with its pretty flower boxes underneath the windows and big bright windows with yellow curtains.

Miranda's house was now complete. Babrea took one last look at everything before walking back across the bridge, where Miranda and Seth waited patiently.

As Babrea approached them, she reached her hands out toward her mother and said, "Come with me, Mother. I want you to see everything. This Orb is my wedding present to you and Seth."

Babrea led the way holding Miranda's hand while Seth followed close behind. As they walked across the bridge, Babrea pointed to the willow trees around the gazebo. Then she asked Miranda, "Does everything look how you envisioned it, Mother?"

Miranda was amazed. She couldn't find the words to speak. She recalled telling Babrea about all the special things she hoped for on her wedding day but never dreamed she would have them.

Looking around, Miranda realized that Babrea had created everything before her from those shared thoughts. This place was exactly how Miranda had visualized a picture-perfect world should look.

Babrea then pointed to the lighthouse and explained, "The beacon shining from it is an Everlight. It will shine forever so that I will always know where you are and forever be able to find my way home to you. No matter where I may wander on my life's journey, I can always return to you because it will shine forever.

Miranda was as excited as a little girl getting her first pony. Seth could only stare at his surroundings in amazement. He was unable to think of anything to say that made sense. Miranda was speechless as well. She hadn't realized it, but she had been holding her breath as Babrea steadily pulled her along, showing her everything, so she was now breathless. As Babrea led her mother through the bubble, she told Miranda, "I hope you like your present, Mother. I've never seen mountains or lakes, only pictures of them and the images you shared with me. The cottage is for you and Seth to share whenever you get married."

Babrea had relied on Miranda's vision of how things should look, and seeing the smile on her mother's face let her know she had gotten it right. Miranda was beyond words. She could only smile and gasp now and then at the beauty of it all. Babrea had created an entire world just for her. It was more beautiful than anything Miranda had ever seen. She had lived in the city all her life and had never seen big trees, only the smaller ones that lined the sidewalks and the short shrubs that grew in the parks. Miranda had only dreamed of mountains and their majestic grandeur. She had hoped to one day see real ones again, even small ones, and now she could gaze upon huge ones every day.

Babrea's mountains were magnificent. They were huge and much prettier than any picture Miranda had ever seen. Everything was so vibrant and picturesque. Miranda felt that she was looking at a watercolor painting, and almost too perfect to be real.

Miranda waited for Seth to catch up because he had fallen behind while admiring his surroundings.

Seth, come touch the water, it's warm, and it feels like silk. It's so clear you can see the rocks on the bottom."

While Seth joined Miranda, Babrea went outside to get Protecus, Solarian, and Tanus. She was ready for them to join Miranda and Seth.

As the three of them followed Babrea across the bridge, Tanus became excited. He had spotted the crystal-clear lake and eagerly asked Babrea, "Is it okay if we swim in the lake?"

"Of course, you can swim in there. The water in the lake is safe, and it will always be warm and inviting."

Seth heard the conversation Babrea was having with Tanus and asked, "Can we eat the fish from the lake?"

Babrea laughed, "Yes, Seth, if you can catch them, you can eat them. You can enjoy the lake in any way you choose. You can catch the fish, eat them, swim, or do whatever you normally do with water that is safe."

Tanus threw off his shirt, then ran and jumped into the water. He began to splash about while the rest of Babrea's family watched him from the beach area.

Babrea told Carver to invite everyone else to join them so they could enjoy the warm sunshine and beautiful water. She wanted them all to enjoy the benefits her gift had to offer.

At first, they were hesitant to leave the courtyard, as they were all aware of the dangers that lurked outside the protection of the Manor walls. Carver reassured them that Babrea was waiting for them and that it was safe inside.

They slowly walked across the bridge and were shocked and amazed at what they saw. They were uncertain if what they were seeing was real or if they were dreaming. Babrea reassured them, saying, "Everything you see is safe and made for you to enjoy."

As the residents gathered inside the bubble, a few began to wade into the water with Tanus. It was pleasingly warm and crystal clear. Fish could be seen swimming around them. There were so many fish that several people were able to simply grab them with their bare hands as they swam by.

Solarian had joined Tanus in the water by then, and they began to splash about like children at play. Everyone was having a splendid time.

Several hours later, after frolicking in the water and fishing in the lake, they started a fire and began cooking the fish they had caught. There was plenty for everyone to eat, so they feasted.

After everyone had their fill and settled down, Babrea asked for their attention. She wanted to make sure they all understood the importance of what she was about to tell them.

"This Orb I have created for my Mother will become not only her new home but a home for everyone. The bubble surrounding it will protect you all from what will come. You must all stay within its confines and never leave it, no matter what temptations try to sway you. Soon the outside world will no longer be able to sustain life. This bubble surrounding the Orb will expand to include all your cottages, the well from which you drink, and the Manor house. That will allow all of you to continue living the way you are accustomed to, but at the same time, keep you safe."

While everyone enjoyed the gifts Babrea provided them, no one noticed the dark shadow that flew into the high tower at the top of the Manor. It went down into the underbelly of the Manor until it reached a secret hatchway. It descended through that entrance and finally into the caves beneath the Manor. It had access to the artesian stream from that cave which flowed freely there. That stream ran the purification system Protecus built to cleanse the only drinking water source for all the residents. Though the creature was unrecognizable in its present form, its sadistic laugh instantly gave away its identity. Then it spoke, "Now, Miranda, let's see how much you like my special wedding present!"

The creature then produced a vial with an ominous-looking liquid inside. After emptying the container into the water purifier, Devant flew out the end of the tunnel, and her menacing shadow disappeared into the night sky. No one ever knew she was there. Silently the poisonous liquid contaminated the purifier, then it slowly filtered down into the drinking water supply without anyone ever knowing.

CHAPTER 18
THE PROPOSAL

While the guests ate, swam, and partook in the festivities, Seth and Miranda went to look at the cottage Babrea had created for them. It was a lovely, welcoming place on its peaceful little island. Miranda was thrilled. She wanted to rush inside and look at everything, but Seth wanted to take in the lovely surroundings first. As they walked through the beautiful garden area, Seth felt there could be no better time to ask Miranda to marry him than at that moment.

He grabbed both her hands in his, bent down on one knee, and said the words he had felt in his heart for a long time. "Miranda, I hope that you know that I love you. I have loved you as long as I can remember, and I should have asked you to marry me long ago, but it took me this long to get up the nerve to say what is in my heart. Babrea knew that we belonged together. She saw it in our hearts. Her giving us this beautiful home fortifies my hope that you will agree to marry me."

His words moved Miranda. After her first husband died, she never thought she would meet another that would touch her heart. Seth warmed her heart in a way no other had done before. She knew she loved Seth the same way and could think of no one she would rather spend the rest of her life with.

"Oh, Seth, I want to be your wife. Yes, I'll marry you."

Seth wanted to share his news with everyone. Since the entire Manor family was gathered by the lake, feasting and enjoying each other's company, he decided to make his declaration public.

Smiling from ear to ear, he grabbed Miranda's hand, saying, "Let's tell everyone our good news."

Miranda agreed, "What a great idea."

Hand in hand, they ran down toward the lake where everyone was gathered. After arriving on the beach, the couple was breathless. When Seth finally caught his breath, he cleared his throat and said, "I have an announcement to make, so can I please have everyone's attention?"

Once everyone quieted and Seth had the floor, he said, "I want to thank Babrea for everything she has so lovingly created for all of us. I especially want to thank her for our wedding present. I can't thank her enough for all of her phenomenal work. Miranda and I are overwhelmed by it all. However, getting the wedding gift before the proposal made me realize how remiss I've been. I should have asked Miranda to marry me long ago, but I've rectified that situation. I just asked her to be my wife, and thankfully, she has accepted my proposal."

Everyone began to clap and cheer at Seth's heartfelt news. They all loved Seth and Miranda and felt they belonged together, so it was no surprise that they wanted to get married. Anybody that knew them, and had seen them together, was well aware of their real feeling toward one another. It was exciting to know they were finally making their love official. The gathering was now indeed a party. Now they all had something special to celebrate. Babrea's gift of a new paradise to share and their favorite pair becoming a couple officially.

One of the older gentlemen in the group brought out a fiddle. Another one produced a guitar, and they began to play. The festivities were now in full swing. Some people started to sing while others danced.

Father Samuel, the resident priest, had been sitting by the fire, telling one of his tall tales, when Seth made the announcement. The jolly old fellow was nearing eighty years of age now but always ready with a smile. As Seth and Miranda approached the fire, Samuel said, "I hear that congratulations are in order for the two of you. Have you thought about a date yet? You know I'm always ready to perform a wedding ceremony."

Miranda looked at Seth, and they both laughed.

"We haven't thought about that yet, Father."

Samuel laughed too and said, "Well, you know, I've always said there is no time better than the present to commit to something you feel deep in your heart."

Seth gave that some thought. Samuel was right. Why not now? Everyone was together, happy, and in a festive mood.

Seth whispered something into Miranda's ear, and she smiled at him, then said, "You know Seth, Father is right. This is a perfect time. I've never really cared for all the frivolous things that usually accompany a wedding anyway. All that matters is that we love one another. Since our friends and family are here to share our special moment with us, today would be a great day for a wedding."

Seth nodded his head that he agreed. There was no better time than the present. Seth once again asked for everyone's attention.

"Could I please have everyone's attention once more? I hate to keep bothering all of you. Father Samuel has suggested he is free tonight, so Miranda and I have decided to say our vows. If everyone would like to gather around the gazebo on Miranda's island, we'll make this shindig officially a wedding ceremony."

Everyone headed toward Miranda's island with excitement in the air.

While everyone gathered on the island, Miranda searched for Solarian and Miranda. Once she spotted them, she signaled to both of them to come to her.

"Since Seth and I have decided to get married today while everyone is here, I want my two special girls to stand up with me while I say my vows."

Both girls were excited for their mother. Babrea wanted all of the decorations Miranda had spoken of in her fantasy wedding to be perfect. Miranda knew that Babrea needed an explanation for the seemingly rushed ceremony, so she tried to explain everything.

"Sweetheart, when a woman plans to get married, she usually takes a lot of time to decide what dress she plans to wear and the flowers she will carry. I had a big wedding when I got married for the first time. I have everything that I want here with me right now. I want you and Solarian, my two most special females, to stand up with me before the Priest. Father Samuel is going to preside over our ceremony. Seth also plans to ask the most important male in his life to stand up with him. Seth and I will then say our vows to one another, our promise of love and devotion for the rest of our lives together. Then, Father Samuel will pronounce us man and wife, and we will seal the promise with a kiss. After that, Seth and I will be man and wife, live in the cottage Babrea made for us, and be a happy couple for the rest of our days."

Babrea smiled and said, "That sounds lovely, Mother, and if that is what you want, that is what we will do."

Babrea then took Miranda's hands in hers, and she smiled because she could tell that her mother was overflowing with happiness.

Samuel walked to the gazebo and waited there for Miranda to arrive. As Miranda and the girls walked toward Samuel, Babrea, and Solarian began to giggle. They were excited.

Once they arrived at the gazebo, Father Samuel said, "When you're ready, Miranda, you and the girls are to stand on my right, and Seth and his party will stand to my left. Once everyone is ready, we can begin."

They all took their places then Miranda whispered to Babrea and Solarian, "Now Seth and I will say our vows to one another. It will be a profession of our love for each other."

Father Samuel explained, "Once both of you say your vows, I will pronounce you man and wife. Then, Seth, you will kiss your bride, and the ceremony will end. After that, you and Seth can go on your honeymoon together. Does either one of you have any questions?"

"I'm ready, Father," Seth was quick to answer.

Miranda said, "I don't have any questions either, Father, and I'm ready too."

Father Samuel then said, "Very good. Let's begin."

All of the Manor family had gathered around for the ceremony. They couldn't wait for Seth and Miranda to tie the bond. Protecus had stationed himself on the bench closest to the area where Samuel had stationed himself. He wanted a front-row seat to the event he considered his daughter's wedding. Protecus had always felt close to Miranda and, until today, didn't realize how close he felt to her. She was his daughter in every sense of the word, and Protecus couldn't feel prouder of her than he did right this minute.

Both girls were so excited they could hardly contain their enthusiasm. They continued to stand where they had been instructed, trying to control their excitement.

Miranda couldn't stop smiling as she proclaimed her love for Seth. He smiled back as he declared his love for her. Father Samuel then pronounced them man and wife. The happy couple hugged, and kissed, then waved goodbye to their loved ones and headed for their red-topped cottage.

After Seth and Miranda left, the feasting and frivolity continued for several more hours until everyone started to wear down. Soon they all began to depart and go to their cottages.

Once the residents had drifted away, Protecus turned to Tanus and said, "It's getting late, Seth, and time to put this old man to bed. Congratulations on catching the best girl in town."

Seth hugged Protecus, then laughing, said, no doubt, sir, but you are one hundred percent correct on that aspect."

Babrea approached Protecus at that instant and said, "Father, I'm tired too, and I think I'm ready to turn in for the night."

"Yes, it's been a long day for both of us, especially for you. I'm sure that you must be completely exhausted."

Babrea yawned, and Protecus chuckled.

Tanus and Solarian were both ready to turn in as well, so as Babrea and Protecus walked away, Tanus said, "We'll be right behind you. I want to make sure the fire is out good first."

While Protecus and Babrea slowly walked toward the Manor, Babrea stopped. She was happy for her mother, but she felt a pain in her heart for some reason, which she didn't make sense. She shared her feelings with her father.

"Father, why do I feel so much sadness whenever I feel nothing but happiness for my mother?"

Protecus understood what she was going through. He stopped, turned to face her, and tried to reassure her by telling her, "You probably feel like you're losing your mother because she and Seth got married. Don't fear that, Sweetheart. You will never lose your Miranda because she will always love you. You have a larger family now than you did before. Seth is a part of your family, and he can love both. One day, a man will enter your life and steal your heart away. Believe me, when that day comes, and it will, you'll understand how your mother is feeling right now about Seth."

Hearing those words made Babrea smile.

The two of them finished walking the rest of the way to the Manor. Tanus and Solarian soon caught up with them, excitedly saying, "That was a great party!"

"Yes, it was, Tanus. Everything was perfect, and I'm so happy for Seth and Miranda. They belong together. I'm going to see the girls to bed, then I'm going to turn in myself. Goodnight, everyone."

Once Protecus knew Babrea and Solarian were safe in their beds, he climbed the stairs to go to his bed.

Babrea fell asleep quickly but tossed and turned so much it woke her. Bad dreams continued to plague her. The words of the evil one speaking to her prevented her from returning to sleep. She couldn't get that voice out of her head. It continued calling her name as it had done many times before. Babrea couldn't shake the feeling that there was a presence in her bedroom besides Solarian. She had to get away from that droning voice.

She rose in bed, and as soon as she did, she woke Bumble. He told her that he, too, felt the presence of something evil and that they should go to her garden to escape it.

Babrea got out of bed, trying not to wake Solarian, and then quietly slipped out the back door and down to the barn. Beauty nickered as Babrea bridled her. The mare knew Babrea had an apple in her pocket because she could smell it. Babrea retrieved the apple and gave it to Beauty. Then Babrea climbed onto the mare's back and told Bumble, "I'm ready, so let's go."

After entering the garden, Babrea asked Bumble to let her be alone for a little while. He nodded that he understood her request and watched as she rode further into the garden. Babrea loved to ride. It was one of her favorite things to do. She loved to let her hair billow freely behind her while Beauty ran. She would close her eyes, turn the reins loose, and let Beauty run free at those times. Tonight, she felt the need to do just that. So, she leaned forward and whispered into the mare's ear, "Fly like the wind, girl."

Beauty began to gallop faster and faster, and Babrea allowed her mind to wander far away. She thought of her mother's smiling face as Seth held her close and kissed her. She wrapped her arms around herself and pretended someone she loved was holding her. Babrea lost herself in her fantasy. She felt as if she were far away, sitting on a cloud of white and silver while being held in the arms of a loving man.

Farther and farther, Babrea rode, reaching an area where she had never been before. Beauty began to slow her pace as they ventured past the fertile region of Babrea's garden.

The horse continued onward, and new things began to appear before her as she walked. Babrea visualized the mountains she had created for her mother. Then she felt herself climbing them and going higher and higher.

Babrea knew she was moving and suddenly found herself in a strange new place she had never been to before. She looked up into a pair of beautiful blue eyes and heard a voice speaking to her.

"Our time is not yet upon us, my Darling, but we will be together soon. For now, though, you must return to your Earthly family. There are many tasks that you have not yet completed."

Babrea could see his face as clearly as if he was directly in front of her. She could even feel his breath on her cheek. She imagined she could feel his touch. At that moment, Babrea was no longer a child, and this man was someone she knew. She could remember loving him and being with him. She wanted to float away now and be with him once again.

"Wake up, Babrea. It's time for you to return to your family now. They are in great need of your help." The voice was very persistent.

When Babrea opened her eyes, she realized she had created the things she had imagined. The most beautiful lake was before her, and beyond it was a cascade of mountains. Each mountain rose higher than the one before it until they seemed to touch the clouds.

The sky was the bluest of blues and filled with beautiful white fluffy clouds dancing everywhere.

"Harwin," she said in a whisper. "I'll do as you say, for now."

Babrea realized that she was no longer riding Beauty. She was lying on the grass in a bed of yellow flowers. She didn't know how she got there. When she looked up, Beauty was beside her, looking down at her. Babrea stood up and climbed onto the horse's back. Then she quickly left the garden.

Babrea didn't know she had been gone from the Manor for two days. In her absence, something tragic had taken place.

As she exited the garden, Bumble caught up with her, and together they rushed to the Manor. As Babrea rode through the Manor gates, Seth wasn't there to meet her. He always met her upon her return. Babrea could hear no happy voices, and not a single person was walking about, which was strange. None of the little people were scurrying about, as they always were. No one was in the courtyard, and the silence was alarming.

Babrea put the mare in the barn and ran across the bridge to her mother's island, but Miranda wasn't home, and neither was Seth. She then went to the kitchen inside the Manor but saw no one there.

Babrea began calling, "Mother, Mother, where are you? Mother, answer me!"

Miranda didn't answer. No one answered.

Then Babrea searched upstairs but found no one there. Then Babrea started to shout as loud as she could, "Where is everybody?"

Receiving no answer, Babrea headed toward her sister's room when she heard a faint groan. She ran into Solarian's bedroom, and once inside, she was stunned by what she saw.

On the floor beside Solarian lay her mother, and beside her was Seth. Tanus was lying in bed, and they were all barely breathing. She touched each one in turn and realized they were burning up with fever. Babrea spoke to them, but no one answered her. A faint moan escaped Miranda's lips, but no one moved. Babrea didn't know what to do for her family.

Protecus was missing, so she went to search for her father. She looked everywhere but couldn't find him. Babrea was frightened. She had always been able to help her family, but now, she felt helpless.

Bumble was at a loss too. He didn't know why everyone was so sick. He could smell a strange odor in the room, though, and when he sniffed the glass of water on the bedside table, he wrinkled his nose. He told Babrea that the odor was bitter smelling and not to drink it. Babrea grabbed her mother's hand and began to cry.

As tears streamed down Babrea's face, Bumble began to hear a high-pitched hum. He followed the sound until he reached its point of origin. It led him to a wall inside the great room of the Manor. He clawed at the loosened stones until they began to fall away. Once he had removed several of them, he discovered, inside the wall, a pendant. He grasped the pendant and quickly took it to Babrea. He knew it was summoning her.

Once Babrea placed the pendant around her neck, it stopped humming and began to glow. She bent down beside her mother and kissed her on the cheek. When she did that, her pendant touched Miranda's lips, and color slowly began to return to her face. Miranda gasped and looked wide-eyed at Babrea. Then in a weak voice, she said, "Help the others. Everyone is sick."

Babrea then repeated touching her pendant to Solarian's lips, Tanus, then Seth, and they began to revive too.

Babrea went in search of her father next. She and Bumble looked everywhere but couldn't find him. Babrea feared if she didn't find him soon, Protecus would surely perish.

Her pendant shot a beam of light toward the floor underneath the table. Babrea pulled the table off the rug and then pulled the carpet back. There, she found a hatchway on the floor that she didn't know existed.

She tried to lift the hatch, but it seemed to be stuck. Bumble helped her by jumping on the covering. He broke through and ended up on the level below the kitchen.

Babrea could see Bumble beneath the opening where he had dropped. He pointed toward a set of stairs that Babrea could use to climb down, but when she reached the bottom, it was too dark to see. Then her pendant began to glow, and she could make out something toward the end of the tunnel on the floor. As she walked toward it, she could see what the object was. It was Protecus. He was lying in a heap on the ground.

She started shouting, "Father, are you all right?" She rushed to his side, but Protecus never moved. Babrea kneeled beside him and kissed him on the cheek. She touched him with her pendant as she had done for the others, but Protecus didn't revive.

That was when Babrea realized her father hadn't been poisoned like everyone else. He was lying in a pool of his own blood.

Blood was everywhere. Protecus must have been lying on that cold ground for several hours with his life's blood slowly ebbing away. His head was bleeding profusely. Babrea staunched the blood flow and then pulled her father into her arms. His life source was weak, but she could feel a slight heartbeat. Protecus was still alive but hanging on by a thread.

He lay in her arms, limp and unresponsive. Babrea didn't know what else to do for him. She felt lost and alone. She began to cry. Between her tears, she spoke aloud, "Father, I will not allow anything ever to touch this water supply again, and I will make our people safe."

Then she reached out and touched the water that led to the well. The water started to shimmer as the flow became visibly more apparent. The glittering water flowed toward the purification filter and then back down to the underground stream from which it originated. The water was clean once again and safe for everyone to drink. Then a bright radiance rose above the water as it flowed. Babrea had created a barrier of protection to surround the stream.

Babrea felt helpless. She had never known pain like this before. She had never felt such sadness or loss and didn't understand the ache she felt down to her core. It hurt her so deeply that she didn't think she could bear it.

Babrea's pain awakened Adolla. She immediately became aware of what took place through the telepathic link they shared. Babrea could then hear Adolla speaking to her telepathically.

Your father has not left you yet, Master, you can save him, but we must hurry. Have Bumble fly him to the garden you created for him. We can then prepare him for the long journey that we must take. Tell your family you will be away for a very long time, but you will return to them.

Babrea told Bumble, "I must tell my family goodbye, for we have to go on a journey far away to save my father. We will be gone for a very long time. Adolla said we should go to the garden to prepare my father for the trip.

Fly Protecus to the end of the tunnel and then wait for me there. I'll catch up with you after I tell my family goodbye. Then we can go to the garden together to prepare Father for the trip."

Bumble gently lifted Protecus and carried him out to the end of the tunnel. There he waited for Babrea to join him as she had instructed.

Babrea returned to her mother's side and explained what had transpired.

"Our water supply was poisoned. That's why everyone got sick and almost died. I've made it safe again for everyone to drink. Tell all the people they can drink from the well. It is now purified and safe to drink. I must leave all of you for now, though, and take my father with me. He will die if I don't save him, and the only way I can do that is to take him to a place far away from here. Father won't be able to return to Earth. I'll be away for a long time, but I'll return to you."

Miranda was still weak from her ordeal with the poisoned water, but she understood what Babrea was saying to her. Protecus was near death, and Miranda knew Babrea had to leave them. Miranda wanted to protest, but she knew how much Babrea loved Protecus, and she had to try if there was any way for her to save his life.

Miranda softly said, "We love you, Babrea, and we'll miss you, but I understand that you must save your father. Seth and I will ensure everyone drinks fresh water from the well. Return to us as soon as you can, Sweetheart."

Babrea believed the evil one had done this to her family. Babrea knew that it would do anything to stop her. The voice had been telling her for months to stop her efforts to revive the world, or dire consequences would befall her. It said that she was to leave this place and never return, or her loved ones would suffer.

Babrea realized now that was a warning. This poisoning event was the result of that threat. She had to protect her family, but having to leave them meant that she wouldn't be around to watch over them. She had to do something to protect them in her absence. Babrea walked to the bedroom door, and then she slowly raised both arms high above her head. As she did this, her pendant began to glow once again. Then, she softly said, "The Orb will protect all of you in my absence until I return."

Orb slowly began to grow. It enveloped the Manor, the courtyard, and all the cottages. It also took in the water well and the underground water source.

Babrea explained to her mother, "Everyone will be safe now if they stay inside the Orb. No one can leave its protection, though, for there is only death and destruction in the world outside. This world can no longer sustain life, so it isn't safe outside. I'm sorry I must leave you all, but my father needs me now. Remember, the evil one is waiting outside, destroying everything of substance. The Orb will provide everyone all that is needed until I return. Please don't worry about me, I won't be alone, and I promise to return to all of you one day."

Miranda and Babrea hugged, with tears streaming down both their faces. Miranda whispered, "Please don't forget us."

"I can never forget you, Mother. As long as the light glows in the lighthouse, you will know I'm thinking of you. The Everlight will always lead me back to you.

Babrea hugged Seth and Tanus, then reached for Solarian to hug her, but Solarian turned away. She wanted to hide her tears from her sister, but as she turned, Babrea saw a small grey cloud of smoke trail behind Solarian's hand as she raised it to wipe away her tears.

Babrea didn't know what the grey smoke meant, but it made her feel cold as she watched it. She reached for Solarian's hand and then slowly waved her hand over the top of it. Once Babrea did that, the smoky vapor disappeared. With a blank look on her face and an odd tone in her voice, Babrea told her family, “You must never leave the protection of the Orb because the evil one wants to destroy all of you. Everyone must stay within the safety of this bubble until I return.”

Babrea then turned Solarian’s hands loose and hugged her sister once more. She smiled at her and walked outside to where she had tied Beauty. She climbed onto the horse's back and rode away. Bumble was invisible as he flew high above her, carrying Protecus to the garden. It appeared that Protecus was free-floating above Babrea as she rode.

Miranda and Seth revived enough from their poisoning ordeal to ensure everyone drank water directly from the well as Babrea instructed. Miranda then tried to explain what had happened to the Manor residents.

“Our water had poison in it, which made us all sick. Babrea cleansed the water for us and made it safe for everyone to drink. However, the poison almost killed Protecus, and the only way that Babrea could save him was to take him to a place where he could heal. Sadly, Protecus will never be able to return to us again. Babrea had to go with him to a faraway site because that was the only way she could help him. She will be gone for a long time, though, and we must all stay inside the Orb until she returns.”

Everyone was glad to be alive but sad that Protecus was gone from them forever. Miranda explained to them that Babrea would be gone for many years, but she would, one day, return to them.

CHAPTER 19
THE AWAKENING

It had been six years since the dreaded day when everyone almost died from drinking poisoned water. Babrea saved her family and the residents at the Manor that day, except her Father. The only way she could save Protecus was to take him to a place far away.

As Seth thought about Babrea, he surmised that she would now be sixteen years old. He missed her as all the Manor residents did. He wondered, at times, what she was doing. Seth knew that Miranda missed her too. He had often walked in on her in the middle of the day and caught her crying. Sometimes she would at a window, staring out at nothing in particular. Seth had learned through time that when one of those episodes was upon her, it was best to leave her alone and give her space. It seemed that attempting to console her only made matters worse.

The day Babrea rescued everyone from near death after drinking poisoned water, her painful cry at finding her father dying awakened Adolla from her deep sleep. Her master needed her. Adolla knew the time of awakening had arrived. The great dragon retrieved the sword from where Protecus had placed it many years earlier, raised her head upwards, and exhaled. Her icy breath froze the top of the cave. When she shot upwards, she burst through the frozen rock, shattering it into shards that looked like a million pieces of broken glass. Adolla then flew to the garden to wait for her master's return.

After Babrea told her family goodbye and safeguarded the Orb, she rode back to meet Bumble. He waited for her as she had instructed him at the cave opening. Babrea urged Beauty into a gallop and headed for the garden. Bumble lifted Protecus and followed Babrea to the garden.

Once there, Bumble laid Protecus on the bench beneath the biggest tree while Babrea dismounted. She unbridled Beauty, patted her neck, gave her another apple, and bid her goodbye. Babrea didn't know if she would ever see the mare again because she was unsure what would come next.

Babrea's baby dragons quietly joined her then and began to encircle the tree. Adolla had already told them what to do, and they were proud to do their part to save Protecus.

Babrea slowly walked between each of them, touching them in turn. Then she raised her arms, and the brightest light emanated from her pendant. The light ray beamed downward, and once it had reached all the baby dragons, they slowly ascended above the treetop. A shower of lights began to sprinkle down from their wings like snow, falling directly onto the bench. The bench gradually became covered by flowering greenery, slowly enveloping Protecus, covering him like a blanket. Once he was completely engulfed, the green covering began to harden and form a solid case with Protecus inside. The entire tree began to glow. The dragons began to fly around the top of the tree, causing the lights to intertwine and form a wall of light.

Babrea began to ascend then, and once she was within the light wall, the dragons flew even faster until the entire wall was glowing.

Babrea gently floated back to the ground, and the dragons landed beside her. Adolla then bowed down for Babrea to climb onto her back. With her powerful claws, the giant dragon grasped the case with Protecus inside and shot upwards like a massive lightning bolt. Within seconds they were out of sight.

The baby dragons watched as their master disappeared into the glittering lights above. Bumble and his brothers would remain in the garden until Babrea returned and summoned them.

When Adolla arrived at her destination far from the Orb and all that Babrea had known, Harwin was there, waiting for them. Adolla carefully laid the case, with Protecus inside, down on the soft grass. The protective covering that had surrounded the case for the long journey began to recede onto the grass beneath it, then slowly disappeared.

Adolla bowed once more, and Babrea dismounted. Then Adolla folded her great wings beside her and stood patiently by her master's side.

Babrea looked intently at Harwin because she felt she recognized him. Then she slowly walked toward him, saying, "You are the man in my dream. I recognize you."

Harwin smiled at her and said, "Yes, you know me very well. All of your memories of me will soon return to you, but for now, we must work together to save your father. We are quickly running out of time, so we must begin."

"What do you need me to do?"

"You must concentrate on your love for your father and clear your mind of everything else."

Babrea concentrated as instructed, unaware of what would happen next.

Harwin was well aware of what was to follow, though. He knew the only way to save Babrea's Earthly father was for him to give all of his power to Protecus. It would drain him, but only briefly, and he would recover. The most important thing to Babrea was to save Protecus. Harwin knew how much her father meant to her.

Harwin removed Babrea's sword from Adolla's side and plunged it into the ground at the head of Protecus's case. Then he drew his sword from its sheath on his side and drove it into the ground near the foot.

Harwin then grasped Babrea's hands, and while they held hands, Harwin instructed her to close her eyes, then he closed his.

Babrea concentrated intently on her love for her father, and her pendant began to glow as it had before. A beam of light from Harwin's medallion and one from Babrea's pendant shot straight toward the case Protecus lay in. Within seconds, Protecus began sitting up, slowly stepping out of the case and standing. When Babrea opened her eyes, Protecus stood before her, smiling. She hugged her father tightly, saying, "Are you really here, or am I just dreaming?"

Protecus looked around at his surroundings and then down at himself. He touched his face and chest and said, "Yes, I'm here and alive? I thought I died. Where am I?"

Harwin stepped forward then and explained to Protecus, "This is your new home and where you must live from now on."

Harwin told Babrea, "Your father will be safe here with me, and I will explain everything to him in time. You must return to Earth now because you've been away for a long time, and they need you. I will see that all of your father's needs are taken care of until it's time for you to return to be with us again. Now, you must save your family and finish your tasks."

Babrea hugged Protecus again and told him. "I'm so happy you are alive, Father. I'll miss you, but I have to leave you now. Our family needs me."

Protecus was still confused but trusted Babrea and said, "You go now and save our loved ones. Finish your destiny, Sweetheart, and don't worry about me. I'll be fine here, and I love you. I'll be waiting for you when you return."

Protecus smiled at her, and then Babrea kissed him on the cheek, saying, "I love you too very much."

Then she turned, climbed on Adolla's back, and instantly, they were no longer in sight.

CHAPTER 20
THE PLAN

Devant knew her plan to rid Earth of Babrea, and destroy her mission to save humanity, would be a short-lived victory because Babrea would soon return. She wasn't sure, however, when that day would be, so she knew she must work fast. Her new plan was a simple one. She would set free many more minions and have them cause far-reaching devastation and chaos worldwide. That would spread Babrea's resources so thin Devant could quickly destroy them.

Devant felt a sense of triumph when Babrea found her father so near death. Protecus did as she expected when everyone started getting sick. He had only drunk a small amount of the poisoned water and thought it tasted and smelled odd, so he quickly spat it out. He felt something might be wrong with the water purification system, so he went to the cave below the Manor to check on it. Devant's devil dogs were waiting for him there. They mauled Protecus so significantly that he almost bled to death. He had fought diligently for his life, but there were three of them, and they were powerful.

Devant had instructed her pets to kill Protecus, but they only wounded him. Protecus was so severely injured he was close to death. Babrea couldn't bring him back from death's door without help. She knew Babrea loved her father and would do anything to save him.

Protecus had successfully forced Babrea to seek advice to save Protecus. Getting rid of her, even briefly, allowed Devant to continue with her plans unhampered. Knowing that Babrea was sad, thrilled Devant, but she wanted more.

After Babrea was gone, Devant made several failed attempts to enter the Orb, with no success. The protective barrier that Babrea had placed around her creation had held steadfast, even in her absence. Everyone inside the giant bubble remained safe.

Devant had tried to send her devil dogs back through the underground cave below the Manor again, where they had successfully poisoned the water and mauled Protecus. Their efforts failed because they ran into a wall of rocks under Babrea's protection.

With the cave entrance sealed and the tower entrance covered, all her people had remained safe, even in her absence.

Devant was more determined than ever to stop Babrea. She had lost all patience, which was in limited supply to begin with. It didn't take much to push Devant over the edge.

After she turned her multitude of minions loose, she moved on to the next step in her devious plan.

Devant knew her best hope of stalling Babrea's progress was through her family. Killing them would only anger Babrea and cause her to act faster, and Devant didn't want that. She needed Babrea to leave and never return, but for now, she would have to settle for slowing down her progress. Hampering Babrea was essential because it would allow Devant's minions more time to wreak havoc. Indeed, it seemed the best plan was to cause pain for Babrea's family.

It was apparent how vital Miranda was to Babrea, so Devant decided to concentrate on how to best harm Miranda.

Devant knew she couldn't go inside the Orb, so she would have to lure Babrea's mother outside.

Babrea loved her mother and would protect her at all costs. Devant hoped that would be her downfall.

Devant felt confident that controlling Miranda would allow her to manipulate Babrea into doing anything she wanted. She would have to be very crafty with her next move, though.

Solarian was Miranda's daughter, and she meant the world to Miranda. Devant decided that she would use Solarian as a pawn to manipulate Miranda. The easiest way to get to Solarian was through Tanus. Devant could have Tanus deceive Solarian. Then she would use Miranda's precious daughter as bait to lure Miranda outside. This idea was good, but she had to time everything perfectly to pull it off. This might be her best chance to come out on top in this battle of wills.

The only fault Devant could see in her plan was that Tanus had no reason to leave the Orb. Everything needed to sustain life was available within that bubble, so he was not motivated to go outside. Babrea had created a beautiful place for her people that would provide for them and protect them forever.

Solarian and Tanus loved each other, so Devant felt they would do anything for one another. Though Solarian was the youngest of the pair, Tanus was extremely impressionable and very curious by nature. For those reasons, he should be easy to tempt. Devant would use his weakness to her advantage.

Luring Tanus outside would be much easier than getting Solarian or Miranda to leave. Maybe with Tanus's help, Solarian could be coaxed out. Once they were trapped outside their protected home, Miranda would no doubt come out to save them. Then Devant would have complete control over all three of them.

Devant bellowed out one of her great devious laughs and said, "Yes, this plan is perfect. I'll then have three bargaining chips."

Solarian would listen to Tanus and follow him wherever he led. Then, Miranda would search for her daughter, and when she couldn't locate her, she would go outside the Orb to look because she couldn't allow Solarian to come to any harm. It would only be a matter of time before Miranda made the fatal mistake and stepped outside.

Devant smiled. Her new plan was so simple yet so effective. Once again, her cynical laugh could be heard echoing throughout her surroundings.

CHAPTER 21
DEAD ZONE

Miranda loved Tanus like a son. He and Solarian had been together since they were small children. It was only natural that they would be drawn to one another as adults.

Devant had watched their relationship unfold through time. Seeing how close they had become made for a great weapon against Babrea. She had an undetectable way of communicating with Tanus through his dreams, as she had done with Babrea for years.

Devant planned to convince him that Solarian was his sister, making it immoral for him to desire any form of sexual relationship with her. She knew his sexual desires were awakening, so she would encourage him to venture outside the Orb to meet new people, and then he would be able to find true love. She coaxed him by reassuring him that Babrea had been wrong and everything outside was completely renewed. She persuaded him to believe that other people survived The Great Disaster and were thriving in the world outside. Each day she would put new thoughts into his head, continuously deceiving him while convincing him that he needed to go out and at least take a look.

"It's been many years since The Great Disaster," the voice would say, "and Earth has now transformed. Everything beyond the walls of the prison you live in has transformed. The new world is waiting for you to come out and enjoy it. Go, venture out there, and see for yourself. You will be amazed at what you will see and who you might meet."

Tanus spent many sleepless nights being disturbed from his slumber by that voice, continuously coaxing him to be brave and venture out. He thought about his love for Solarian, and he ached. He had loved Solarian for a long time, so to hear what he had desired for so long had been wrong devastated him. Tanus knew deep down that Solarian wasn't his sister but couldn't stop thinking his feelings for her were inappropriate.

One day, while Tanus was fishing, the voice entered his thoughts. He was wide awake and hearing the voices, so it seemed he couldn't escape them, whether asleep or awake. He threw his fishing pole down on the ground and began to pace. Before he realized it, he had walked to the edge of the Orb. Ironically this was the spot where he had found himself many times before. Today, however, it felt like something was pulling him forward. Some unknown force of nature was drawing him to exit the Orb.

Tanus knew it was wrong to leave the Orb and the protection Babrea had built for them, but it felt like he was destined to move forward.

Before he realized it, Tanus stepped outside of his protective perimeters. Astonishingly, the voices he had been hearing were right. Everything outside the Orb was the same as it was inside. The air was clear and fresh. The sky was the brightest of blues, and lush green grass was everywhere. Large, mature trees dotted the entire area, and they were all full of leaves.

Tanus was excited and could hardly wait to tell his brother about all the new things he had discovered. He ran back inside the Orb to find Seth as quickly as possible. When he found Seth, Tanus excitedly told him what he had witnessed outside. Seth was amazed but hesitant at what he was hearing.

He questioned Tanus, "Babrea told us never to leave the Orb. Why did you step outside?"

Tanus feared telling Seth about the voices that had led him to leave the Orb, so instead, he was simply curious and needed to know.

Tanus was insistent that Seth come to look for himself. He started pulling his brother away from what he was doing and guided him toward the exit point he had used to walk outside. When Tanus arrived where he had stepped outside their perimeter before, Seth could see what Tanus had described but was confused. He didn't understand how he could see outside the Orb, which had never been possible. The Orb had always been defined by its barrier walls of mountains, making it easy to know where their safe area ended.

Tanus had brought Seth to a place he had been many times before. However, today everything appeared different. Seth knew the Orb well. He had been all over it, up to the base of every mountain, and knew it well. He had never seen this willow before, nor the images he could see behind it.

Before him, the giant willow seemed to form a curtain, albeit a doorway to the new area. Through the draping limbs of the willow, Seth could see a section of the garden that had never been visible before.

Perhaps Babrea's Orb had continued growing after she left, and this new extension was another part of their safe area. Seth was unsure because he had been here many times before and never saw this willow tree. The expanse before him appeared safe, and with Tanus so insistent Seth come with him, Seth followed his brother through the limbs of the willow to see for himself.

When they exited the safety of the Orb, Seth was amazed at what he saw. As far as Seth could see, everything appeared renewed. The vision before him was that of a world untouched as if no catastrophe had ever occurred. Tanus was right.

Lush green grass was everywhere, and trees full of green leaves were all about the entire area. The sky was the bluest of blues and almost too clear to look real. But something struck Seth as odd. He wasn't sure precisely what it was, but suddenly he felt very uneasy as he surveyed the landscape before him. He could not pinpoint what was bothering him, but suddenly he was very uncomfortable.

The beautiful surroundings enthralled Tanus. He couldn't stop pointing out all the new things he saw. The richness of everything fascinated him.

Tanus was too young when The Great Disaster occurred to remember trees or grass. He had only seen pictures of how things were in books, but what was before him now was far more impressive than those pictures.

Seth remembered, though. In his youth, he had witnessed real trees, sky, and grass and remembered how they looked. What he saw now, however, didn't seem right in some way. Something was off.

Seth told his Tanus, "We should not be out here. We need to return inside the Orb, where it's safe."

Tanus would have protested, but Seth persisted, saying, "Let's talk about this some more back home. Miranda has dinner ready, and she's waiting for us."

Seth knew he could get Tanus's attention with the mention of food, and sure enough, he did. Tanus shrugged his shoulders, nodded in agreement, and obediently followed his brother back inside the Orb. However, once they were back inside the safety of the Orb, Tanus was too excited to think about eating, even though he was hungry. He couldn't wait to tell Solarian about his discovery.

Tanus turned to Seth and said, "I've got to find Solarian to tell her about everything we saw. Tell Miranda I'll go find Solarian, then we'll come to eat later."

Tanus wanted to show Solarian everything he had seen but would wait until later to take her there.

Seth knew Tanus's real intentions and would have protested, but Tanus was already out the door. When Tanus was anxious about something, there was no talking to him. Hopefully, Solarian would see the danger that Tanus wanted to expose them to and tell him she wanted no part of it.

Seth shared the news with Miranda of the renewed state of the world outside that Tanus had discovered. He shared with her that he felt very uncomfortable being out in that area. Miranda immediately became alarmed.

"Seth, we are not supposed to leave the Orb for any reason. Don't you remember what Babrea told us before she left? She warned us there would be temptations and we shouldn't be fooled by them. Babrea said leaving the Orb would mean certain death. What were you thinking? Don't let Tanus tell Solarian about that area, and please don't let him take her there. Seth, I'm begging you. Explain the importance of staying inside the Orb and not venturing to that area again.

"I'm sorry, Miranda, but Tanus is convinced he found a way out of the Orb into our real world, and it was safe. I'm afraid he's wrong, and as Babrea told us, he is being tempted. If he continues to step outside, I fear he won't be able to return to us."

Miranda then asked Seth, "Did he go to find Solarian to tell her?"

"I'm afraid Tanus will tell Solarian, and she will go with him."

Miranda then shouted at Seth, "Why didn't you stop him. We have to find Tanus and stop him!"

Miranda flew past Seth and out the door but found herself almost immediately amid a crowd. The entire Manor family had gathered to hear what Tanus had to share. He had called everyone into the courtyard, saying he had an announcement. Miranda fought her way to the head of the crowd. She was almost breathless by the time she finally reached Solarian. Solarian was standing beside Tanus, hinged on his every word.

Miranda raised her hands and shouted, "Everyone needs to listen to me. No one is to go outside! Babrea warned us before she left that we should stay inside this

Orb until her return. She said that it was unsafe for anyone to go outside."

Tanus would have argued with Miranda, but Seth had caught up with her by then and said, "Miranda is right, Tanus. Everyone should listen to her. Babrea told us before she left that there would be many temptations but that we were never to leave the protection of the Orb. She said only death awaits us outside, and there was urgency in her voice when she said it."

Miranda spoke again, "Babrea was very specific with her instructions for us when she left. She told us that something out there wants us all dead, so we must stay in the Orb until she returns."

Seth recalled what Babrea said the day she left, and he felt uneasy about what was happening. He knew something was wrong outside. He just couldn't pinpoint it. Seth then announced his thoughts to the crowd that had gathered around Tanus.

"I've been outside The Orb with Tanus, and I know something isn't right out there. I can't figure it out, but I'm begging everyone not to go outside. Babrea knew there would be temptations, and she warned us against it."

Tanus argued, "Babrea has deserted us, and she is never coming back. It's been over five years since she left us, and she hasn't sent any word to let us know when she plans to return. Everything out there looks new. The world has healed itself. The air is breathable again, and green living plants and trees are everywhere. Why should we remain prisoners in this bubble when we can be free out there? Our new world awaits us, everyone. Come join me and see for yourself. I'll prove to you that it's safe out there."

Seth tried to stop Tanus from leading everyone outside the Orb, but talking didn't seem to work, so he grabbed his arm. Tanus angrily jerked away from his brother's grip, saying, "You want to keep me here forever, locked away. I'm tired of being a prisoner. I'm no longer a child, Seth, and I want to leave, so don't try to stop me!"

Seth heard malice in Tanus's voice that he had never heard before. He didn't sound like his brother. He sounded like someone Seth didn't know.

Tanus was still holding Solarian's hand, but hearing her mother's pleas not to go outside, Solarian attempted to pull free from him, but his grip only tightened. She couldn't get her hand free from Tanus, so she begged him, "Please, Tanus, let me go. I can't leave with you. I won't go against my mother's wishes, so please let go of me."

Seth had had enough. He stepped in front of Tanus, blocking his path. Then said, "I can't let you take Solarian with you. If you insist on going outside again, then you go but leave Solarian here.

Seth's bold move angered Tanus. He drew back and punched Seth in the face. That action took Seth by surprise, but with Tanus preoccupied, Solarian was able to free herself from his grip. She then fled to her mother's side, visibly shaken. She had never seen Tanus act so aggressively before. It frightened her.

Solarian couldn't understand why Tanus was so angry and acting so strangely. It was almost as if he were possessed. Seeing Solarian was free of Tanus' grip, Seth repositioned himself between Solaria and Tanus.

"Brother, I'm only going to say this to you one more time. If you're determined to go outside, you go. I won't stop you, but you won't force Solarian to go with you. I wish you would rethink going yourself. Something out there isn't right. I'm not sure what it is, but Babrea warned us to stay inside for a reason. I'm afraid that going outside will end badly for everyone that goes out there."

Tanus gave Solarian one final hateful stare and exited outside the Orb. Most of the residents adhered to

Miranda and Seth's pleas to stay put and not go outside. However, a few of them decided to follow Tanus outside. They were excited to see their world renewed.

Even though Seth had cared for everyone for years, their desire to see what existed outside overpowered their sensibilities. The residents that followed Tanus outside immediately found themselves in complete amazement at what they saw. Tanus had been right. Everything was renewed. Things appeared normal again as they had been before that dreadful day when tragedy struck. As everyone perused their new outdoor surroundings, they began discussing their possibilities. With the world seemingly back to normal again, their options seemed limitless. Some considered leaving the Orb and seeking out their previous homes. Some of their family members could have survived, and they might be able to find them. Perhaps others had survived as well. Sixteen years had passed since The Great Disaster occurred, and many things could have happened in that time.

After walking around outside, looking at everything, and discussing the changes they saw, everyone started to get hungry. They all drifted back inside the Orb, debating the changes outside as they walked. While they ate, they deliberated on what they might do next. A few residents decided they wanted to leave the Orb and try their luck on the outside. Most chose to stay put and follow Babrea's instructions.

Seth had desperately continued trying to dissuade those that decided to leave, as did Miranda. Their discussions went on through the night and into the early morning hours. However, there were still some residents that insisted on leaving. Seth and Miranda fought a hard battle, but exhaustion finally set in, and they gave in. Everyone returned to their cottages at that time. After resting overnight, those that intended to leave packed for their trip.

The next day everyone that planned to leave the Orb promised Seth, faithfully, they would send word back just as soon as they could so Seth would know they arrived at their intended destination and were alright.

Miranda continued to plead with those that intended to leave. Her pleas fell on deaf ears, though. With all their personal belonging packed, along with food and water, they set out. Leaving the safety of the Orb for the unknown was frightening, but they knew the risks.

Still worried but at a loss as to what to do, Miranda begged Seth to do something. She knew that everything about this situation was wrong. In her heart, she felt what Babrea had said to them was true. If anyone left the Orb, they would surely perish.

Seth tried to comfort her, saying, “We both pleaded with every one of them. We’ve tried reasoning as best we could, but they insist on going. They’ve made up their minds, and that’s final.”

Seth agreed with Miranda but knew there was nothing more they could do. Babrea had said before she left that as long as they stayed inside, they were protected. Seth continued to be uneasy about their newfound world on the outside. Something was just not right.

The next day, Seth watched as two more families he had always felt were part of his own family left the Orb. It was hard to watch them go because Seth feared he would never see them again. He bid them farewell and watched as they walked into the unknown.

Several weeks later, there was still no word from anyone that had left. Seth hoped they all made it to their intended destination. However, he didn’t hold out much hope for them.

Even though no one had heard from the group that left, a few more residents decided they wanted to venture out into their newfound world.

Seth once again pleaded with them to wait, "Don't go! At least wait until we get word back from someone that they made it safely where they were going. I've been out there and know something isn't right."

Preston, one of the Manor residents, argued in defense of his desire to leave, "Just because we haven't heard back from anyone doesn't necessarily mean that anything bad happened to them. They may not have had enough time to make it to their destination or been able to send word back that they made it, and they're all fine."

Miranda tried again to discourage them from leaving by pointing out some crucial facts. "That's true, Preston, but you live much farther from here than any of the others. It will take you much longer to reach your hometown state, and that is if you can make that long journey. Please wait at least another couple of weeks or so. Surely by that time, we will hear something back from the others, and then we will know that making the journey is at least possible."

Miranda doubted they would ever hear news from the residents who left. She honestly felt they were all dead. She hated to be the one destroying everyone's hope that maybe, some of their loved ones had survived.

Preston had a small son, Billy, and Miranda felt sure that if they left, all three of them would perish. The only thing she could do was to detain them for as long as she could in hopes that Babrea would return soon.

Those who wanted to leave wouldn't listen to any of the arguments she and Seth presented. They were too excited about the possibilities and anxious to return to their homelands. All reasoning was wasted on Preston as he continued to prepare his little family for the long trip ahead of them. They wanted to see the new world for themselves and all that it held in store for them.

Just thinking about that little boy being cold, wet, and hungry made Miranda want to cry. She could see him and his family wandering in the wilderness until they starved.

It was evident to Miranda that there was nothing more she could say or do to change their minds. The evil presence that Babrea had warned them about was about to destroy her loved ones in her absence.

CHAPTER 22
THE UNKNOWN

Since the first day, Tanus discovered the renewed world outside, Seth had been closely watching him. He feared Tanus would eventually slip out again, and Seth would lose him forever. Seth had fought his uneasy feeling about the newly refreshed world outside, but something about all of it still bothered him. The changes that had taken place were far too perfect.

Seth couldn't explain his uneasiness, but his duty was to protect his family, as he had always done.

Early one morning, several weeks after Preston left with his family, Tanus managed to slip away from his brother's hovering attention. Against Seth's wishes, he left the safety of the Orb.

This time, Tanus walked further than he had gone before. He was intrigued by all the changes that had taken place and wanted to see everything. Tanus had been trapped in the bubble all his life. He wanted to feel the freedom his dreams craved.

It had been a long time since the world outside could sustain life. Tanus figured that time was probably the healing factor for Earth. That was the only possible explanation for the beauty he was witnessing.

Protecus had taught Tanus a lot about science. He had told Tanus that Earth could cleanse itself over time, but with the damage it had suffered, it would take thousands of years for that process to occur.

Protecus knew the damages to our sun were irreversible, so it would continue to degrade. Yet, as Tanus looked up at the sun, it was remarkably bright and vibrant.

Tanus continued to walk further from the Orb, checking out his new surroundings. His attention was drawn to a horse pulling a small wagon coming straight toward him. Perched upon the driver's seat were two people. Tanus purposefully walked in their direction. As they neared Tanus, he saw a man with a young girl on the seat beside him. When they reached Tanus, the man stopped the horse. Tanus spoke first, saying, "Good afternoon."

These were the first people Tanus had ever seen outside the Manor. He was surprised, excited, and bursting with questions. As he contemplated what to ask first, the young girl said, "Good afternoon to you too. With whom do I have the pleasure of speaking to?"

Tanus felt himself stumbling over what to say next. Then suddenly, the words came spilling forth. "I'm Tanus, and what is your name?"

"I'm sorry, where are my manners, I'm Kaley, and this is my dad. We've traveled for several days and are very thirsty. We need water to drink and some for our horse. Do you know where we might find some around here?"

Without hesitation, Tanus said, "Yes, I do. We have plenty of water, and I would be happy to share some with you. Follow me, and I'll show you the way in."

Kaley vehemently refused to go with Tanus, almost shouting at him, "No, we can't go with you. My father doesn't socialize with anyone, especially people he doesn't know. You will have to bring the water here to us. He can't help you because he is too weak, and I broke my arm, so I can't help you. You'll have to get someone else to help you bring the water to us."

Tanus wanted Kaley to come with him, even if she couldn't help carry the water. He wanted to prove to everyone in the Orb that people existed outside.

"I can bring you water, but I would love for you to come with me. You can meet my family."

Kaley quickly responded, saying, "I can't leave my dad. He isn't in good health. I'll have to stay here and wait for you."

Tanus realized he wasn't going to convince Kaley to come with him, so he shrugged it off and told Kaley, "It's no problem. I'll find some buckets and bring the water back to you."

"We planned to pitch camp here for the night anyway because we've traveled all day and are tired. We'll wait for you here to bring the water back to us."

Tanus was excited. He was the first to discover the new world outside and had definitive proof that the world outside the Orb could sustain life. These people were living proof of that.

Kaley and her father appeared healthy, and they had traveled some distance and were just fine. If it was safe outside for a young girl and an old man to travel about, then it was probably safe for anyone to move around. That was great news because anyone wanting to leave Babrea's Orb could survive.

Tanus rushed back to get buckets to bring Kaley water from their well. He could hardly contain his excitement. He wanted everyone to know what he had discovered. He wanted to prove to Seth that he was right after all.

On his way back, however, Tanus started to think that Seth might not be happy with him after discovering he had disobeyed his orders. Seth had begged Tanus not to leave the Orb again and never to take Solarian outside.

For now, he would get water for Kaley and her father and keep their presence a secret. Tanus would question the two of them more about where they had traveled from and what they encountered. Then he would share his newfound friends and their information with this family. Tanus wanted to know all about the world outside the Orb. He had so many questions.

After re-entering the Orb, Tanus took a quick look around. Once he was sure no one was in the courtyard, he quickly filled the buckets with water. Checking again to ensure no one had seen him, Tanus felt it was safe to leave again.

Tanus hadn't been undetected, though. Solarian had seen him at the well filling the buckets and was about to approach him when he hurriedly left. She decided to follow him. When Tanus exited the Orb, Solarian approached the spot where she saw him disappear but could see nothing outside. She had never been outside and was hesitant to do it now. She remembered what Seth said to them about never leaving the Orb, or they would die. She wanted to see the things Tanus had spoken of out there, but all she could see was total blackness, which made her fearful. Her hesitation also made her remember her mother's words. Solarian lowered her head in shame because she knew she couldn't go against her mother's wishes, no matter what.

Solarian decided to wait for Tanus to return, so she sat down on the ground by the spot where he had exited and waited.

Tanus returned with the water, and Kaley questioned why he came alone and had only brought two buckets. "That's not enough water for us and our horse. Why didn't you get help? We need more than that; you will have to go back and get more, and this time get help."

Tanus hesitated to explain why he couldn't ask for help because he didn't want her to know he wasn't supposed to be there. He quickly said, "No one was available to help me this evening. I'll get someone to help me tomorrow and bring you more water."

Kaley seemed appeased with his explanation and encouraged him to stay and visit her for a while. She and Tanus spent the entire afternoon talking about everything. He was most curious about the condition of the rest of the world. He wanted to know if Kaley had any news from the outside world. She told him that since the world had healed itself, everything looked like before The Great Disaster. People were traveling again all over the place.

Kaley encouraged Tanus to tell everyone about the new changes and have them venture out to see for themselves. She told him to invite all his friends to come to visit her and she would tell them about the world. Kaley said they only planned to stay at this campsite for a couple more days, and then they would be on their way again. They planned to visit other family members in another part of the country.

Tanus knew it had to be getting late because he was hungry. His stomach's dinner bell had already called for food more than once, so he must have been away for quite a while. Strangely enough, the sun still appeared quite high in the sky. It was still burning brightly. It seemed to be in the same spot that it was in when he first arrived, which must have been several hours earlier.

Tanus was about to mention this oddity to Kaley when she questioned him about his family and friends. He quickly forgot his train of thought as he answered her questions.

Kaley then asked Tanus to please bring his sisters to meet her, "Perhaps you could even invite them to come and eat lunch with us tomorrow. I am an excellent cook, and we have plenty to eat."

Tanus stayed a little longer, but he knew it was time for him to get back home. He told Kaley he would return the next day and bring more water, but he probably couldn't bring his sisters. He explained that Solarian might be willing to come, but Babrea was away. Kaley asked about Babrea's absence, "Do you know when she is coming back?"

"No, we aren't sure. Babrea is off on a mission."

"Do you think that Babrea has deserted all of you?"

"No, Babrea would never desert us. She loves us. I'm sure that she will return soon."

Kaley was about to say something else when Tanus broke her off by saying, "It's getting late, and I have to get home."

Once again, Kaley begged Tanus not to forget to return the next day and bring his sister. He promised to return and try to persuade Solarian to come too. Then he left the campsite and returned to the Orb.

When Tanus returned to the Orb, he found Solarian still waiting for him. She had waited all day for him and finally fell asleep on the grass. It was beginning to get dark inside the Orb when he eventually returned. Solarian woke when she heard him rustling the bushes beside her as he entered. The second Tanus saw Solarian, he began to ramble about his day with Kaley. He went to great lengths to tell her how much he enjoyed himself and everything they discussed. He was so busy telling Solarian about his enjoyable day with Kaley that he failed to notice Solarian was upset. She had waited for him all day, and when he finally returned, all he could talk about was what a good time he had all day with another girl.

As Solarian watched the ever-changing expressions on his face while unfolding the events of his day, Solarian realized that she was jealous.

Solarian had never admitted to anyone, not even herself, her true feelings for Tanus. At that instant, she realized how much she truly cared for him. Hearing him talk about how he had spent the entire day with another woman and explain just how much he had enjoyed himself doing it infuriated her.

When Tanus finally shut up, Solarian was fuming and getting angrier by the second. When she finally got a word in edgewise, all her pent-up feelings burst forth.

Before she realized what she was saying, the words passed her lips. I'm glad you had a great time with your new girlfriend today. I spent the entire day worrying about whether you were injured or dead." Each word beat like a hammer pounding away at her heart.

Tanus had never seen Solarian so angry before. It caught him off guard. When he tried to make light of the situation, it only made things worse. He quickly found out that Solarian was not kidding around. She was agitated. Tanus had never seen this side of Solarian before. The way her hands were placed on her hips in such an emphatic manner almost made him laugh. But he caught himself in time not to make that mistake. He realized he had already angered her enough for one day.

Solarian was cute when she was mad. Tanus didn't realize he was smiling as he looked at her until she stopped short, "Oh, so you think all of this is funny? Well, it's not funny at all to me. The next time you decide to run off with some strange girl, why don't you stay with her and not bother to come home at all."

When Solarian finally finished her tirade, she turned her back on Tanus and was about to walk away from him when he reached out and grabbed her. Tanus hadn't thought about what he wanted to say to her before he spoke, so he once again put his foot in his mouth.

"She's just a girl I met today. Her name is Kaley, and I took water to her and her father." Tanus quickly realized that Solarian didn't care about the girl's name or the reason for his visit. All that statement succeeded in doing was making her angrier. He tried to smooth over his bungles of the day by saying, "She invited me to spend the day with her and her father, so I did, but all we did all day was talk." All he did with that statement was to make matters worse. Tanus could tell by the expression on Solarian's face that he had said nothing to repair the damage he had caused. He knew now that he had to attempt somehow to calm her down.

"Kaley and her father traveled a long way to get here. They needed water, so I took them some. She's anxious to meet you, Solarian. She asked me several times to bring you to her camp. She's about your age, and she and her father have traveled all over. You would enjoy talking to her."

Tanus then asked, in the most contrite voice he could muster, "Please come with me tomorrow to meet her. She said they were leaving tomorrow around noon. You can see for yourself that other people have survived besides us. You will see that it is possible to survive outside this prison that Babrea has created for us."

Tanus felt that he was beginning to make some headway with Solarian up to that point. Saying her home was a prison, though, upset her again.

"Babrea saved our lives, Tanus. I guess you forgot about that! We would have all died if it hadn't been for her. She didn't imprison us here. She gave us a beautiful home that has protected us all these years. She gave us everything that any human being could ever need or want. I'm amazed that you don't remember any of this. We almost died, and Babrea saved us."

"Yes, Solarian, I remember all that, but we can leave now and live a normal life again in the real world."

"Babrea only left us to save her father. I miss her more than anything, and I know she will return to us one day. All you can think about is leaving. It's like you don't even love us anymore. You seem to want to be with strangers more than you want to be with the ones that love you. You just met that girl, but you act like you would rather be with her than with your family. We should matter more to you. I should matter the most to you."

Solarian began to cry. All of her pent-up emotions started to flood forward. Tanus finally realized how much he had upset her and tried to apologize. He knew she was right about everything she said and apologized for his comment. He reached out and held her as he tried to comfort her.

"I'm sorry I called our home a prison. You're right, Babrea did save us, and this is a wonderful place. It's beautiful, and it provides everything we need. I only wanted to see more of the world. I've never been anywhere else but here. For my entire life, this place is all I've ever known. It's not that I don't appreciate everything Babrea did for us. I just needed to see what was out there. Please come with me tomorrow. You'll be amazed at all of the changes outside. The world has truly remade itself. Everything out there is just as perfect as the world that Babrea created for us here."

Solarian knew she shouldn't leave the protection of the Orb, but she also knew Tanus was going back out there again, with or without her. She didn't want him to go alone, but she also wanted to see everything he had spoken of for herself.

Solarian finally told Tanus, "I'll go with you in the morning. Meet me outside the kitchen door but say nothing to no one. My mother can't know, and we must be quiet and not let anyone see us leave."

Tanus was excited. He could hardly wait until morning to show Solarian all of his discoveries and, of course, introduce her to Kaley.

Solarian was nervous about their upcoming adventure. Going out into the unknown was exciting, but at the same time, she was fearful of what discoveries might be in store for them. Solarian also wasn't ready to face her mother's wrath. She knew if Miranda found out that she had disobeyed her, she would be very disappointed. It had never been Solarian's nature to go against her mother's wishes. Plus, she kept remembering the words she said when she reminded everyone about the importance of never leaving the safety of the Orb. That part of the unknown was what frightened Solarian the most.

CHAPTER 23
THE RETURN

After Solarian and Tanus finished dinner at Miranda and Seth's cottage that evening, they all settled down for the night. After parting company, Tanus and Solarian headed toward the Manor to their rooms for the night.

While Miranda cleaned the kitchen, she once again got a faraway look on her face, which she seemed to be doing a lot lately. Seth could tell that she was thinking about Babrea as she often did. Miranda missed Babrea terribly. She never voiced her woes to Seth, but he knew she was worried.

Seth thought about Babrea often as well. He wondered where she was and what she was doing. Seth was proud of all Babrea had provided them and knew she would return to them if she could.

As Seth looked out the window, he gazed up at the perpetual light emanating from the lighthouse. It reassured him that as long as that light was burning, Babrea would one day return to them. Seth didn't understand how that light continued to glow because it had no fuel source. He knew it was somehow an extension of Babrea, and she was alive as long as it shone brightly.

Miranda saw Seth looking up at the lighthouse and asked, "Were you thinking about Babrea?"

"Yes, I was. I know Babrea is out there, somewhere, and I'm sure she's thinking about us too. I know she's desperately trying to return to us."

"I'm sure you're right, and as soon as she can return to us, I know she will."

Seth knew Miranda was right. Babrea would return to them one day. Thankfully, for the time being, at least, it seemed that Tanus was content to stay put. Seth had drilled his brother about the dangers of leaving their protected area. He was hopeful he had gotten through to Tanus. Seth reminded Tanus that not one of the residents that left the Orb had returned so far. They all promised to send word about what they found, but no one had done that. Seth knew that if they had been able to, surely, by this time, they would have done so. It was like they had all perished.

Tanus remained belligerent, which made Seth uneasy about what he planned to do next. Seth knew Tanus was still intent on going outside the Orb. He feared Tanus would step outside again one day and never return. Seth feared Tanus would disappear forever, just like all the others had done.

Miranda tried to reassure Seth that his brother loved him very much and would never leave him, but Miranda didn't see the look in Tanus's eyes when he stood up to Seth. She hadn’t felt the ire in his voice when he spoke of leaving.

Tanus was sincere when he had vehemently said, "If I decide that I'm going to leave this place, there is nothing that you or anyone else can do to stop me."

Since that day, Seth had secretly kept an almost constant vigil on Tanus. He needed to keep his brother safe. That had always been his responsibility as the big brother. It was his promise to his mother the day she died.

Tanus had been influenced somehow, and that had changed his brother. Seth had spent many sleepless nights worrying about what Tanus would do next.

Seth had thought a lot about the changes that appeared to be happening on the outside. He had even considered going back out there himself, if for nothing more than to prove or disprove his doubts. Seth needed to clear his conscience of all the uncertainties running through his mind. What if he had misjudged what he had seen? Seth had only been out there for a short while.

What if he returned and stayed longer to better understand everything. Seth felt he could have misjudged the outside world and should give it another look. What if, even in Babrea's absence, she had somehow caused all of the wonderful changes that had taken place? He shook his head to bring himself back to reality. That reasoning was hard for Seth to accept, though, because he remembered very well the look on Babrea's face when she had uttered those cautioning words to them just before she left,

Never leave the protection of the Orb because the evil one wants all of you dead. Stay inside the safety of this place until I return. I will come back because I have more tasks to perform.

Seth could only pray that Tanus remained inside the protected Orb.

Early the next morning, Tanus awoke excited about what the new day held for them. He grabbed his clothes and dressed quickly, then headed for the kitchen. Solarian was there waiting for him as she had promised. She didn't sleep well because she couldn't stop worrying about what they planned to do today. Solarian had never gone against her mother's wishes, so she felt ill at ease doing it this time.

After Tanus joined her, he gave her his usual crooked smile and reached for her hand. Without saying a word, he began to lead the way. As they walked, they didn't talk. When they neared the edge of the Orb, Solarian pulled him to an abrupt stop. She hesitated before speaking, but her words came out stilted when she finally said, "Are you sure it's safe for us to do this?"

Tanus smiled and reassured her, "I've been out there several times without incident. I spent the entire day out there yesterday, and nothing terrible happened. Don't be afraid. I'll take care of you.

Solarian took a deep breath and pursed her lips as she hesitated a little longer. She then cautiously continued to walk in the direction Tanus was steering her toward. Solarian stopped one last time as they were about to exit behind the willow tree. She felt compelled to tell Tanus something she had wanted to share with him for a long time. She needed him to know her true feelings in case something happened to them, and she needed to say it at that moment.

"Tanus, there's something that I need to tell you before we go out there. I've wanted to tell you this for a long time but couldn't think of the right words. If something happens to either of us, I need you to know that I love you. Tanus, I've loved you for a long time. Not like how a sister loves her brother, but more than that, much more than that. You may not feel the same way about me as I do you, and that's okay. I'll understand if you don't feel the same, but I've held this inside me for a long time, and I needed to let you know before we go out there."

Tanus was slightly surprised by her confession but knew he felt the same way about her. Hearing her say the words out loud made them seem more real. Tanus gave her his silly half-smile, which Solarian had come to love so much, and then he made his profession of love.

"Solarian, I feel the same way about you. I love you and have loved you for a long time. I don't know when I first realized it, but it's true. You mean the world to me, and I would do anything for you. I swear to you that I would never put you in harm's way. I won't let anything happen to you, I promise. I will protect you for as long as I live."

After hearing that, Solarian smiled at him, took hold of his hand, and said, "Let's go see your new world together."

They stepped outside together, and Solarian gasped. She was amazed at all of the beauty surrounding them. Tanus was right. Everything outside had renewed itself. The outside world was as perfect as the world inside their Orb. As Tanus led Solarian further from the Orb and in the direction he knew Kaley and her father had camped, he began to ramble.

Tanus was pointing at things while taking her farther from the safety of her home.

Solarian had always been aware of her surroundings, so she immediately noticed something wrong. The sun was very high in the sky for this early hour. It was sitting where it should be if it were closer to noon. It should only be just starting to rise. With no timepiece to tell time anymore, Solarian had learned to tell time by the sun, and its current position was wrong.

She questioned Tanus, "The sun is sitting too high in the sky at this early hour. Don't you find that strange?"

Her question caused Tanus to stop dead in his tracks. He immediately remembered Seth repeatedly saying that there was something wrong outside. He had been unable to pinpoint what it was, but Solarian pointed it out.

Alarm bells went off in his head. She was right. The sun was far too high in the sky. Why was the sun so high? Tanus looked up again and realized that the sun was in the same spot as the day before. He remembered noticing that oddity on his last visit but ignored it.

Tanus wanted his discovery to be real so badly he ignored the obvious. Seth told him something was wrong. He just hadn't been out here long enough to figure it out.

Tanus's senses began to shout at once, turn around, and go back. You are both in danger.

Tanus didn't want to frighten Solarian, but he was responsible for bringing her out here, and in doing that, he had put her life in danger.

Solarian could tell that Tanus was frightened about something. She asked him, "What's wrong?"

Tanus heard her words, but his mind was racing. He recalled other oddities about this place from his previous visits. He had seen and heard other strange things but hadn't allowed his mind to register them. Now, everything came flooding back to him. He recalled Kaley asking him about his two sisters. How did she know he had sisters? Tanus knew that he hadn't mentioned having sisters, nor had he ever told her their names, so how did Kaley know about them. Plus, she was aware that Babrea was away and unusually curious about when she was supposed to return. Tanus now realized how bizarre all of that was. Why didn't he pay more attention?

Suddenly Tanus realized that he had allowed himself to be deceived, and now he had led Solarian into the same deception. Tanus felt his skin begin to crawl. He had to get Solarian back into the safety of the Orb quickly.

He turned around while still holding Solarian's hand and quickly walked back toward the Orb.

Solarian could tell that Tanus was acting strangely, and it alarmed her. She asked, "Tanus, what's wrong?"

Tanus tried not to further alarm Solarian by saying, "I've changed my mind. We're not going to do this today."

He continued to pull her hurriedly back toward the direction they had come in. However, Tanus stopped dead in his tracks when he realized he didn't recognize his surroundings.

Somehow he had lost his bearings and gotten completely turned around. Tanus didn't see any landmarks and couldn't remember his way back. He then began to panic.

Solarian realized that Tanus was acting confused. She reached up and placed her hands on his face to get his full attention.

"Tanus, look at me. Calm down! What is wrong?"

Tanus calmed down somewhat, but then he noticed a man walking toward them. He was speaking to them, saying, "Howdy you two youngsters. Are you lost?"

When Tanus didn't answer, Solarian said, "No, sir, we're fine. Thank you anyway." The older man continued walking toward them, but as he neared them, he seemed to lunge toward Tanus. He placed his hands on Tanus' shoulders and smiled oddly when he turned him loose. The elderly man grabbed Solarian's hand, saying, "You come with me, little girl. I will take you to where you need to go.'

Tanus would have prevented the man from taking Solarian away, but he was numb and couldn't move. He tried but was unable. He felt paralyzed. Then he realized that he was unable to speak as well.

The man continued to pull Solarian along while she tried to pull free from his grip. She didn't want to be impolite, but the man was scaring her. She told him, "I don't want to go with you. Please let me go!"

He continued pulling her along, ignoring her protests, so she kept trying to escape his grip. Solarian quickly realized she couldn't escape the old man's grasp, so she protested even louder, "Let me go! I don't want to go with you."

Solarian could see Tanus watching her as the man pulled her away, but she couldn't understand why he wasn't helping her. He just stared at her and never spoke a word. She began to fight against the man's grip, raking her fingernails across his arm. He immediately turned loose of her and let out a shrill screech. Solarian had managed to free herself, then she ran to Tanus.

She began to vigorously pull Tanus's arm, trying to prompt him to run while crying and begging him to please move. However, Tanus never moved. Solarian couldn't understand why he wouldn't move and began to panic.

When the man finally stopped screeching, he seemed to rise off the ground growing taller. He started to change physically. He began to morph into something that wasn't human. He expanded in height and bulk until he towered above Tanus and Solarian.

Solarian knew they had to escape this dreaded creature, but Tanus wouldn't move. She hadn't realized that Tanus was unable to move. The man's touch had paralyzed Tanus.

Solarian cried out for help, but no one could hear her pleas. She feared for their lives.

After the creature expanded in size, it grew wings, then flew upwards, hovering above them. Solarian knew it would descend up them any moment and, from the expression on Tanus's face, feared the worst.

Tanus wished he had only listened to his brother because he was about to pay the ultimate price for his foolhardiness. He would lose his life and the life of the only person he had ever loved. He regretted that he had convinced Solarian to come with him. She could see in his eyes that he was apologizing to her for his fatal mistake. With tears streaming down her face, she whispered to him, "I know you didn't mean for any of this to happen, and I forgive you. No matter what happens to us, I love you and always will."

The sky above them began to darken. The bright sunshine that had been so prevalent earlier had now turned a dull grey, and the air that had been so clean and fresh had become thin and difficult to breathe. Tanus wanted Solarian to leave him and run to safety, but she refused to leave his side. The creature would return soon and, no doubt, kill them both. Being paralyzed, Tanus could do nothing to prevent that from happening.

Solarian then heard the loud flapping of its wings as the creature returned. She hesitantly looked up and saw it coming straight toward them. It was screeching now so loudly it was almost deafening. Solarian knew they were both about to die, so she tightly wrapped her arms around Tanus, then closed her eyes. The last thing she remembered telling him was, "I love you very much."

Adolla appeared at that moment like a bolt of lightning. Babrea was standing on her back with her sword high above her head. As the creature dove straight toward Solarian and Tanus, with its claws outstretched, Babrea sliced through the air with her sword. One of the creature's wings fell to the ground, followed by the beast. Adolla then landed, and Babrea climbed down. She ran to Tanus, and Solarian, ensuring they were both alright. She touched Tanus, and his paralysis was absolved.

Once Adolla was sure Babrea's sister and brother were unharmed, she turned on the disgusting thing that had tried to kill them, grabbed it with her claws, and in a flash, they disappeared. She flew straight to her cave, where she had slept for many years, and there she dropped the hideous creature. As it descended into the depths of the cave, it could be heard laughing a most cynical laugh. Then it said, "Dragon, you can't kill me."

Adolla answered, "I didn't intend to kill you, odious one. I only need to place you where you can do no more harm. Here you will be lost within the maze of these tunnels, and as long as this rock remains solid, it shall be your tomb.

As Devant plummeted down into the darkness below, she continued to laugh. Adolla exhaled and swept across the entire top of her lair with her fiery breath, melting the rocks like butter. As she gazed downward one last time to inspect her work, she nodded her giant head with approval.

It was now time for her to return to her master's side. They had many more tasks to complete before their day of rest.

BOOKS BY RC DRAKE

Where Is She Now
Let's Find a Toy for Moo Moo the Mutdog
Crystal Clear a Supernatural Mystery
Roxi Needs A Home
A Moment Missed
Rebirth Legion of Dragons Book I
Escutcheon Legion of Dragons Book II

DEDICATION

I dedicate this book to my sons and husband with all my love. Without whom, this book would have probably never gotten finished.

www.ingramcontent.com/pod-product-compliance
Lightning Source LLC
LaVergne TN
LVHW010052170826
845678LV00012B/2121

9781075088322